Kahlil Gibran

The Collection Vol. 2 - (7 Books)

The Prophet,
Sand and Foam,
Jesus the Son of Man,
Lazarus and his Beloved,
The Earth Gods,
The Wanderer,
The Garden of the Prophet.

2017 by McAllister Editions (MCALLISTEREDITIONS@GMAIL.COM). This book is a classic, and a product of its time. It does not reflect the same views on race, gender, sexuality, ethnicity, and interpersonal relations as it would if it was written today.

CONTENTS

BOOK ONE. THE PROPHET 7
BOOK TWO. SAND AND FOAM 47
BOOK THREE. JESUS THE SON OF MAN 78
    JAMES, THE SON OF ZEBEDEE 78
    ANNA, THE MOTHER OF MARY 81
    ASSAPH, CALLED THE ORATOR OF TYRE 83
    MARY MAGDALENE 84
    PHILEMON, A GREEK APOTHECARY 87
    SIMON, WHO WAS CALLED PETER 88
    CAIAPHAS, *THE HIGH PRIEST* 91
    JOANNA, THE WIFE OF HEROD'S STEWARD 92
    RAFCA, *The Bride of Cana* 92
    A PERSIAN PHILOSOPHER IN DAMASCUS 95
    DAVID, ONE OF HIS FOLLOWERS 96
    LUKE 96
    MATTHEW 98
    JOHN, THE SON OF ZEBEDEE 100
    A YOUNG PRIEST OF CAPERNAUM 102
    A RICH LEVI, IN THE NEIGHBOURHOOD OF NAZARETH ... 103
    A SHEPHERD IN SOUTH LEBANON 104
    JOHN THE BAPTIST 105
    JOSEPH OF ARIMATHEA 106
    NATHANIEL 110
    SABA OF ANTIOCH 111
    SALOME TO A WOMAN FRIEND 112
    RACHAEL, A WOMAN DISCIPLE 113
    CLEOPAS OF BETHROUNE 115
    NAAMAN OF THE GADARENES 116
    THOMAS 117
    ELMADAM THE LOGICIAN 118
    ONE OF THE MARYS 119
    RUMANOUS, A GREEK POET 119
    LEVI, A DISCIPLE 121
    A WIDOW IN GALILEE 122
    JUDAS, THE COUSIN OF JESUS 123

THE MAN FROM THE DESERT	126
PETER	127
MELACHI OF BABYLON, AN ASTRONOMER	127
A PHILOSOPHER	129
URIAH, AN OLD MAN OF NAZARETH	130
NICODEMUS THE POET	131
JOSEPH OF ARIMETHEA	133
GEORGUS OF BEIRUT	133
MARY MAGDALENE	134
JOTHAM OF NAZARETH, TO A ROMAN	135
EPHRAIM OF JERICHO	136
BARCA, A MERCHANT OF TYRE	137
PHUMIAH, THE HIGH PRIESTESS OF SIDON	138
BENJAMIN THE SCRIBE	139
ZACCHAEUS	140
JONATHAN	142
HANNAH OF BETHSAIDA	143
MANASSEH	145
JEPHTHA OF CAESAREA	146
JOHN THE BELOVED DISCIPLE	147
MANNUS THE POMPEIIAN, TO A GREEK	148
PONTIUS PILATUS	149
BARTHOLOMEW IN EPHESUS	151
MATTHEW	153
ANDREW	153
A RICH MAN	155
JOHN AT PATMOS	156
PETER	158
A COBBLER IN JERUSALEM	159
SUZANNAH OF NAZARETH	159
JOSEPH SURNAMED JUSTUS	165
PHILIP	166
BIRBARAH OF YAMMOUNI	167
PILATE'S WIFE TO A ROMAN LADY	167
A MAN OUTSIDE OF JERUSALEM	168
SARKIS, AN OLD GREEK SHEPHERD, CALLED THE MADMAN	170

ANNAS THE HIGH PRIEST	173
A WOMAN, ONE OF MARY'S NEIGHBOURS	174
AHAZ THE PORTLY	175
BARABBAS	176
CLAUDIUS, A ROMAN SENTINEL	178
JAMES, THE BROTHER OF THE LORD	179
SIMON THE CYRENE	183
CYBOREA	184
THE WOMAN OF BYBLOS	185
MARY MAGDALEN, THIRTY YEARS LATER	186
A MAN FROM LEBANON	187
BOOK FOUR. THE EARTH GODS	193
BOOK FIVE. THE WANDERER	215
HIS PARABLES AND HIS SAYINGS	215
THE WANDERER	215
GARMENTS	215
THE EAGLE AND THE SKYLARK	216
THE LOVE SONG	217
TEARS AND LAUGHTER	217
AT THE FAIR	217
THE TWO PRINCESSES	218
THE LIGHTNING FLASH	218
THE HERMIT AND THE BEASTS	219
THE PROPHET AND THE CHILD	219
THE PEARL	220
BODY AND SOUL	220
THE KING	221
UPON THE SAND	223
THE THREE GIFTS	223
PEACE AND WAR	224
THE DANCER	224
THE TWO GUARDIAN ANGELS	225
THE STATUE	226
THE EXCHANGE	226
LOVE AND HATE	227
DREAMS	227

THE MADMAN	227
THE FROGS	228
LAWS AND LAW-GIVING	229
YESTERDAY, TODAY AND TOMORROW	229
THE PHILOSOPHER AND THE COBBLER	230
BUILDERS OF BRIDGES	231
THE FIELD OF ZAAD	231
THE GOLDEN BELT	232
THE RED EARTH	233
THE FULL MOON	233
THE HERMIT PROPHET	233
THE OLD, OLD WINE	233
THE TWO POEMS	234
LADY RUTH	235
THE MOUSE AND THE CAT	235
THE CURSE	236
THE POMEGRANATES	236
GOD AND MANY GODS	237
SHE WHO WAS DEAF	237
THE QUEST	238
THE SCEPTRE	239
THE PATH	239
THE WHALE AND THE BUTTERFLY	240
THE SHADOW	240
PEACE CONTAGIOUS	241
SEVENTY	241
FINDING GOD	242
THE RIVER	242
THE TWO HUNTERS	243
THE OTHER WANDERER	243
BOOK SIX. THE GARDEN OF THE PROPHET	245

THE TIMELESS WISDOM COLLECTION

Emerson once said: *"Consider what you have in the smallest chosen library. A company of the wisest and wittiest men that could be picked out of all civil countries in a thousand years, have set in best order the results of their learning and wisdom. The men themselves were hid and inaccessible, solitary, impatient of interruptions, fenced by etiquette; but the thought which they did not uncover to their bosom friend is here written out in transparent words to us, the strangers of another age."*

TWC is YOUR small library. Thousands of individual books and anthologies, the best of the best in fiction and non-fiction from the 19th and 20th Centuries, written by men and women whose lives were committed to enlighten the world with the wisdom of the ages.

Our fiction features names as Hemingway, Faulkner, Wells, Orwell, Huxley, Doyle, Twain, Burroughs, Chesterton, Alcott, C. S. Lewis, J. M. Barrie, Edgar Wallace, and hundreds more... Authors who have enriched our lives and forever enlarged our capacity to dream, to get enamored by the characters, to suffer their pain, tragedies, and triumphs as if they were ours; as if they were true...

In self-development and positive-thinking, our authors include Napoleon Hill, Dale Carnegie, Charles Haanel, William Atkinson, Orison Swett Marden, Wallace Wattles, James Allen, Christian D. Larson, Florence Scovell-Shinn, Robert Collier and many more.

In Psychology, we have the works of Freud, Jung, Coué, Coriat, Adler, etc.; and in philosophy, the works of Kant, Russell, Whitehead and Eucken, among others. In theosophy and mysticism, our authors include Blavatsky, Bulwer, Besant, Leadbeater, and Sinnet. We feature the works of scientists as Eddington, Darwin, and J.W.Dunne; successful industrialists as Henry Ford, Andrew Carnegie and Charles Schwab; and Economists as John Maynard Keynes...

Thousands of carefully selected masterpieces that have brilliantly captured the essence of life, are now being placed in your hands. *The results of the learning and wisdom of the greatest minds, set in best order,* as Emerson would say. Books for enlightenment, learning, illumination... that will provide the seeker –the one who is ready and is paying attention–, some of the deepest answers to life.

Mauricio Chaves-Mesén, Author of
12 Laws of Successful Entrepreneurs;
Think Success, **and** *The Knights of Nostradamus*

BOOK ONE.
THE PROPHET

ALMUSTAFA, the chosen and the beloved, who was a dawn unto his own day, had waited twelve years in the city of Orphalese for his ship that was to return and bear him back to the isle of his birth.

And in the twelfth year, on the seventh day of Ielool, the month of reaping, he climbed the hill without the city walls and looked seaward; and he beheld his ship coming with the mist.

Then the gates of his heart were flung open, and his joy flew far over the sea. And he closed his eyes and prayed in the silences of his soul.

But as he descended the hill, a sadness came upon him, and he thought in his heart:

How shall I go in peace and without sorrow? Nay, not without a wound in the spirit shall I leave this city.

Long were the days of pain I have spent within its walls, and long were the nights of aloneness; and who can depart from his pain and his aloneness without regret?

Too many fragments of the spirit have I scattered in these streets, and too many are the children of my longing that walk naked among these hills, and I cannot withdraw from them without a burden and an ache.

It is not a garment I cast off this day, but a skin that I tear with my own hands.

Nor is it a thought I leave behind me, but a heart made sweet with hunger and with thirst.

Yet I cannot tarry longer.

The sea that calls all things unto her calls me, and I must embark.

For to stay, though the hours burn in the night, is to freeze and crystallize and be bound in a mould.

Fain would I take with me all that is here. But how shall I?

A voice cannot carry the tongue and the lips that gave it wings. Alone must it seek the ether.

And alone and without his nest shall the eagle fly across the sun.

Now when he reached the foot of the hill, he turned again towards the sea, and he saw his ship approaching the harbour, and upon her prow the mariners, the men of his own land.

And his soul cried out to them, and he said:

Sons of my ancient mother, you riders of the tides,

How often have you sailed in my dreams.

And now you come in my awakening, which is my deeper dream.

Ready am I to go, and my eagerness with sails full set awaits the wind.

Only another breath will I breathe in this still air, only another loving look cast backward,

And then I shall stand among you, a seafarer among seafarers.

And you, vast sea, sleeping mother,

Who alone are peace and freedom to the river and the stream,

Only another winding will this stream make, only another murmur in this glade,

And then I shall come to you, a boundless drop to a boundless ocean.

And as he walked he saw from afar men and women leaving their fields and their vineyards and hastening towards the city gates.

And he heard their voices calling his name, and shouting from field to field telling one another of the coming of his ship.

And he said to himself:

Shall the day of parting be the day of gathering?

And shall it be said that my eve was in truth my dawn?

And what shall I give unto him who has left his slough in midfurrow, or to him who has stopped the wheel of his winepress?

Shall my heart become a tree heavy-laden with fruit that I may gather and give unto them?

And shall my desires flow like a fountain that I may fill their cups?

Am I a harp that the hand of the mighty may touch me, or a flute that his breath may pass through me?

A seeker of silences am I, and what treasure have I found in silences that I may dispense with confidence?

If this is my day of harvest, in what fields have I sowed the seed, and in what unremembered seasons?

If this indeed be the hour in which I lift up my lantern, it is not my flame that shall burn therein.

Empty and dark shall I raise my lantern, And the guardian of the night shall fill it with oil and he shall light it also.

These things he said in words. But much in his heart remained unsaid. For he himself could not speak his deeper secret.

And when he entered into the city all the people came to meet him, and they were crying out to him as with one voice.

And the elders of the city stood forth and said:

Go not yet away from us.

A noontide have you been in our twilight, and your youth has given us dreams to dream.

No stranger are you among us, nor a guest, but our son and our dearly beloved.

Suffer not yet our eyes to hunger for your face.

And the priests and the priestesses said unto him:

Let not the waves of the sea separate us now, and the years you have spent in our midst become a memory.

You have walked among us a spirit, and your shadow has been a light upon our faces.

Much have we loved you. But speechless was our love, and with veils has it been veiled.

Yet now it cries aloud unto you, and would stand revealed before you.

And ever has it been that love knows not its own depth until the hour of separation.

And others came also and entreated him. But he answered them not. He only bent his head; and those who stood near saw his tears falling upon his breast.

And he and the people proceeded towards the great square before the temple.

And there came out of the sanctuary a woman whose name was Almitra. And she was a seeress.

And he looked upon her with exceeding tenderness, for it was she who had first sought and believed in him when he had been but a day in their city.

And she hailed him, saying:

Prophet of God, in quest of the uttermost, long have you searched the distances for your ship.

And now your ship has come, and you must needs go.

Deep is your longing for the land of your memories and the dwelling-place of your greater desires; and our love would not bind you nor our needs hold you.

Yet this we ask ere you leave us, that you speak to us and give us of your truth.

And we will give it unto our children, and they unto their children, and it shall not perish.

In your aloneness you have watched with our days, and in your wakefulness you have listened to the weeping and the laughter of our sleep.

Now therefore disclose us to ourselves, and tell us all that has been shown you of that which is between birth and death.

And he answered:

People of Orphalese, of what can I speak save of that which is even now moving within your souls?

*

THEN said Almitra, Speak to us of Love.

And he raised his head and looked upon the people, and there fell a stillness upon them. And with a great voice he said:

When love beckons to you, follow him,

Though his ways are hard and steep.

And When his wings enfold you yield to him,

Though the sword hidden among his pinions may wound you.

And When he speaks to you believe in him,

Though his voice may shatter your dreams as the north wind lays waste the garden.

For even as love crowns you so shall he crucify you.

Even as he is for your growth so is he for your pruning.

Even as he ascends to your height and caresses your tenderest branches that quiver in the sun,

So shall he descend to your roots and shake them in their clinging to the earth.

Like sheaves of corn he gathers you unto himself.

He threshes you to make you naked.

He sifts you to free you from your husks.

He grinds you to whiteness.

He kneads you until you are pliant;

And then he assigns you to his sacred fire, that you may become sacred bread for God's sacred feast.

All these things shall love do unto you that you may know the secrets of your heart, and in that knowledge become a fragment of Life's heart.

But if in your fear you would seek only love's peace and love's pleasure,

Then it is better for you that you cover your nakedness and pass out of love's threshing-floor,

Into the seasonless world where you shall laugh, but not all of your laughter, and weep, but not all of your tears.

Love gives naught but itself and takes naught but from itself.

Love possesses not nor would it be possessed;

For love is sufficient unto love.

When you love you should not say, "God is in my heart," but rather, "I am in the heart of God."

And think not you can direct the course of love, for love, if it finds you worthy, directs your course.

Love has no other desire but to fulfill itself.

But if you love and must needs have desires, let these be your desires:

To melt and be like a running brook that sings its melody to the night.

To know the pain of too much tenderness.

To be wounded by your own understanding of love;

And to bleed willingly and joyfully.

To wake at dawn with a winged heart and give thanks for another day of loving;

To rest at the noon hour and meditate love's ecstasy;

To return home at eventide with gratitude;

And then to sleep with a prayer for the beloved in your heart and a song of praise upon your lips.

*

THEN Almitra spoke again and said, And what of Marriage, master?

And he answered saying:

You were born together, and together you shall be for evermore.

You shall be together when the white wings of death scatter your days.

Aye, you shall be together even in the silent memory of God.

But let there be spaces in your togetherness.

And let the winds of the heavens dance between you.

Love one another, but make not a bond of love:

Let it rather be a moving sea between the shores of your souls.

Fill each other's cup but drink not from one cup.

Give one another of your bread but eat not from the same loaf.

Sing and dance together and be joyous, but let each one of you be alone,

Even as the strings of a lute are alone though they quiver with the same music.

Give your hearts, but not into each other's keeping.

For only the hand of Life can contain your hearts.

And stand together yet not too near together:

For the pillars of the temple stand apart,

And the oak tree and the cypress grow not in each other's shadow.

*

AND a woman who held a babe against her bosom said, Speak to us of Children.

And he said:

Your children are not your children.

They are the sons and daughters of Life's longing for itself.

They come through you but not from you,

And though they are with you yet they belong not to you.

You may give them your love but not your thoughts,

For they have their own thoughts.

You may house their bodies but not their souls,

For their souls dwell in the house of to-morrow, which you cannot visit, not even in your dreams.

You may strive to be like them, but seek not to make them like you.

For life goes not backward nor tarries with yesterday.

You are the bows from which your children as living arrows are sent forth.

The archer sees the mark upon the path of the infinite, and He bends you with His might that His arrows may go swift and far.

Let your bending in the Archer's hand be for gladness;

For even as He loves the arrow that flies, so He loves also the bow that is stable.

*

THEN said a rich man, Speak to us of Giving.

And he answered:

You give but little when you give of your possessions.

It is when you give of yourself that you truly give.

For what are your possessions but things you keep and guard for fear you may need them to morrow?

And to-morrow, what shall to-morrow bring to the over-prudent dog burying bones in the trackless sand as he follows the pilgrims to the holy city?

And what is fear of need but need itself?

Is not dread of thirst when your well is full, the thirst that is unquenchable?

There are those who give little of the much which they have – and they give it for recognition and their hidden desire makes their gifts unwholesome.

And there are those who have little and give it all.

These are the believers in life and the bounty of life, and their coffer is never empty.

There are those who give with joy, and that joy is their reward.

And there are those who give with pain, and that pain is their baptism.

And there are those who give and know not pain in giving, nor do they seek joy, nor give with mindfulness of virtue;

They give as in yonder valley the myrtle breathes its fragrance into space.

Through the hands of such as these God speaks, and from behind their eyes He smiles upon the earth.

IT is well to give when asked, but it is better to give unasked, through understanding;

And to the open-handed the search for one who shall receive is joy greater than giving.

And is there aught you would withhold?

All you have shall some day be given;

Therefore give now, that the season of giving may be yours and not your inheritors'.

You often say, "I would give, but only to the deserving."

The trees in your orchard say not so, nor the flocks in your pasture.

They give that they may live, for to withhold is to perish.

Surely he who is worthy to receive his days and his nights is worthy of all else from you.

And he who has deserved to drink from the ocean of life deserves to fill his cup from your little stream.

And what desert greater shall there be, than that which lies in the courage and the confidence, nay the charity, of receiving?

And who are you that men should rend their bosom and unveil their pride, that you may see their worth naked and their pride unabashed?

See first that you yourself deserve to be a giver, and an instrument of giving.

For in truth it is life that gives unto life-while you, who deem yourself a giver, are but a witness.

And you receivers – and you are all receivers – assume no weight of gratitude, lest you lay a yoke upon yourself and upon him who gives.

Rather rise together with the giver on his gifts as on wings;

For to be overmindful of your debt is to doubt his generosity who has the free-hearted earth for mother, and God for father.

*

THEN an old man, a keeper of an inn, said, Speak to us of Eating and Drinking.

And he said:

Would that you could live on the fragrance of the earth, and like an air plant be sustained by the light.

But since you must kill to eat, and rob the newly born of its mother's milk to quench your thirst, let it then be an act of worship,

And let your board stand an altar on which the pure and the innocent of forest and plain are sacrificed for that which is purer and still more innocent in man.

When you kill a beast say to him in your heart:

"By the same power that slays you, I too am slain; and I too shall be consumed.

For the law that delivered you into my hand shall deliver me into a mightier hand.

Your blood and my blood is naught but the sap that feeds the tree of heaven."

And when you crush an apple with your teeth, say to it in your heart:

"Your seeds shall live in my body,

And the buds of your to-morrow shall blossom in my heart,

And your fragrance shall be my breath,

And together we shall rejoice through all the seasons."

And in the autumn, when you gather the grapes of your vineyards for the winepress, say in your heart:

"I too am a vineyard, and my fruit shall be gathered for the winepress,

And like new wine I shall be kept in eternal vessels."

And in winter, when you draw the wine, let there be in your heart a song for each cup;

And let there be in the song a remembrance for the autumn days, and for the vineyard, and for the winepress.

*

THEN a ploughman said, Speak to us of Work.

And he answered, saying:

You work that you may keep pace with the earth and the soul of the earth.

For to be idle is to become a stranger unto the seasons, and to step out of life's procession that marches in majesty and proud submission towards the infinite.

When you work you are a flute through whose heart the whispering of the hours turns to music.

Which of you would be a reed, dumb and silent, when all else sings together in unison?

Always you have been told that work is a curse and labour a misfortune.

But I say to you that when you work you fulfill a part of earth's furthest dream, assigned to you when that dream was born,

And in keeping yourself with labour you are in truth loving life,

And to love life through labour is to be intimate with life's inmost secret.

But if you in your pain call birth an affliction and the support of the flesh a curse written upon your brow, then I answer that naught but the sweat of your brow shall wash away that which is written.

You have been told also that life is darkness, and in your weariness you echo what was said by the weary.

And I say that life is indeed darkness save when there is urge,

And all urge is blind save when there is know ledge.

And all knowledge is vain save when there is work,

And all work is empty save when there is love;

And when you work with love you bind your self to yourself, and to one another, and to God.

And what is it to work with love?

It is to weave the cloth with threads drawn from your heart, even as if your beloved were to wear that cloth.

It is to build a house with affection, even as if your beloved were to dwell in that house.

It is to sow seeds with tenderness and reap the harvest with joy, even as if your beloved were to eat the fruit.

It is to charge all things your fashion with a breath of your own spirit,

And to know that all the blessed dead are standing about you and watching.

Often have I heard you say, as if speaking in sleep, "He who works in marble, and finds the shape of his own soul in the stone, is nobler than he who ploughs the soil.

And he who seizes the rainbow to lay it on a cloth in the likeness of man, is more than he who makes the sandals for our feet."

But I say, not in sleep, but in the overwakefulness of noontide, that the wind speaks not more sweetly to the giant oaks than to the least of all the blades of grass;

And he alone is great who turns the voice of the wind into a song made sweeter by his own loving.

Work is love made visible. And if you cannot work with love but only with distaste, it is better that you should leave your work and sit at the gate of the temple and take alms of those who work with joy.

For if you bake bread with indifference, you bake a bitter bread that feeds but half man's hunger.

And if you grudge the crushing of the grapes, your grudge distills a poison in the wine.

And if you sing though as angels, and love not the singing, you muffle man's ears to the voices of the day and the voices of the night.

*

THEN a woman said, Speak to us of Joy and Sorrow.

And he answered:

Your joy is your sorrow unmasked.

And the selfsame well from which your laughter rises was oftentimes filled with your tears.

And how else can it be?

The deeper that sorrow carves into your being, the more joy you can contain.

Is not the cup that holds your wine the very cup that was burned in the potter's oven?

And is not the lute that soothes your spirit the very wood that was hollowed with knives?

When you are joyous, look deep into your heart and you shall find it is only that which has given you sorrow that is giving you joy.

When you are sorrowful, look again in your heart, and you shall see that in truth you are weeping for that which has been your delight.

Some of you say, "Joy is greater than sorrow," and others say, "Nay, sorrow is the greater."

But I say unto you, they are inseparable.

Together they come, and when one sits alone with you at your board, remember that the other is asleep upon your bed.

Verily you are suspended like scales between your sorrow and your joy.

Only when you are empty are you at standstill and balanced.

When the treasure-keeper lifts you to weigh his gold and his silver, needs must your joy or your sorrow rise or fall.

*

THEN a mason came forth and said, Speak to us of Houses.

And he answered and said:

Build of your imaginings a bower in the wilderness ere you build a house within the city walls.

For even as you have home-comings in your twilight, so has the wanderer in you, the ever distant and alone.

Your house is your larger body.

It grows in the sun and sleeps in the stillness of the night; and it is not dreamless.

Does not your house dream? and dreaming, leave the city for grove or hilltop?

Would that I could gather your houses into my hand, and like a sower scatter them in forest and meadow.

Would the valleys were your streets, and the green paths your alleys, that you might seek one another through vineyards, and come with the fragrance of the earth in your garments.

But these things are not yet to be.

In their fear your forefathers gathered you too near together.

And that fear shall endure a little longer.

A little longer shall your city walls separate your hearths from your fields.

And tell me, people of Orphalese, what have you in these houses?

And what is it you guard with fastened doors?

Have you peace, the quiet urge that reveals your power?

Have you remembrances, the glimmering arches that span the summits of the mind?

Have you beauty, that leads the heart from things fashioned of wood and stone to the holy mountain?

Tell me, have you these in your houses?

Or have you only comfort, and the lust for comfort, that stealthy thing that enters the house a guest, and then becomes a host, and then a master?

Ay, and it becomes a tamer, and with hook and scourge makes puppets of your larger desires.

Though its hands are silken, its heart is of iron.

It lulls you to sleep only to stand by your bed and jeer at the dignity of the flesh.

It makes mock of your sound senses, and lays them in thistledown like fragile vessels.

Verily the lust for comfort murders the passion of the soul, and then walks grinning in the funeral.

But you, children of space, you restless in rest, you shall not be trapped nor tamed.

Your house shall be not an anchor but a mast.

It shall not be a glistening film that covers a wound, but an eyelid that guards the eye.

You shall not fold your wings that you may pass through doors, nor bend your heads that they strike not against a ceiling, nor fear to breathe lest walls should crack and fall down.

You shall not dwell in tombs made by the dead for the living.

And though of magnificence and splendour, your house shall not hold your secret nor shelter your longing.

For that which is boundless in you abides in the mansion of the sky, whose door is the morning mist, and whose windows are the songs and the silences of night.

*

AND the weaver said, Speak to us of Clothes.

And he answered:

Your clothes conceal much of your beauty, yet they hide not the unbeautiful.

And though you seek in garments the freedom of privacy you may find in them a harness and a chain.

Would that you could meet the sun and the wind with more of your skin and less of your raiment.

For the breath of life is in the sunlight and the hand of life is in the wind.

Some of you say, "It is the north wind who has woven the clothes we wear."

And I say, Aye, it was the north wind,

But shame was his loom, and the softening of the sinews was his thread.

And when his work was done he laughed in the forest.

Forget not that modesty is for a shield against the eye of the unclean.

And when the unclean shall be no more, what were modesty but a fetter and a fouling of the mind?

And forget not that the earth delights to feel your bare feet and the winds long to play with your hair.

*

AND a merchant said, Speak to us of Buying and Selling.

And he answered and said:

To you the earth yields her fruit, and you shall not want if you but know how to fill your hands.

It is in exchanging the gifts of the earth that you shall find abundance and be satisfied.

Yet unless the exchange be in love and kindly justice it will but lead some to greed and others to hunger.

When in the market-place you toilers of the sea and fields and vineyards meet the weavers and the potters and the gatherers of spices, –

Invoke then the master spirit of the earth, to come into your midst and sanctify the scales and the reckoning that weighs value against value.

And suffer not the barren-handed to take part in your transactions, who would sell their words for your labour.

To such men you should say:

"Come with us to the field, or go with our brothers to the sea and cast your net;

For the land and the sea shall be bountiful to you even as to us."

And if there come the singers and the dancers and the flute players, – buy of their gifts also.

For they too are gatherers of fruit and frankincense, and that which they bring, though fashioned of dreams, is raiment and food for your soul.

And before you leave the market-place, see that no one has gone his way with empty hands.

For the master spirit of the earth shall not sleep peacefully upon the wind till the needs of the least of you are satisfied.

*

THEN one of the judges of the city stood forth and said, Speak to us of Crime and Punishment.

And he answered, saying:

It is when your spirit goes wandering upon the wind,

That you, alone and unguarded, commit a wrong unto others and therefore unto yourself.

And for that wrong committed must you knock and wait a while unheeded at the gate of the blessed.

Like the ocean is your god-self;

It remains for ever undefiled.

And like the ether it lifts but the winged.

Even like the sun is your god-self;

It knows not the ways of the mole nor seeks it the holes of the serpent.

But your god-self dwells not alone in your being.

Much in you is still man, and much in you is not yet man,

But a shapeless pigmy that walks asleep in the mist searching for its own awakening.

And of the man in you would I now speak.

For it is he and not your god-self nor the pigmy in the mist that knows crime and the punishment of crime.

Oftentimes have I heard you speak of one who commits a wrong as though he were not one of you, but a stranger unto you and an intruder upon your world.

But I say that even as the holy and the righteous cannot rise beyond the highest which is in each one of you,

So the wicked and the weak cannot fall lower than the lowest which is in you also.

And as a single leaf turns not yellow but with the silent knowledge of the whole tree,

So the wrong-doer cannot do wrong without the hidden will of you all.

Like a procession you walk together towards your god-self.

You are the way and the wayfarers.

And when one of you falls down he falls for those behind him, a caution against the stumbling stone.

Aye, and he falls for those ahead of him, who, though faster and surer of foot, yet removed not the stumbling stone.

And this also, though the word lie heavy upon your hearts:

The murdered is not unaccountable for his own murder,

And the robbed is not blameless in being robbed.

The righteous is not innocent of the deeds of the wicked,

And the white-handed is not clean in the doings of the felon.

Yea, the guilty is oftentimes the victim of the injured,

And still more often the condemned is the burden bearer for the guiltless and unblamed.

You cannot separate the just from the unjust and the good from the wicked;

For they stand together before the face of the sun even as the black thread and the white are woven together.

And when the black thread breaks, the weaver shall look into the whole cloth, and he shall examine the loom also.

IF any of you would bring to judgment the unfaithful wife,

Let him also weigh the heart of her husband in scales, and measure his soul with measurements.

And let him who would lash the offender look unto the spirit of the offended.

And if any of you would punish in the name of righteousness and lay the axe unto the evil tree, let him see to its roots;

And verily he will find the roots of the good and the bad, the fruitful and the fruitless, all entwined together in the silent heart of the earth.

And you judges who would be just.

What judgment pronounce you upon him who though honest in the flesh yet is a thief in spirit?

What penalty lay you upon him who slays in the flesh yet is himself slain in the spirit?

And how prosecute you him who in action is a deceiver and an oppressor,

Yet who also is aggrieved and outraged?

And how shall you punish those whose remorse is already greater than their misdeeds?

Is not remorse the justice which is administered by that very law which you would fain serve?

Yet you cannot lay remorse upon the innocent nor lift it from the heart of the guilty.

Unbidden shall it call in the night, that men may wake and gaze upon themselves.

And you who would understand justice, how shall you unless you look upon all deeds in the fullness of light?

Only then shall you know that the erect and the fallen are but one man standing in twilight between the night of his pigmy-self and the day of his god self,

And that the corner-stone of the temple is not higher than the lowest stone in its foundation.

*

THEN a lawyer said, But what of our Laws, master?

And he answered:

You delight in laying down laws,

Yet you delight more in breaking them.

Like children playing by the ocean who build sand-towers with constancy and then destroy them with laughter.

But while you build your sand-towers the ocean brings more sand to the shore,

And when you destroy them the ocean laughs with you.

Verily the ocean laughs always with the innocent.

But what of those to whom life is not an ocean, and man-made laws are not sand-towers,

But to whom life is a rock, and the law a chisel with which they would carve it in their own likeness?

What of the cripple who hates dancers?

What of the ox who loves his yoke and deems the elk and deer of the forest stray and vagrant things?

What of the old serpent who cannot shed his skin, and calls all others naked and shameless?

And of him who comes early to the wedding feast, and when over-fed and tired goes his way saying that all feasts are violation and all feasters law-breakers?

What shall I say of these save that they too stand in the sunlight, but with their backs to the sun?

They see only their shadows, and their shadows are their laws.

And what is the sun to them but a caster of shadows?

And what is it to acknowledge the laws but to stoop down and trace their shadows upon the earth?

But you who walk facing the sun, what images drawn on the earth can hold you?

You who travel with the wind, what weather vane shall direct your course?

What man's law shall bind you if you break your yoke but upon no man's prison door?

What laws shall you fear if you dance but stumble against no man's iron chains?

And who is he that shall bring you to judgment if you tear off your garment yet leave it in no man's path?

People of Orphalese, you can muffle the drum, and you can loosen the strings of the lyre, but who shall command the skylark not to sing?

*

AND an orator said, Speak to us of Freedom.

And he answered:

At the city gate and by your fireside I have seen you prostrate yourself and worship your own freedom,

Even as slaves humble themselves before a tyrant and praise him though he slays them.

Aye, in the grove of the temple and in the shadow of the citadel I have seen the freest among you wear their freedom as a yoke and a handcuff.

And my heart bled within me; for you can only be free when even the desire of seeking freedom becomes a harness to you, and when you cease to speak of freedom as a goal and a fulfillment.

You shall be free indeed when your days are not without a care nor your nights without a want and a grief,

But rather when these things girdle your life and yet you rise above them naked and unbound.

And how shall you rise beyond your days and nights unless you break the chains which you at the dawn of your understanding have fastened around your noon hour?

In truth that which you call freedom is the strongest of these chains, though its links glitter in the sun and dazzle your eyes.

And what is it but fragments of your own self you would discard that you may become free?

If it is an unjust law you would abolish, that law was written with your own hand upon your own forehead.

You cannot erase it by burning your law books nor by washing the foreheads of your judges, though you pour the sea upon them.

And if it is a despot you would dethrone, see first that his throne erected within you is destroyed.

For how can a tyrant rule the free and the proud, but for a tyranny in their own freedom and a shame in their own pride?

And if it is a care you would cast off, that care has been chosen by you rather than imposed upon you.

And if it is a fear you would dispel, the seat of that fear is in your heart and not in the hand of the feared.

Verily all things move within your being in constant half embrace, the desired and the dreaded, the repugnant and the cherished, the pursued and that which you would escape.

These things move within you as lights and shadows in pairs that cling.

And when the shadow fades and is no more, the light that lingers becomes a shadow to another light.

And thus your freedom when it loses its fetters becomes itself the fetter of a greater freedom.

*

And the priestess spoke again and said: Speak to us of Reason and Passion.

And he answered, saying:

Your soul is oftentimes a battlefield, upon which your reason and your judgment wage war against your passion and your appetite.

Would that I could be the peacemaker in your soul, that I might turn the discord and the rivalry of your elements into oneness and melody.

But how shall I, unless you yourselves be also the peacemakers, nay, the lovers of all your elements?

Your reason and your passion are the rudder and the sails of your seafaring soul.

If either your sails or your rudder be broken, you can but toss and drift, or else be held at a standstill in mid-seas.

For reason, ruling alone, is a force confining; and passion, unattended, is a flame that burns to its own destruction.

Therefore let your soul exalt your reason to the height of passion, that it may sing;

And let it direct your passion with reason, that your passion may live through its own daily resurrection, and like the phoenix rise above its own ashes.

I would have you consider your judgment and your appetite even as you would two loved guests in your house.

Surely you would not honour one guest above the other; for he who is more mindful of one loses the love and the faith of both.

Among the hills, when you sit in the cool shade of the white poplars, sharing the peace and serenity of distant fields and meadows – then let your heart say in silence, "God rests in reason."

And when the storm comes, and the mighty wind shakes the forest, and thunder and lightning proclaim the majesty of the sky, – then let your heart say in awe, "God moves in passion."

And since you are a breath in God's sphere, and a leaf in God's forest, you too should rest in reason and move in passion.

*

AND a woman spoke, saying, Tell us of Pain.

And he said:

Your pain is the breaking of the shell that encloses your understanding.

Even as the stone of the fruit must break, that its heart may stand in the sun, so must you know pain.

And could you keep your heart in wonder at the daily miracles of your life, your pain would not seem less wondrous than your joy;

And you would accept the seasons of your heart, even as you have always accepted the seasons that pass over your fields.

And you would watch with serenity through the winters of your grief.

Much of your pain is self-chosen.

It is the bitter potion by which the physician within you heals your sick self.

Therefore trust the physician, and drink his remedy in silence and tranquillity:

For his hand, though heavy and hard, is guided by the tender hand of the Unseen,

And the cup he brings, though it burn your lips, has been fashioned of the clay which the Potter has moistened with His own sacred tears.

*

And a man said, Speak to us of Self-Knowledge.

And he answered, saying:

Your hearts know in silence the secrets of the days and the nights.

But your ears thirst for the sound of your heart's knowledge.

You would know in words that which you have always known in thought.

You would touch with your fingers the naked body of your dreams.

And it is well you should.

The hidden well-spring of your soul must needs rise and run murmuring to the sea;

And the treasure of your infinite depths would be revealed to your eyes.

But let there be no scales to weigh your unknown treasure;

And seek not the depths of your knowledge with staff or sounding line.

For self is a sea boundless and measureless.

Say not, "I have found the truth," but rather, "I have found a truth."

Say not, "I have found the path of the soul." Say rather, "I have met the soul walking upon my path."

For the soul walks upon all paths.

The soul walks not upon a line, neither does it grow like a reed.

The soul unfolds itself, like a lotus of countless petals.

*

THEN said a teacher, Speak to us of Teaching.

And he said:

No man can reveal to you aught but that which already lies half asleep in the dawning of your knowledge.

The teacher who walks in the shadow of the temple, among his followers, gives not of his wisdom but rather of his faith and his lovingness.

If he is indeed wise he does not bid you enter the house of his wisdom, but rather leads you to the threshold of your own mind.

The astronomer may speak to you of his understanding of space, but he cannot give you his understanding.

The musician may sing to you of the rhythm which is in all space, but he cannot give you the ear which arrests the rhythm, nor the voice that echoes it.

And he who is versed in the science of numbers can tell of the regions of weight and measure, but he cannot conduct you thither.

For the vision of one man lends not its wings to another man.

And even as each one of you stands alone in God's knowledge, so must each one of you be alone in his knowledge of God and in his understanding of the earth.

*

AND a youth said, Speak to us of Friendship.

And he answered, saying:

Your friend is your needs answered.

He is your field which you sow with love and reap with thanksgiving.

And he is your board and your fireside.

For you come to him with your hunger, and you seek him for peace.

When your friend speaks his mind you fear not the "nay" in your own mind, nor do you with hold the "aye."

And when he is silent your heart ceases not to listen to his heart;

For without words, in friendship, all thoughts, all desires, all expectations are born and shared, with joy that is unclaimed.

when you part from your friend, you grieve not;

For that which you love most in him may be clearer in his absence, as the mountain to the climber is clearer from the plain.

And let there be no purpose in friendship save the deepening of the spirit.

For love that seeks aught but the disclosure of its own mystery is not love but a net cast forth: and only the unprofitable is caught.

And let your best be for your friend.

If he must know the ebb of your tide, let him know its flood also.

For what is your friend that you should seek him with hours to kill?

Seek him always with hours to live.

For it is his to fill your need, but not your emptiness.

And in the sweetness of friendship let there be laughter, and sharing of pleasures.

For in the dew of little things the heart finds its morning and is refreshed.

*

And then a scholar said, Speak of Talking.

And he answered, saying:

You talk when you cease to be at peace with your thoughts;

And when you can no longer dwell in the solitude of your heart you live in your lips, and sound is a diversion and a pastime.

And in much of your talking, thinking is half murdered. For thought is a bird of space, that in a cage of words may indeed unfold its wings but cannot fly.

There are those among you who seek the talkative through fear of being alone.

The silence of aloneness reveals to their eyes their naked selves and they would escape.

And there are those who talk, and without knowledge or forethought reveal a truth which they themselves do not understand.

And there are those who have the truth within them, but they tell it not in words.

In the bosom of such as these the spirit dwells in rhythmic silence.

When you meet your friend on the roadside or in the market-place, let the spirit in you move your lips and direct your tongue.

Let the voice within your voice speak to the ear of his ear;

For his soul will keep the truth of your heart as the taste of the wine is remembered.

When the colour is forgotten and the vessel is no more.

*

And an astronomer said, "Master, what of Time?"

And he answered:

You would measure time the measureless and the immeasurable.

You would adjust your conduct and even direct the course of your spirit according to hours and seasons.

Of time you would make a stream upon whose bank you would sit and watch its flowing.

Yet the timeless in you is aware of life's timelessness,

And knows that yesterday is but to-day's memory and to-morrow is to-day's dream.

And that which sings and contemplates in you is still dwelling within the bounds of that first moment which scattered the stars into space.

Who among you does not feel that his power to love is boundless?

And yet who does not feel that very love, though boundless, encompassed within the centre of his being, and moving not from love thought to love thought, nor from love deeds to other love deeds?

And is not time even as love is, undivided and paceless?

But if in your thought you must measure time into seasons, let each season encircle all the other seasons,

And let to-day embrace the past with remembrance and the future with longing.

*

And one of the elders of the city said, Speak to us of Good and Evil.

And he answered:

Of the good in you I can speak, but not of the evil.

For what is evil but good tortured by its own hunger and thirst?

Verily when good is hungry it seeks food even in dark caves, and when it thirsts it drinks even of dead waters.

You are good when you are one with yourself.

Yet when you are not one with yourself you are not evil.

For a divided house is not a den of thieves; it is only a divided house.

And a ship without rudder may wander aimlessly among perilous isles yet sink not to the bottom.

You are good when you strive to give of yourself.

Yet you are not evil when you seek gain for yourself.

For when you strive for gain you are but a root that clings to the earth and sucks at her breast.

Surely the fruit cannot say to the root, "Be like me, ripe and full and ever giving of your abundance."

For to the fruit giving is a need, as receiving is a need to the root.

You are good when you are fully awake in your speech.

Yet you are not evil when you sleep while your tongue staggers without purpose.

And even stumbling speech may strengthen a weak tongue.

You are good when you walk to your goal firmly and with bold steps.

Yet you are not evil when you go thither limping.

Even those who limp go not backward.

But you who are strong and swift, see that you do not limp before the lame, deeming it kindness.

You are good in countless ways, and you are not evil when you are not good,

You are only loitering and sluggard.

Pity that the stags cannot teach swiftness to the turtles.

IN your longing for your giant self lies your goodness: and that longing is in all of you.

But in some of you that longing is a torrent rushing with might to the sea, carrying the secrets of the hillsides and the songs of the forest.

And in others it is a flat stream that loses itself in angles and bends and lingers before it reaches the shore.

But let not him who longs much say to him who longs little, "Wherefore are you slow and halting?"

For the truly good ask not the naked, "Where is your garment?" nor the houseless, "What has befallen your house?"

*

Then a priestess said, "Speak to us of Prayer."

And he answered, saying:

You pray in your distress and in your need; would that you might pray also in the fullness of your joy and in your days of abundance.

For what is prayer but the expansion of your self into the living ether?

And if it is for your comfort to pour your darkness into space, it is also for your delight to pour forth the dawning of your heart.

And if you cannot but weep when your soul summons you to prayer, she should spur you again and yet again, though weeping, until you shall come laughing.

When you pray you rise to meet in the air those who are praying at that very hour, and whom save in prayer you may not meet.

Therefore let your visit to that temple invisible be for naught but ecstasy and sweet communion.

For if you should enter the temple for no other purpose than asking you shall not receive:

And if you should enter into it to humble yourself you shall not be lifted:

Or even if you should enter into it to beg for the good of others you shall not be heard.

It is enough that you enter the temple invisible.

I cannot teach you how to pray in words.

God listens not to your words save when He Himself utters them through your lips.

And I cannot teach you the prayer of the seas and the forests and the mountains.

But you who are born of the mountains and the forests and the seas can find their prayer in your heart,

And if you but listen in the stillness of the night you shall hear them saying in silence:

"Our God, who art our winged self, it is thy will in us that willeth.

"It is thy desire in us that desireth.

"It is thy urge in us that would turn our nights, which are thine, into days, which are thine also.

"We cannot ask thee for aught, for thou knowest our needs before they are born in us:

"Thou art our need; and in giving us more of thyself thou givest us all."

*

THEN a hermit, who visited the city once a year, came forth and said, Speak to us of Pleasure.

And he answered, saying:

Pleasure is a freedom-song,

But it is not freedom.

It is the blossoming of your desires,

But it is not their fruit.

It is a depth calling unto a height,

But it is not the deep nor the high.

It is the caged taking wing,

But it is not space encompassed.

Aye, in very truth, pleasure is a freedom-song.

And I fain would have you sing it with fullness of heart; yet I would not have you lose your hearts in the singing.

Some of your youth seek pleasure as if it were all, and they are judged and rebuked.

I would not judge nor rebuke them. I would have them seek.

For they shall find pleasure, but not her alone;

Seven are her sisters, and the least of them is more beautiful than pleasure.

Have you not heard of the man who was digging in the earth for roots and found a treasure?

And some of your elders remember pleasures with regret like wrongs committed in drunkenness.

But regret is the beclouding of the mind and not its chastisement.

They should remember their pleasures with gratitude, as they would the harvest of a summer.

Yet if it comforts them to regret, let them be comforted.

And there are among you those who are neither young to seek nor old to remember;

And in their fear of seeking and remembering they shun all pleasures, lest they neglect the spirit or offend against it.

But even in their foregoing is their pleasure.

And thus they too find a treasure though they dig for roots with quivering hands.

But tell me, who is he that can offend the spirit?

Shall the nightingale offend the stillness of the night, or the firefly the stars?

And shall your flame or your smoke burden the wind?

Think you the spirit is a still pool which you can trouble with a staff?

Oftentimes in denying yourself pleasure you do but store the desire in the recesses of your being.

Who knows but that which seems omitted to day, waits for to-morrow?

Even your body knows its heritage and its rightful need and will not be deceived.

And your body is the harp of your soul,

And it is yours to bring forth sweet music from it or confused sounds.

And now you ask in your heart, "How shall we distinguish that which is good in pleasure from that which is not good?"

Go to your fields and your gardens, and you shall learn that it is the pleasure of the bee to gather honey of the flower,

But it is also the pleasure of the flower to yield its honey to the bee.

For to the bee a flower is a fountain of life,

And to the flower a bee is a messenger of love,

And to both, bee and flower, the giving and the receiving of pleasure is a need and an ecstasy.

People of Orphalese, be in your pleasures like the flowers and the bees.

*

AND a poet said, Speak to us of Beauty.

And he answered:

Where shall you seek beauty, and how shall you find her unless she herself be your way and your guide?

And how shall you speak of her except she be the weaver of your speech?

The aggrieved and the injured say, "Beauty is kind and gentle.

"Like a young mother half-shy of her own glory she walks among us."

And the passionate say, "Nay, beauty is a thing of might and dread.

"Like the tempest she shakes the earth beneath us and the sky above us."

The tired and the weary say, "Beauty is of soft whisperings.

"She speaks in our spirit.

"Her voice yields to our silences like a faint light that quivers in fear of the shadow."

But the restless say, "We have heard her shouting among the mountains,

"And with her cries came the sound of hoofs, and the beating of wings and the roaring of lions."

At night the watchmen of the city say, "Beauty shall rise with the dawn from the east."

And at noontide the toilers and the wayfarers say, "We have seen her leaning over the earth from the windows of the sunset."

In winter say the snow-bound, "She shall come with the spring leaping upon the hills."

And in the summer heat the reapers say, "We have seen her dancing with the autumn leaves, and we saw a drift of snow in her hair."

All these things have you said of beauty,

Yet in truth you spoke not of her but of needs unsatisfied,

And beauty is not a need but an ecstasy.

It is not a mouth thirsting nor an empty hand stretched forth,

But rather a heart inflamed and a soul enchanted.

It is not the image you would see nor the song you would hear,

But rather an image you see though you close your eyes and a song you hear though you shut your ears.

It is not the sap within the furrowed bark, nor a wing attached to a claw,

But rather a garden for ever in bloom and a flock of angels for ever in flight.

People of Orphalese, beauty is life when life unveils her holy face.

But you are life and you are the veil.

Beauty is eternity gazing at itself in a mirror.

But you are eternity and you are the mirror.

*

And an old priest said, "Speak to us of Religion."

And he said:

Have I spoken this day of aught else?

Is not religion all deeds and all reflection,

And that which is neither deed nor reflection, but a wonder and a surprise ever springing in the soul, even while the hands hew the stone or tend the loom?

Who can separate his faith from his actions, or his belief from his occupations?

Who can spread his hours before him, saying,

"This for God and this for myself;

"This for my soul and this other for my body"?

All your hours are wings that beat through space from self to self.

He who wears his morality but as his best garment were better naked.

The wind and the sun will tear no holes in his skin.

And he who defines his conduct by ethics imprisons his song-bird in a cage.

The freest song comes not through bars and wires.

And he to whom worshipping is a window, to open but also to shut, has not yet visited the house of his soul whose windows are from dawn to dawn.

Your daily life is your temple and your religion.

When ever you enter into it take with you your all.

Take the slough and the forge and the mallet and the lute,

The things you have fashioned in necessity or for delight.

For in reverie you cannot rise above your achievements nor fall lower than your failures.

And take with you all men:

For in adoration you cannot fly higher than their hopes nor humble yourself lower than their despair.

And if you would know God, be not therefore a solver of riddles.

Rather look about you and you shall see Him playing with your children.

And look into space; you shall see Him walking in the cloud, outstretching His arms in the lightning and descending in rain.

You shall see Him smiling in flowers, then rising and waving His hands in trees.

*

THEN Almitra spoke, saying, "We would ask now of Death."

And he said:

You would know the secret of death.

But how shall you find it unless you seek it in the heart of life?

The owl whose night-bound eyes are blind unto the day cannot unveil the mystery of light.

If you would indeed behold the spirit of death, open your heart wide unto the body of life.

For life and death are one, even as the river and the sea are one.

IN the depth of your hopes and desires lies your silent knowledge of the beyond;

And like seeds dreaming beneath the snow your heart dreams of spring.

Trust the dreams, for in them is hidden the gate to eternity.

Your fear of death is but the trembling of the shepherd when he stands before the king whose hand is to be laid upon him in honour.

Is the shepherd not joyful beneath his trembling, that he shall wear the mark of the king?

Yet is he not more mindful of his trembling?

For what is it to die but to stand naked in the wind and to melt into the sun?

And what is it to cease breathing but to free the breath from its restless tides, that it may rise and expand and seek God unencumbered?

Only when you drink from the river of silence shall you indeed sing.

And when you have reached the mountain top, then you shall begin to climb.

And when the earth shall claim your limbs, then shall you truly dance.

*

And now it was evening.

And Almitra the seeress said, "Blessed be this day and this place and your spirit that has spoken."

And he answered,

Was it I who spoke?

Was I not also a listener?

Then he descended the steps of the Temple and all the people followed him.

And he reached his ship and stood upon the deck.

And facing the people again, he raised his voice and said:

People of Orphalese, the wind bids me leave you.

Less hasty am I than the wind, yet I must go.

We wanderers, ever seeking the lonelier way, begin no day where we have ended another day; and no sunrise finds us where sunset left us.

Even while the earth sleeps we travel.

We are the seeds of the tenacious plant, and it is in our ripeness and our fullness of heart that we are given to the wind and are scattered.

Brief were my days among you, and briefer still the words I have spoken.

But should my voice fade in your ears, and my love vanish in your memory, then I will come again,

And with a richer heart and lips more yielding to the spirit will I speak.

Yea, I shall return with the tide,

And though death may hide me, and the greater silence enfold me, yet again will I seek your under standing.

And not in vain will I seek.

If aught I have said is truth, that truth shall reveal itself in a clearer voice, and in words more kin to your thoughts.

I go with the wind, people of Orphalese, but not down into emptiness;

And if this day is not a fulfillment of your needs and my love, then let it be a promise till another day.

Man's needs change, but not his love, nor his desire that his love should satisfy his needs.

Know, therefore, that from the greater silence I shall return.

The mist that drifts away at dawn, leaving but dew in the fields, shall rise and gather into a cloud and then fall down in rain.

And not unlike the mist have I been.

In the stillness of the night I have walked in your streets, and my spirit has entered your houses,

And your heart-beats were in my heart, and your breath was upon my face, and I knew you all.

Aye, I knew your joy and your pain, and in your sleep your dreams were my dreams.

And oftentimes I was among you a lake among the mountains.

I mirrored the summits in you and the bending slopes, and even the passing flocks of your thoughts and your desires.

And to my silence came the laughter of your children in streams, and the longing of your youths in rivers.

And when they reached my depth the streams and the rivers ceased not yet to sing.

But sweeter still than laughter and greater than longing came to me.

It was the boundless in you;

The vast man in whom you are all but cells and sinews;

He in whose chant all your singing is but a soundless throbbing.

It is in the vast man that you are vast,

And in beholding him that I beheld you and loved you.

For what distances can love reach that are not in that vast sphere?

What visions, what expectations and what presumptions can outsoar that flight?

Like a giant oak tree covered with apple blossoms is the vast man in you.

His might binds you to the earth, his fragrance lifts you into space, and in his durability you are deathless.

You have been told that, even like a chain, you are as weak as your weakest link.

This is but half the truth.

You are also as strong as your strongest link.

To measure you by your smallest deed is to reckon the power of ocean by the frailty of its foam.

To judge you by your failures is to cast blame upon the seasons for their inconstancy.

Ay, you are like an ocean,

And though heavy-grounded ships await the tide upon your shores, yet, even like an ocean, you cannot hasten your tides.

And like the seasons you are also,

And though in your winter you deny your spring,

Yet spring, reposing within you, smiles in her drowsiness and is not offended.

Think not I say these things in order that you may say the one to the other,

"He praised us well.

"He saw but the good in us."

I only speak to you in words of that which you yourselves know in thought.

And what is word knowledge but a shadow of wordless knowledge?

Your thoughts and my words are waves from a sealed memory that keeps records of our yesterdays,

And of the ancient days when the earth knew not us nor herself,
And of nights when earth was upwrought with confusion.
Wise men have come to you to give you of their wisdom.
I came to take of your wisdom:
And behold I have found that which is greater than wisdom.
It is a flame spirit in you ever gathering more of itself,
While you, heedless of its expansion, bewail the withering of your days.
It is life in quest of life in bodies that fear the grave.
There are no graves here.
These mountains and plains are a cradle and a stepping-stone.

When ever you pass by the field where you have laid your ancestors look well thereupon, and you shall see yourselves and your children dancing hand in hand.

Verily you often make merry without knowing.

Others have come to you to whom for golden promises made unto you faith you have given but riches and power and glory.

Less than a promise have I given, and yet more generous have you been to me.

You have given me my deeper thirsting after life.

Surely there is no greater gift to a man than that which turns all his aims into parching lips and all life into a fountain.

And in this lies my honour and my reward, –

That when ever I come to the fountain to drink I find the living water itself thirsty;

And it drinks me while I drink it.

Some of you have deemed me proud and over shy to receive gifts.

Too proud indeed am I to receive wages, but not gifts.

And though I have eaten berries among the hills when you would have had me sit at your board,

And slept in the portico of the temple when you would gladly have sheltered me,

Yet it was not your loving mindfulness of my days and my nights that made food sweet to my mouth and girdled my sleep with visions?

For this I bless you most:

You give much and know not that you give at all.

Verily the kindness that gazes upon itself in a mirror turns to stone,

And a good deed that calls itself by tender names becomes the parent to a curse.

And some of you have called me aloof, and drunk with my own aloneness,

And you have said,

"He holds council with the trees of the forest, but not with men.

"He sits alone on hill-tops and looks down upon our city."

True it is that I have climbed the hills and walked in remote places.

How could I have seen you save from a great height or a great distance?

How can one be indeed near unless he be far?

And others among you called unto me, not in words, and they said:

"Stranger, stranger, lover of unreachable heights, why dwell you among the summits where eagles build their nests?

"Why seek you the unattainable?

"What storms would you trap in your net,

"And what vaporous birds do you hunt in the sky?

"Come and be one of us.

"Descend and appease your hunger with our bread and quench your thirst with our wine."

In the solitude of their souls they said these things;

But were their solitude deeper they would have known that I sought but the secret of your joy and your pain,

And I hunted only your larger selves that walk the sky.

But the hunter was also the hunted;

For many of my arrows left my bow only to seek my own breast.

And the flier was also the creeper;

For when my wings were spread in the sun their shadow upon the earth was a turtle.

And I the believer was also the doubter;

For often have I put my finger in my own wound that I might have the greater belief in you and the greater knowledge of you.

And it is with this belief and this knowledge that I say,

You are not enclosed within your bodies, nor confined to houses or fields.

That which is you dwells above the mountain and roves with the wind.

It is not a thing that crawls into the sun for warmth or digs holes into darkness for safety,

But a thing free, a spirit that envelops the earth and moves in the ether.

If these be vague words, then seek not to clear them.

Vague and nebulous is the beginning of all things, but not their end,

And I fain would have you remember me as a beginning.

Life, and all that lives, is conceived in the mist and not in the crystal.

And who knows but a crystal is mist in decay?

This would I have you remember in remembering me:

That which seems most feeble and bewildered in you is the strongest and most determined.

Is it not your breath that has erected and hardened the structure of your bones?

And is it not a dream which none of you remember having dreamt, that built your city and fashioned all there is in it?

Could you but see the tides of that breath you would cease to see all else,

And if you could hear the whispering of the dream you would hear no other sound.

But you do not see, nor do you hear, and it is well.

The veil that clouds your eyes shall be lifted by the hands that wove it,

And the clay that fills your ears shall be pierced by those fingers that kneaded it.

And you shall see.

And you shall hear.

Yet you shall not deplore having known blindness, nor regret having been deaf.

For in that day you shall know the hidden purposes in all things,

And you shall bless darkness as you would bless light.

After saying these things he looked about him, and he saw the pilot of his ship standing by the helm and gazing now at the full sails and now at the distance.

And he said:

Patient, over patient, is the captain of my ship.

The wind blows, and restless are the sails;

Even the rudder begs direction;

Yet quietly my captain awaits my silence.

And these my mariners, who have heard the choir of the greater sea, they too have heard me patiently.

Now they shall wait no longer.

I am ready.

The stream has reached the sea, and once more the great mother holds her son against her breast.

Fare you well, people of Orphalese.

This day has ended.

It is closing upon us even as the water-lily upon its own to-morrow.

What was given us here we shall keep,

And if it suffices not, then again must we come together and together stretch our hands unto the giver.

Forget not that I shall come back to you.

A little while, and my longing shall gather dust and foam for another body.

A little while, a moment of rest upon the wind, and another woman shall bear me.

Farewell to you and the youth I have spent with you.

It was but yesterday we met in a dream.

You have sung to me in my aloneness, and I of your longings have built a tower in the sky.

But now our sleep has fled and our dream is over, and it is no longer dawn.

The noontide is upon us and our half waking has turned to fuller day, and we must part.

If in the twilight of memory we should meet once more, we shall speak again together and you shall sing to me a deeper song.

And if our hands should meet in another dream we shall build another tower in the sky.

So saying he made a signal to the seamen, and straightaway they weighed anchor and cast the ship loose from its moorings, and they moved eastward.

And a cry came from the people as from a single heart, and it rose into the dusk and was carried out over the sea like a great trumpeting.

Only Almitra was silent, gazing after the ship until it had vanished into the mist.

And when all the people were dispersed she still stood alone upon the sea-wall, remembering in her heart his saying:

"A little while, a moment of rest upon the wind, and another woman shall bear me."

The End

BOOK TWO.
SAND AND FOAM

I AM FOREVER walking upon these shores,
Betwixt the sand and the foam,
The high tide will erase my foot-prints,
And the wind will blow away the foam.
But the sea and the shore will remain
Forever.

*

Once I filled my hand with mist.

Then I opened it and lo, the mist was a worm.

And I closed and opened my hand again, and behold there was a bird.

And again I closed and opened my hand, and in its hollow stood a man with a sad face, turned upward.

And again I closed my hand, and when I opened it there was naught but mist.

But I heard a song of exceeding sweetness.

*

It was but yesterday I thought myself a fragment quivering without rhythm in the sphere of life.

Now I know that I am the sphere, and all life in rhythmic fragments moves within me.

*

They say to me in their awakening, "You and the world you live in are but a grain of sand upon the infinite shore of an infinite sea."

And in my dream I say to them, "I am the infinite sea, and all worlds are but grains of sand upon my shore."

*

Only once have I been made mute. It was when a man asked me, "Who are you?"

*

The first thought of God was an angel.

The first word of God was a man.

*

We were fluttering, wandering, longing creatures a thousand thousand years before the sea and the wind in the forest gave us words.

Now how can we express the ancient of days in us with only the sounds of our yesterdays?

*

The Sphinx spoke only once, and the Sphinx said, "A grain of sand is a desert, and a desert is a grain of sand; and now let us all be silent again."

I heard the Sphinx, but I did not understand.

*

Long did I lie in the dust of Egypt, silent and unaware of the seasons.

Then the sun gave me birth, and I rose and walked upon the banks of the Nile,

Singing with the days and dreaming with the nights.

And now the sun threads upon me with a thousand feet that I may lie again in the dust of Egypt.

But behold a marvel and a riddle!

The very sun that gathered me cannot scatter me.

Still erect am I, and sure of foot do I walk upon the banks of the Nile.

*

Remembrance is a form of meeting.

*

Forgetfulness is a form of freedom.

*

We measure time according to the movement of countless suns; and they measure time by little machines in their little pockets.

Now tell me, how could we ever meet at the same place and the same time?

*

Space is not space between the earth and the sun to one who looks down from the windows of the Milky Way.

*

Humanity is a river of light running from the ex-eternity to eternity.
*

Do not the spirits who dwell in the ether envy man his pain?
*

On my way to the Holy City I met another pilgrim and I asked him, "Is this indeed the way to the Holy City?"

And he said, "Follow me, and you will reach the Holy City in a day and a night."

And I followed him. And we walked many days and many nights, yet we did not reach the Holy City.

And what was to my surprise he became angry with me because he had misled me.
*

Make me, oh God, the prey of the lion, ere You make the rabbit my prey.
*

One may not reach the dawn save by the path of the night.
*

My house says to me, "Do not leave me, for here dwells your past."

And the road says to me, "Come and follow me, for I am your future."

And I say to both my house and the road, "I have no past, nor have I a future. If I stay here, there is a going in my staying; and if I go there is a staying in my going. Only love and death will change all things."
*

How can I lose faith in the justice of life, when the dreams of those who sleep upon feathers are not more beautiful than the dreams of those who sleep upon the earth? Strange, the desire for certain pleasures is a part of my pain.
*

Seven times have I despised my soul:

The first time when I saw her being meek that she might attain height.

The second time when I saw her limping before the crippled.

The third time when she was given to choose between the hard and the easy, and she chose the easy.

The fourth time when she committed a wrong, and comforted herself that others also commit wrong.

The fifth time when she forbore for weakness, and attributed her patience to strength.

The sixth time when she despised the ugliness of a face, and knew not that it was one of her own masks.

And the seventh time when she sang a song of praise, and deemed it a virtue.

*

I AM IGNORANT of absolute truth. But I am humble before my ignorance and therein lies my honor and my reward.

*

There is a space between man's imagination and man's attainment that may only be traversed by his longing.

*

Paradise is there, behind that door, in the next room; but I have lost the key.

Perhaps I have only mislaid it.

*

You are blind and I am deaf and dumb, so let us touch hands and understand.

*

The significance of man is not in what he attains, but rather in what he longs to attain.

*

Some of us are like ink and some like paper.

And if it were not for the blackness of some of us, some of us would be dumb;

And if it were not for the whiteness of some of us, some of us would be blind.

*

Give me an ear and I will give you a voice.

*

Our mind is a sponge; our heart is a stream.

Is it not strange that most of us choose sucking rather than running?

*

When you long for blessings that you may not name, and when you grieve knowing not the cause, then indeed you are growing with all things that grow, and rising toward your greater self.

*

When one is drunk with a vision, he deems his faint expression of it the very wine.

*

You drink wine that you may be intoxicated; and I drink that it may sober me from that other wine.

*

When my cup is empty I resign myself to its emptiness; but when it is half full I resent its half-fulness.

*

The reality of the other person is not in what he reveals to you, but in what he cannot reveal to you.

Therefore, if you would understand him, listen not to what he says but rather to what he does not say.

*

Half of what I say is meaningless; but I say it so that the other half may reach you.

*

A sense of humour is a sense of proportion.

*

My loneliness was born when men praised my talkative faults and blamed my silent virtues.

*

When Life does not find a singer to sing her heart she produces a philosopher to speak her mind.

*

A truth is to be known always, to be uttered sometimes.

*

The real in us is silent; the acquired is talkative.

*

The voice of life in me cannot reach the ear of life in you; but let us talk that we may not feel lonely.

*

When two women talk they say nothing; when one woman speaks she reveals all of life.

*

Frogs may bellow louder than bulls, but they cannot drag the plough in the field not turn the wheel of the winepress, and of their skins you cannot make shoes.

*

Only the dumb envy the talkative.

*

If winter should say, "Spring is in my heart," who would believe winter?

*

Every seed is a longing.

*

Should you really open your eyes and see, you would behold your image in all images.

And should you open your ears and listen, you would hear your own voice in all voices.

*

It takes two of us to discover truth: one to utter it and one to understand it.

*

Though the wave of words is forever upon us, yet our depth is forever silent.

*

Many a doctrine is like a window pane. We see truth through it but it divides us from truth.

*

Now let us play hide and seek. Should you hide in my heart it would not be difficult to find you. But should you hide behind your own shell, then it would be useless for anyone to seek you. A woman may veil her face with a smile.

*

How noble is the sad heart who would sing a joyous song with joyous hearts.

*

He who would understand a woman, or dissect genius, or solve the mystery of silence is the very man who would wake from a beautiful dream to sit at a breakfast table.

*

I would walk with all those who walk. I would not stand still to watch the procession passing by.

*

You owe more than gold to him who serves you. Give him of your heart or serve him.

*

Nay, we have not lived in vain. Have they not built towers of our bones?

*

Let us not be particular and sectional. The poet's mind and the scorpion's tail rise in glory from the same earth.

*

Every dragon gives birth to a St. George who slays it.

*

Trees are poems that the earth writes upon the sky. We fell them down and turn them into paper that we may record our emptiness.

*

Should you care to write (and only the saints know why you should) you must needs have knowledge and art and music – the knowledge of the music of words, the art of being artless, and the magic of loving your readers.

*

They dip their pens in our hearts and think they are inspired.

*

Should a tree write its autobiography it would not be unlike the history of a race.

*

If I were to choose between the power of writing a poem and the ecstasy of a poem unwritten, I would choose the ecstasy. It is better poetry.

But you and all my neighbors agree that I always choose badly.

*

Poetry is not an opinion expressed. It is a song that rises from a bleeding wound or a smiling mouth.

*

Words are timeless. You should utter them or write them with a knowledge of their timelessness.

*

A POET IS a dethroned king sitting among the ashes of his palace trying to fashion an image out of the ashes.

*

Poetry is a deal of joy and pain and wonder, with a dash of the dictionary.

*

In vain shall a poet seek the mother of the songs of his heart.

*

Once I said to a poet, "We shall not know your worth until you die."

And he answered saying, "Yes, death is always the revealer. And if indeed you would know my worth it is that I have more in my heart than upon my tongue, and more in my desire than in my hand."

*

If you sing of beauty though alone in the heart of the desert you will have an audience.

*

Poetry is wisdom that enchants the heart.
Wisdom is poetry that sings in the mind.
If we could enchant man's heart and at the same time sing in his mind,
Then in truth he would live in the shadow of God.

*

Inspiration will always sing; inspiration will never explain.
*

We often sing lullabies to our children that we ourselves may sleep.
*

All our words are but crumbs that fall down from the feast of the mind.
*

Thinking is always the stumbling stone to poetry.
*

A great singer is he who sings our silences.
*

How can you sing if your mouth be filled with food?
How shall your hand be raised in blessing if it is filled with gold?
*

They say the nightingale pierces his bosom with a thorn when he sings his love song.
So do we all. How else should we sing?
*

Genius is but a robin's song at the beginning of a slow spring.
*

Even the most winged spirit cannot escape physical necessity.
*

A madman is not less a musician than you or myself; only the instrument on which he plays is a little out of tune.
*

The song that lies silent in the heart of a mother sings upon the lips of her child.
*

No longing remains unfulfilled.
*

I have never agreed with my other self wholly. The truth of the matter seems to lie between us.
*

Your other self is always sorry for you. But your other self grows on sorrow; so all is well.

*

There is no struggle of soul and body save in the minds of those whose souls are asleep and whose bodies are out of tune.

*

When you reach the heart of life you shall find beauty in all things, even in the eyes that are blind to beauty.

*

We live only to discover beauty. All else is a form of waiting.

*

Sow a seed and the earth will yield you a flower. Dream your dream to the sky and it will bring you your beloved.

*

The devil died the very day you were born.

Now you do not have to go through hell to meet an angel.

*

Many a woman borrows a man's heart; very few could possess it.

*

If you would possess you must not claim.

*

When a man's hand touches the hand of a woman they both touch the heart of eternity.

*

Love is the veil between lover and lover.

*

Every man loves two women; the one is the creation of his imagination, and the other is not yet born.

*

Men who do not forgive women their little faults will never enjoy their great virtues.

*

Love that does not renew itself every day becomes a habit and in turn a slavery.

*

Lovers embrace that which is between them rather than each other.
*

Love and doubt have never been on speaking terms.
*

Love is a word of light, written by a hand of light, upon a page of light.
*

Friendship is always a sweet responsibility, never an opportunity.
*

If you do not understand your friend under all conditions you will never understand him.
*

Your most radiant garment is of the other person's weaving;

You most savory meal is that which you eat at the other person's table;

Your most comfortable bed is in the other person's house.

Now tell me, how can you separate yourself from the other person?
*

Your mind and my heart will never agree until your mind ceases to live in numbers and my heart in the mist.
*

We shall never understand one another until we reduce the language to seven words.
*

HOW SHALL MY heart be unsealed unless it be broken?
*

Only great sorrow or great joy can reveal your truth.

If you would be revealed you must either dance naked in the sun, or carry your cross.
*

Should nature heed what we say of contentment no river would seek the sea, and no winter would turn to Spring. Should she heed all we say of thrift, how many of us would be breathing this air?
*

You see but your shadow when you turn your back to the sun.

*

You are free before the sun of the day, and free before the stars of the night;

And you are free when there is no sun and no moon and no star.

You are even free when you close your eyes upon all there is.

But you are a slave to him whom you love because you love him,

And a slave to him who loves you because he loves you.

*

We are all beggars at the gate of the temple, and each one of us receives his share of the bounty of the King when he enters the temple, and when he goes out.

But we are all jealous of one another, which is another way of belittling the King.

*

You cannot consume beyond your appetite. The other half of the loaf belongs to the other person, and there should remain a little bread for the chance guest.

*

If it were not for your guests all houses would be graves.

*

Said a gracious wolf to a simple sheep, "Will you not honor our house with a visit?"

And the sheep answered, "We would have been honored to visit your house if it were not in your stomach."

*

I stopped my guest on the threshold and said, "Nay, wipe not your feet as you enter, but as you go out."

*

Generosity is not in giving me that which I need more than you do, but it is in giving me that which you need more than I do.

*

You are indeed charitable when you give, and while giving, turn your face away so that you may not see the shyness of the receiver.

*

The difference between the richest man and the poorest is but a day of hunger and an hour of thirst.

*

We often borrow from our tomorrows to pay our debts to our yesterdays.

*

I too am visited by angels and devils, but I get rid of them.
When it is an angel I pray an old prayer, and he is bored;
When it is a devil I commit an old sin, and he passes me by.

*

After all this is not a bad prison; but I do not like this wall between my cell and the next prisoner's cell;

Yet I assure you that I do not wish to reproach the warder not the Builder of the prison.

*

Those who give you a serpent when you ask for a fish, may have nothing but serpents to give. It is then generosity on their part.

*

Trickery succeeds sometimes, but it always commits suicide.

*

You are truly a forgiver when you forgive murderers who never spill blood, thieves who never steal, and liars who utter no falsehood.

*

He who can put his finger upon that which divides good from evil is he who can touch the very hem of the garment of God.

*

If your heart is a volcano how shall you expect flowers to bloom in your hands?

*

A strange form of self-indulgence! There are times when I would be wronged and cheated, that I may laugh at the expense of those who think I do not know I am being wronged and cheated.

*

What shall I say of him who is the pursuer playing the part of the pursued?

*

Let him who wipes his soiled hands with your garment take your garment. He may need it again; surely you would not.

*

It is a pity that money-changers cannot be good gardeners.

*

Please do not whitewash your inherent faults with your acquired virtues. I would have the faults; they are like mine own.

*

How often have I attributed to myself crimes I have never committed, so that the other person may feel comfortable in my presence.

*

Even the masks of life are masks of deeper mystery.

*

You may judge others only according to your knowledge of yourself.
Tell me now, who among us is guilty and who is unguilty?

*

The truly just is he who feels half guilty of your misdeeds.

*

Only an idiot and a genius break man-made laws; and they are the nearest to the heart of God.

*

It is only when you are pursued that you become swift.

*

I have no enemies, O God, but if I am to have an enemy
Let his strength be equal to mine,
That truth alone may be the victor.

*

You will be quite friendly with your enemy when you both die.

*

Perhaps a man may commit suicide in self-defense.

*

Long ago there lived a Man who was crucified for being too loving and too lovable.

And strange to relate I met him thrice yesterday.

The first time He was asking a policeman not to take a prostitute to prison; the second time He was drinking wine with an outcast; and the third time He was having a fist-fight with a promoter inside a church.

*

If all they say of good and evil were true, then my life is but one long crime.

*

Pity is but half justice.

*

THE ONLY ONE who has been unjust to me is the one to whose brother I have been unjust.

*

When you see a man led to prison say in your heart, "Mayhap he is escaping from a narrower prison."

And when you see a man drunken say in your heart, "Mayhap he sought escape from something still more unbeautiful."

*

Oftentimes I have hated in self-defense; but if I were stronger I would not have used such a weapon.

*

How stupid is he who would patch the hatred in his eyes with the smile of his lips.

*

Only those beneath me can envy or hate me.

I have never been envied nor hated; I am above no one.

Only those above me can praise or belittle me.

I have never been praised nor belittled; I am below no one.

*

Your saying to me, "I do not understand you," is praise beyond my worth, and an insult you do not deserve. How mean am I when life gives me gold and I give you silver, and yet I deem myself generous.

*

When you reach the heart of life you will find yourself not higher than the felon, and not lower than the prophet.

*

Strange that you should pity the slow-footed and not the slow-minded,
And the blind-eyed rather than the blind-hearted.

*

It is wiser for the lame not to break his crutches upon the head of his enemy.

*

How blind is he who gives you out of his pocket that he may take out of your heart.

*

Life is a procession. The slow of foot finds it too swift and he steps out;
And the swift of foot finds it too slow and he too steps out.

*

If there is such a thing as sin some of us commit it backward following our forefathers' footsteps;
And some of us commit it forward by overruling our children.

*

The truly good is he who is one with all those who are deemed bad.

*

We are all prisoners but some of us are in cells with windows and some without.

*

Strange that we all defend our wrongs with more vigor than we do our rights.

*

Should we all confess our sins to one another we would all laugh at one another for our lack of originality.
Should we all reveal our virtues we would also laugh for the same cause.

*

An individual is above man-made laws until he commits a crime against man-made conventions; After that he is neither above anyone nor lower than anyone.

*

Government is an agreement between you and myself. You and myself are often wrong.

*

Crime is either another name of need or an aspect of a disease.

*

Is there a greater fault than being conscious of the other person's faults?

*

If the other person laughs at you, you can pity him; but if you laugh at him you may never forgive yourself.

If the other person injures you, you may forget the injury; but if you injure him you will always remember.

In truth the other person is your most sensitive self given another body.

*

How heedless you are when you would have men fly with your wings and you cannot even give them a feather.

*

Once a man sat at my board and ate my bread and drank my wine and went away laughing at me.

Then he came again for bread and wine, and I spurned him;

And the angels laughed at me.

*

Hate is a dead thing. Who of you would be a tomb?

*

It is the honor of the murdered that he is not the murderer.

*

The tribune of humanity is in its silent heart, never its talkative mind.

*

They deem me mad because I will not sell my days for gold;

And I deem them mad because they think my days have a price.

*

They spread before us their riches of gold and silver, of ivory and ebony, and we spread before them our hearts and our spirits.;

And yet they deem themselves the hosts and us the guests.

*

I would not be the least among men with dreams and the desire to fulfill them, rather than the greatest with no dreams and no desires.

*

The most pitiful among men is he who turns his dreams into silver and gold.

*

We are all climbing toward the summit of our hearts' desire. Should the other climber steal your sack and your purse and wax fat on the one and heavy on the other, you should pity him;

The climbing will be harder for his flesh, and the burden will make his way longer.

And should you in your leanness see his flesh puffing upward, help him a step; it will add to your swiftness.

*

You cannot judge any man beyond your knowledge of him, and how small is your knowledge.

*

I would not listen to a conqueror preaching to the conquered.

*

The truly free man is he who bears the load of the bond slave patiently.

*

A thousand years ago my neighbor said to me, "I hate life, for it is naught but a thing of pain."

And yesterday I passed by a cemetery and saw life dancing upon his grave.

*

Strife in nature is but disorder longing for order.

*

Solitude is a silent storm that breaks down all our dead branches;

Yet it sends our living roots deeper into the living heart of the living earth.

*

Once I spoke of the sea to a brook, and the brook thought me but an imaginative exaggerator;

And once I spoke of a brook to the sea, and the sea thought me but a depreciative defamer.

*

How narrow is the vision that exalts the busyness of the ant above the singing of the grasshopper.

*

The highest virtue here may be the least in another world.

*

The deep and the high go to the depth or to the height in a straight line; only the spacious can move in circles.

*

IF IT WERE not for our conception of weights and measures we would stand in awe of the firefly as we do before the sun.

*

A scientist without imagination is a butcher with dull knives and out-worn scales.

But what would you, since we are not all vegetarians?

*

When you sing the hungry hears you with his stomach.

*

Death is not nearer to the aged than to the new-born; neither is life.

*

If indeed you must be candid, be candid beautifully; otherwise keep silent, for there is a man in our neighborhood who is dying.

*

Mayhap a funeral among men is a wedding feast among the angels.

*

A forgotten reality may die and leave in its will seven thousand actualities and facts to be spent in its funeral and the building of a tomb.

*

In truth we talk only to ourselves, but sometimes we talk loud enough that others may hear us.

*

The obvious is that which is never seen until someone expresses it simply.

*

If the Milky Way were not within me how should I have seen it or known it?

*

Unless I am a physician among physicians they would not believe that I am an astronomer.

*

Perhaps the sea's definition of a shell is the pearl.
Perhaps time's definition of coal is the diamond.

*

Fame is the shadow of passion standing in the light.

*

A root is a flower that disdains fame.

*

There is neither religion nor science beyond beauty.

*

Every great man I have known had something small in his make-up; and it was that small something which prevented inactivity or madness or suicide.

*

The truly great man is he who would master no one, and who would be mastered by none.

*

I would not believe that a man is mediocre simply because he kills the criminals and the prophets.

*

Tolerance is love sick with the sickness of haughtiness.
*

Worms will turn; but is it not strange that even elephants will yield?
*

A disagreement may be the shortest cut between two minds.
*

I am the flame and I am the dry bush, and one part of me consumes the other part.
*

We are all seeking the summit of the holy mountain; but shall not our road be shorter if we consider the past a chart and not a guide?
*

Wisdom ceases to be wisdom when it becomes too proud to weep, too grave to laugh, and too self-ful to seek other than itself.
*

Had I filled myself with all that you know what room should I have for all that you do not know?
*

I have learned silence from the talkative, toleration from the intolerant, and kindness from the unkind; yet strange, I am ungrateful to these teachers.
*

A bigot is a stone-leaf orator.
*

The silence of the envious is too noisy.
*

When you reach the end of what you should know, you will be at the beginning of what you should sense.
*

An exaggeration is a truth that has lost its temper.
*

If you can see only what light reveals and hear only what sound announces,
Then in truth you do not see nor do you hear.

*

A fact is a truth unsexed.

*

You cannot laugh and be unkind at the same time.

*

The nearest to my heart are a king without a kingdom and a poor man who does not know how to beg.

*

A shy failure is nobler than an immodest success.

*

Dig anywhere in the earth and you will find a treasure, only you must dig with the faith of a peasant.

*

Said a hunted fox followed by twenty horsemen and a pack of twenty hounds, "Of course they will kill me. But how poor and how stupid they must be. Surely it would not be worth while for twenty foxes riding on twenty asses and accompanied by twenty wolves to chase and kill one man."

*

It is the mind in us that yields to the laws made by us, but never the spirit in us.

*

A traveler am I and a navigator, and every day I discover a new region within my soul.

*

A woman protested saying, "Of course it was a righteous war. My son fell in it."

*

I said to Life, "I would hear Death speak."

And Life raised her voice a little higher and said, "You hear him now."

*

When you have solved all the mysteries of life you long for death, for it is but another mystery of life.

*

Birth and death are the two noblest expressions of bravery.

*

My friend, you and I shall remain strangers unto life,
And unto one another, and each unto himself,
Until the day when you shall speak and I shall listen
Deeming your voice my own voice;
And when I shall stand before you
Thinking myself standing before a mirror.

*

They say to me, "Should you know yourself you would know all men."
And I say, "Only when I seek all men shall I know myself."

*

MAN IS TWO men; one is awake in darkness, the other is asleep in light.

*

A hermit is one who renounces the world of fragments that he may enjoy the world wholly and without interruption.

*

There lies a green field between the scholar and the poet; should the scholar cross it he becomes a wise man; should the poet cross it, he becomes a prophet.

*

Yestereve I saw philosophers in the market-place carrying their heads in baskets, and crying aloud, "Wisdom! Wisdom for sale!"

Poor philosophers! They must needs sell their heads to feed their hearts. Said a philosopher to a street sweeper, "I pity you. Yours is a hard and dirty task."

And the street sweeper said, "Thank you, sir. But tell me what is your task?"

And the philosopher answered saying, "I study man's mind, his deeds and his desires."

Then the street sweeper went on with his sweeping and said with a smile, "I pity you too."

*

He who listens to truth is not less than he who utters truth.

*

No man can draw the line between necessities and luxuries. Only the angels can do that, and the angels are wise and wistful.

Perhaps the angels are our better thought in space.

*

He is the true prince who finds his throne in the heart of the dervish.

*

Generosity is giving more than you can, and pride is taking less than you need.

*

In truth you owe naught to any man. You owe all to all men.

*

All those who have lived in the past live with us now. Surely none of us would be an ungracious host.

*

He who longs the most lives the longest.

*

They say to me, "A bird in the hand is worth ten in the bush."

But I say, "A bird and a feather in the bush is worth more than ten birds in the hand."

Your seeking after *that feather* is life with winged feet; nay, it is life itself.

*

There are only two elements here, beauty and truth; beauty in the hearts of lovers, and truth in the arms of the tillers of the soil.

*

Great beauty captures me, but a beauty still greater frees me even from itself.

*

Beauty shines brighter in the heart of him who longs for it than in the eyes of him who sees it.

*

I admire him who reveals his mind to me; I honor him who unveils his dreams. But why am I shy, and even a little ashamed before him who serves me?

*

The gifted were once proud in serving princes.

Now they claim honor in serving paupers.

*

The angels know that too many practical men eat their bread with the sweat of the dreamer's brow.

*

Wit is often a mask. If you could tear it you would find either a genius irritated or cleverness juggling.

*

The understanding attributes to me understanding and the dull, dullness. I think they are both right.

*

Only those with secrets in their hearts could divine the secrets in our hearts.

*

He who would share your pleasure but not your pain shall lose the key to one of the seven gates of Paradise.

*

Yes, there is a Nirvanah; it is in leading your sheep to a green pasture, and in putting your child to sleep, and in writing the last line of your poem.

*

We choose our joys and our sorrows long before we experience them.

*

Sadness is but a wall between two gardens.

*

When either your joy or your sorrow becomes great the world becomes small.

*

Desire is half of life; indifference is half of death.

*

The bitterest thing in our today's sorrow is the memory of our yesterday's joy.

*

They say to me, "You must needs choose between the pleasures of this world and the peace of the next world."

And I say to them "I have chosen both the delights of this world and the peace of the next. For I know in my heart that the Supreme Poet wrote but one poem, and it scans perfectly, and it also rhymes perfectly."

*

Faith is an oasis in the heart which will never be reached by the caravan of thinking.

*

When you reach your height you shall desire but only for desire; and you shall hunger, for hunger; and you shall thirst for greater thirst.

*

If you reveal your secrets to the wind you should not blame the wind for revealing them to the trees.

*

The flowers of spring are winter's dreams related at the breakfast table of the angels.

*

Said a skunk to a tube-rose, "See how swiftly I run, while you cannot walk nor even creep."

Said the tube-rose to the skunk, "Oh, most noble swift runner, please run swiftly!"

*

Turtles can tell more about roads than hares.

*

Strange that creatures without backbones have the hardest shells.

*

The most talkative is the least intelligent, and there is hardly a difference between an orator and an auctioneer.

*

Be grateful that you do not have to live down the renown of a father nor the wealth of an uncle.

But above all be grateful that no one will have to live down either your renown or your wealth.

*

Only when a juggler misses catching his ball does he appeal to me.

*

The envious praises me unknowingly.

*

Long were you a dream in your mother's sleep, and then she woke to give you birth.

*

The germ of the race is in your mother's longing.

*

My father and mother desired a child and they begot me.

And I wanted a mother and a father and I begot night and the sea.

*

Some of our children are our justifications and some are but our regrets.

*

When night comes and you too are dark, lie down and be dark with a will.

And when morning comes and you are still dark stand up and say to the day with a will, "I am still dark."

It is stupid to play a role with the night and the day.

They would both laugh at you.

*

The mountain veiled in mist is not a hill; an oak tree in the rain is not a weeping willow.

*

Behold here is a paradox; the deep and high are nearer to one another than the mid-level to either.

*

When I stood a clear mirror before you, you gazed into me and saw your image.

Then you said, "I love you."

But in truth you loved yourself in me.

*

When you enjoy loving your neighbor it ceases to be a virtue.

*

Love which is not always springing is always dying.

*

You cannot have youth and the knowledge of it at the same time;

For youth is too busy living to know, and knowledge is too busy seeking itself to live. You may sit at your window watching the passersby. And watching you may see a nun walking toward your right hand, and a prostitute toward your left hand.

And you may say in your innocence, "How noble is the one and how ignoble is the other."

But should you close your eyes and listen awhile you would hear a voice whispering in the ether, "One seeks me in prayer, and the other in pain. And in the spirit of each there is a bower for my spirit."

*

Once every hundred years Jesus of Nazareth meets Jesus of the Christian in a garden among the hills of Lebanon. And they talk long; and each time Jesus of Nazareth goes away saying to Jesus of the Christian, "My friend, I fear we shall never, never agree."

*

May God feed the over-abundant!

*

A great man has two hearts; one bleeds and the other forbears.

*

Should one tell a lie which does not hurt you nor anyone else, why not say in your heart that the house of his facts is too small for his fancies, and he had to leave it for larger space?

*

Behind every closed door is a mystery sealed with seven seals.

*

Waiting is the hoofs of time.

*

What if trouble should be a new window in the Eastern wall of your house?

*

You may forget the one with whom you have laughed, but never the one with whom you have wept.

*

There must be something strangely sacred in salt. It is in our tears and in the sea.

*

Our God in His gracious thirst will drink us all, the dewdrop and the tear.

*

You are but a fragment of your giant self, a mouth that seeks bread, and a blind hand that holds the cup for a thirsty mouth.

*

If you would rise but a cubit above race and country and self you would indeed become godlike.

*

If I were you I would not find fault with the sea at low tide.

It is a good ship and our Captain is able; it is only your stomach that is in disorder.

*

Should you sit upon a cloud you would not see the boundary line between one country and another, nor the boundary stone between a farm and a farm.

It is a pity you cannot sit upon a cloud.

*

Seven centuries ago seven white doves rose from a deep valley flying to the snow-white summit of the mountain. One of the seven men who watched the flight said, "I see a black spot on the wing of the seventh dove."

Today the people in that valley tell of seven black doves who flew to the summit of the snowy mountain.

*

In the autumn I gathered all my sorrows and buried them in my garden.

And when April returned and spring came to wed the earth, there grew in my garden beautiful flowers unlike all other flowers.

And my neighbors came to behold them, and they all said to me, "When autumn comes again, at seeding time, will you not give us of the seeds of these flowers that we may have them in our gardens?"

*

It is indeed misery if I stretch an empty hand to men and receive nothing; but it is hopelessness if I stretch a full hand and find none to receive.

*

I long for eternity because there I shall meet my unwritten poems and my unpainted pictures.

*

Art is a step from nature toward the Infinite.

*

A work of art is a mist carved into an image.

*

Even the hands that make crowns of thorns are better than idle hands.

*

Our most sacred tears never seek our eyes.

*

Every man is the descendant of every king and every slave that ever lived.

*

If the great-grandfather of Jesus had known what was hidden within him, would he not have stood in awe of himself?

*

Was the love of Judas' mother of her son less than the love of Mary for Jesus?

*

There are three miracles of our Brother Jesus not yet recorded in the Book: the first that He was a man like you and me, the second that He had a sense of humour, and the third that He knew He was a conqueror though conquered.

*

Crucified One, you are crucified upon my heart; and the nails that pierce your hands pierce the walls of my heart.

And tomorrow when a stranger passes by this Golgotha he will not know that two bled here.

He will deem it the blood of one man.

*

You may have heard of the Blessed Mountain.

It is the highest mountain in our world.

Should you reach the summit you would have only one desire, and that to descend and be with those who dwell in the deepest valley.

That is why it is called the Blessed Mountain.

*

Every thought I have imprisoned in expression I must free by my deeds.

*

BOOK THREE.
JESUS THE SON OF MAN

His words and His deeds as told and recorded by those who knew Him

JAMES, THE SON OF ZEBEDEE

On the Kingdoms of the World

Upon a day in the spring of the year Jesus stood in the market-place of Jerusalem and He spoke to the multitudes of the kingdom of heaven.

And He accused the scribes and the Pharisees of setting snares and digging pitfalls in the path of those who long after the kingdom; and He denounced them.

Now amongst the crowd was a company of men who defended the Pharisees and the scribes, and they sought to lay hands upon Jesus and upon us also.

But He avoided them and turned aside from them, and walked towards the north gate of the city.

And He said to us, "My hour has not yet come. Many are the things I have still to say unto you, and many are the deeds I shall yet perform ere I deliver myself up to the world."

Then He said, and there was joy and laughter in His voice, "Let us go into the North Country and meet the spring. Come with me to the hills, for winter is past and the snows of Lebanon are descending to the valleys to sing with the brooks.

"The fields and the vineyards have banished sleep and are awake to greet the sun with their green figs and tender grapes."

And He walked before us and we followed Him, that day and the next.

And upon the afternoon of the third day we reached the summit of Mount Hermon, and there He stood looking down upon the cities of the plains.

And His face shone like molten gold, and He outstretched His arms and He said to us, "Behold the earth in her green raiment, and see how the streams have hemmed the edges of her garments with silver.

"In truth the earth is fair and all that is upon her is fair.

"But there is a kingdom beyond all that you behold, and therein I shall rule. And if it is your choice, and if it is indeed your desire, you too shall come and rule with me.

"My face and your faces shall not be masked; our hand shall hold neither sword nor sceptre, and our subjects shall love us in peace and shall not be in fear of us."

Thus spoke Jesus, and unto all the kingdoms of the earth I was blinded, and unto all the cities of walls and towers; and it was in my heart to follow the Master to His kingdom.

Then just at that moment Judas of Iscariot stepped forth. And he walked up to Jesus, and spoke and said, "Behold, the kingdoms of the world are vast, and behold the cities of David and Solomon shall prevail against the Romans. If you will be the king of the Jews we shall stand beside you with sword and shield and we shall overcome the alien."

But when Jesus heard this He turned upon Judas, and His face was filled with wrath. And He spoke in a voice terrible as the thunder of the sky and He said, "Get you behind me, Satan. Think you that I came down the years to rule an ant-hill for a day?

"My throne is a throne beyond your vision. Shall he whose wings encircle the earth seek shelter in a nest abandoned and forgotten?

"Shall the living be honoured and exalted by the wearer of shrouds?"

"My kingdom is not of this earth, and my seat is not builded upon the skulls of your ancestors.

"If you seek aught save the kingdom of the spirit then it were better for you to leave me here, and go down to the caves of your dead, where the crowned heads of yore hold court in their tombs and may still be bestowing honours upon the bones of your forefathers.

"Dare you tempt me with a crown of dross, when my forehead seeks the Pleiades, or else your thorns?

"Were it not for a dream dreamed by a forgotten race I would not suffer your sun to rise upon my patience, nor your moon to throw my shadow across your path.

"Were it not for a mother's desire I would have stripped me of the swaddling-clothes and escaped back to space.

"And were it not for sorrow in all of you I would not have stayed to weep.

"Who are you and what are you, Judas Iscariot? And why do you tempt me?

"Have you in truth weighed me in the scale and found me one to lead legions of pygmies, and to direct chariots of the shapeless against an enemy that encamps only in your hatred and marches nowhere but in your fear?

"Too many are the worms that crawl about me feet, and I will give them no battle. I am weary of the jest, and weary of pitying the creepers who deem me coward because I will not move among their guarded walls and towers.

"Pity it is that I must needs pity to the very end. Would that I could turn my steps towards a larger world where larger men dwell. But how shall I?

"Your priest and your emperor would have my blood. They shall be satisfied ere I go hence. I would not change the course of the law. And I would not govern folly.

"Let ignorance reproduce itself until it is weary of its own offspring.

"Let the blind lead the blind to the pitfall.

"And let the dead bury the dead till the earth be choked with its own bitter fruit.

"My kingdom is not of the earth. My kingdom shall be where two or three of you shall meet in love, and in wonder at the loveliness of life, and in good cheer, and in remembrance of me."

Then of a sudden He turned to Judas, and He said, "Get you behind me, man. Your kingdoms shall never be in my kingdom."

And now it was twilight, and He turned to us and said, "Let us go down. The night is upon us. Let us walk in light while the light is with us."

Then He went down from the hills and we followed Him. And Judas followed afar off.

And when we reached the lowland it was night.

And Thomas, the son of Diophanes, said unto Him, "Master, it is dark now, and we can no longer see the way. If it is in your will, lead us to the lights of yonder village where we may find meat and shelter."

And Jesus answered Thomas, and He said, "I have led you to the heights when you were hungry, and I have brought you down to the plains with a greater hunger. But I cannot stay with you this night. I would be alone."

Then Simon Peter stepped forth, and said:

Master, suffer us not to go alone in the dark. Grant that we may stay with you even here on this byway. The night and the shadows of the night will not linger, and the morning shall soon find us if you will but stay with us."

And Jesus answered, "This night the foxes shall have their holes, and the birds of the air their nests, but the Son of Man has not where on earth to lay His head. And indeed I would now be alone. Should you desire me you will find me again by the lake where I found you."

Then we walked away from Him with heavy hearts, for it was not in our will to leave Him.

Many times did we stop and turn our faces towards Him, and we saw him in lonely majesty, moving westward.

The only man among us who did not turn to behold Him in His aloneness was Judas Iscariot.

And from that day Judas became sullen and distant. And methought there was danger in the sockets of his eyes.

ANNA, THE MOTHER OF MARY

On the Birth of Jesus

Jesus the son of my daughter, was born here in Nazareth in the month of January. And the night that Jesus was born we were visited by men from the East. They were Persians who came to Esdraelon with the caravans of the Midianites on their way to Egypt. And because they did not find rooms at the inn they sought shelter in our house.

And I welcomed them and I said, "My daughter has given birth to a son this night. Surely you will forgive me if I do not serve you as it behoves a hostess."

Then they thanked me for giving them shelter. And after they had supped they said to me: "We would see the new-born."

Now the Son of Mary was beautiful to behold, and she too was comely.

And when the Persians beheld Mary and her babe, they took gold and silver from their bags, and myrrh and frankincense, and laid them all at the feet of the child.

Then they fell down and prayed in a strange tongue which we did not understand.

And when I led them to the bedchamber prepared for them they walked as if they were in awe at what they had seen.

When morning was come they left us and followed the road to Egypt.

But at parting they spoke to me and said, "The child is not but a day old, yet we have seen the light of our God in His eyes and the smile of our God upon His mouth.

"We bid you protect Him that He may protect you all."

And so saying, they mounted their camels and we saw them no more.

Now Mary seemed not so much joyous in her first-born, as full of wonder and surprise.

She would look upon her babe, and then turn her face to the window and gaze far away into the sky as if she saw visions.

And there were valleys between her heart and mine.

And the child grew in body and in spirit, and He was different from other children. He was aloof and hard to govern, and I could not lay my hand upon Him.

But He was beloved by everyone in Nazareth, and in my heart I knew why.

Oftentimes He would take away our food to give to the passer-by. And He would give other children the sweetmeat I had given Him, before He had tasted it with His own mouth.

He would climb the trees of my orchard to get the fruits, but never to eat them Himself.

And He would race with other boys, and sometimes, because He was swifter of foot, He would delay so that they might pass the stake ere He should reach it.

And sometimes when I led Him to His bed He would say, "Tell my mother and the others that only my body will sleep. My mind will be with them till their mind come to my morning."

And many other wondrous words He said when He was a boy, but I am too old to remember.

Now they tell me I shall see Him no more. But how shall I believe what they say?

I still hear His laughter, and the sound of His running about my house. And whenever I kiss the cheek of my daughter His fragrance returns to my heart, and His body seems to fill my arms.

But is it not passing strange that my daughter does not speak of her first-born to me?

Sometimes it seems that my longing for Him is greater than hers. She stands as firm before the day as if she were a bronzen image, while my heart melts and runs into streams.

Perhaps she knows what I do not know. Would that she might tell me also.

ASSAPH,
CALLED THE ORATOR OF TYRE

On the Speech of Jesus

What shall I say of His speech? Perhaps something about His person lent power to His words and swayed those who heard Him. For He was comely, and the sheen of the day was upon His countenance.

Men and women gazed at Him more than they listened to His argument. But at times He spoke with the power of a spirit, and that spirit had authority over those who heard Him.

In my youth I had heard the orators of Rome and Athens and Alexandria. The young Nazarene was unlike them all.

They assembled their words with an art to enthral the ear, but when you heard Him your heart would leave you and go wandering into regions not yet visited.

He would tell a story or relate a parable, and the like of His stories and parables had never been heard in Syria. He seemed to spin them out of the seasons, even as time spins the years and the generations.

He would begin a story thus: "The ploughman went forth to the field to sow his seeds."

Or, "Once there was a rich man who had many vineyards."

Or, "A shepherd counted his sheep at eventide and found that one sheep was missing."

And such words would carry His listeners into their simpler selves, and into the ancient of their days.

At heart we are all ploughmen, and we all love the vineyard. And in the pastures of our memory there is a shepherd and a flock and the lost sheep.

And there is the plough-share and the winepress and the threshing-floor.

He knew the source of our older self, and the persistent thread of which we are woven.

The Greek and the Roman orators spoke to their listeners of life as it seemed to the mind. The Nazarene spoke of a longing that lodged in the heart.

They saw life with eyes only a little clearer than yours and mine. He saw life in the light of God.

I often think that He spoke to the crowd as a mountain would speak to the plain.

And in His speech there was a power that was not commanded by the orators of Athens or of Rome.

MARY MAGDALENE

On Meeting Jesus for the First Time

It was in the month of June when I saw Him for the first time. He was walking in the wheat field when I passed by with my handmaidens, and He was alone.

The rhythm of His steps was different from other men's, and the movement of His body was like naught I had seen before.

Men do not pace the earth in that manner. And even now I do not know whether He walked fast or slow.

My handmaidens pointed their fingers at Him and spoke in shy whispers to one another. And I stayed my steps for a moment, and raised my hand to hail Him. But He did not turn His face, and He did not look at me. And I hated Him. I was swept back into myself, and I was as cold as if I had been in a snow-drift. And I shivered.

That night I beheld Him in my dreaming; and they told me afterward that I screamed in my sleep and was restless upon my bed.

It was in the month of August that I saw Him again, through my window. He was sitting in the shadow of the cypress tree across my garden, and He was still as if He had been carved out of stone, like the statues in Antioch and other cities of the North Country.

And my slave, the Egyptian, came to me and said, "That man is here again. He is sitting there across your garden."

And I gazed at Him, and my soul quivered within me, for He was beautiful.

His body was single and each part seemed to love every other part.

Then I clothed myself with raiment of Damascus, and I left my house and walked towards Him.

Was it my aloneness, or was it His fragrance, that drew me to Him? Was it a hunger in my eyes that desired comeliness, or was it His beauty that sought the light of my eyes?

Even now I do not know.

I walked to Him with my scented garments and my golden sandals, the sandals the Roman captain had given me, even these sandals. And when I reached Him, I said, "Good-morrow to you."

And He said, "Good-morrow to you, Miriam."

And He looked at me, and His night-eyes saw me as no man had seen me. And suddenly I was as if naked, and I was shy.

Yet He had only said, "Good-morrow to you."

And then I said to Him, "Will you not come to my house?"

And He said, "Am I not already in your house?"

I did not know what He meant then, but I know now.

And I said, "Will you not have wine and bread with me?"

And He said, "Yes, Miriam, but not now."

Not now, not now, He said. And the voice of the sea was in those two words, and the voice of the wind and the trees. And when He said them unto me, life spoke to death.

For mind you, my friend, I was dead. I was a woman who had divorced her soul. I was living apart from this self which you now see. I belonged to all men, and to none. They called me harlot, and a woman possessed of seven devils. I was cursed, and I was envied.

But when His dawn-eyes looked into my eyes all the stars of my night faded away, and I became Miriam, only Miriam, a woman lost to the earth she had known, and finding herself in new places.

And now again I said to Him, "Come into my house and share bread and wine with me."

And He said, "Why do you bid me to be your guest?"

And I said, "I beg you to come into my house." And it was all that was sod in me, and all that was sky in me calling unto Him.

Then He looked at me, and the noontide of His eyes was upon me, and He said, "You have many lovers, and yet I alone love you. Other men love themselves in your nearness. I love you in your self. Other men see a beauty in you that shall fade away sooner than their own years. But I see in you a beauty that shall not fade away, and in the autumn of your days that beauty shall not be afraid to gaze at itself in the mirror, and it shall not be offended.

"I alone love the unseen in you."

Then He said in a low voice, "Go away now. If this cypress tree is yours and you would not have me sit in its shadow, I will walk my way."

And I cried to Him and I said, "Master, come to my house. I have incense to burn for you, and a silver basin for your feet. You are a stranger and yet not a stranger. I entreat you, come to my house."

Then He stood up and looked at me even as the seasons might look down upon the field, and He smiled. And He said again: "All men love you for themselves. I love you for yourself."

And then He walked away.

But no other man ever walked the way He walked. Was it a breath born in my garden that moved to the east? Or was it a storm that would shake all things to their foundations?

I knew not, but on that day the sunset of His eyes slew the dragon in me, and I became a woman, I became Miriam, Miriam of Mijdel.

PHILEMON, A GREEK APOTHECARY

On Jesus the Master Physician

The Nazarene was the Master Physician of His people. No other man knew so much of our bodies and of their elements and properties.

He made whole those who were afflicted with diseases unknown to the Greeks and the Egyptians. They say He even called back the dead to life. And whether this be true or not true, it declares His power; for only to him who has wrought great things is the greatest ever attributed.

They say also that Jesus visited India and the Country between the Two Rivers, and that there the priests revealed to Him the knowledge of all that is hidden in the recesses of our flesh.

Yet that knowledge may have been given to Him direct by the gods, and not through the priests. For that which has remained unknown to all men for an eon may be disclosed to one man in but a moment. And Apollo may lay his hand on the heart of the obscure and make it wise.

Many doors were open to the Tyrians and the Thebans, and to this man also certain sealed doors were opened. He entered the temple of the soul, which is the body; and He beheld the evil spirits that conspire against our sinews, and also the good spirits that spin the threads thereof.

Methinks it was by the power of opposition and resistance that He healed the sick, but in a manner unknown to our philosophers. He astonished fever with His snow-like touch and it retreated; and He surprised the hardened limbs with His own calm and they yielded to Him and were at peace.

He knew the ebbing sap within the furrowed bark – but how He reached the sap with His fingers I do not know. He knew the sound steel underneath the rust – but how He freed the sword and made it shine no man can tell.

Sometimes it seems to me that He heard the murmuring pain of all things that grow in the sun, and that then He lifted them up and supported them, not only by His own knowledge, but also by disclosing to them their own power to rise and become whole.

Yet He was not much concerned with Himself as a physician. He was rather preoccupied with the religion and the politics of this land. And this I regret, for first of all things we must needs be sound of body.

But these Syrians, when they are visited by an illness, seek an argument rather than medicine.

And pity it is that the greatest of all their physicians chose rather to be but a maker of speeches in the market-place.

SIMON, WHO WAS CALLED PETER

When He and His Brother were Called

I was on the shore of the Lake of Galilee when I first beheld Jesus my Lord and my Master.

My brother Andrew was with me and we were casting out net into the waters.

The waves were rough and high and we caught but few fish. And our hearts were heavy.

Suddenly Jesus stood near us, as if He had taken form that very moment, for we had not seen Him approaching.

He called us by our names, and He said, "If you will follow me I will lead you to an inlet where the fishes are swarming."

And as I looked at His face the net fell from my hands, for a flame kindled within me and I recognized Him.

And my brother Andrew spoke and said, "We know all the inlets upon these shores, and we know also that on a windy day like this the fish seek a depth beyond our nets."

And Jesus answered, "Follow me to the shores of a greater sea. I shall make you fishers of men. And your net shall never be empty."

And we abandoned our boat and our net and followed Him.

I myself was drawn by a power, viewless, that walked beside His person.

I walked near Him, breathless and full of wonder, and my brother Andrew was behind us, bewildered and amazed.

And as we walked on the sand I made bold and said unto Him, "Sir, I and my brother will follow your footsteps, and where you go we too will go. But if it please you to come to our house this night, we shall be graced by your visit. Our house is not large and our ceiling not high, and you will sit at but a frugal meal. Yet if you will abide in our hovel it will be to us a palace.

And would you break bread with us, we in your presence were to be envied by the princes of the land."

And He said, "Yea, I will be your guest this night."

And I rejoiced in my heart. And we walked behind Him in silence until we reached our house.

And as we stood at the threshold Jesus said, "Peace be to this house, and to those who dwell in it."

Then He entered and we followed Him.

My wife and my wife's mother and my daughter stood before Him and they worshipped Him; then they knelt before Him and kissed the hem of His sleeve.

They were astonished that He, the chosen and the well beloved, had come to be our guest; for they had already seen Him by the River Jordan when John the Baptist had proclaimed Him before the people.

And straightway my wife and my wife's mother began to prepare the supper.

My brother Andrew was a shy man, but his faith in Jesus was deeper than my faith.

And my daughter, who was then but twelve year old, stood by Him and held His garment as if she were in fear He would leave us and go out again into the night. She clung to Him like a lost sheep that has found its shepherd.

Then we sat at the board, and He broke the bread and poured the wine; and He turned to us saying, "My friends, grace me now in sharing this food with me, even as the Father has graced us in giving it unto us."

These words He said ere He touched a morsel, for He wished to follow an ancient custom that the honoured guest becomes the host.

And as we sat with Him around the board we felt as if we were sitting at the feast of the great King.

My daughter Petronelah, who was young and unknowing, gazed at His face and followed the movements of His hands. And I saw a veil of tears in her eyes.

When He left the board we followed Him and sat about Him in the vine-arbour.

And He spoke to us and we listened, and our hearts fluttered within us like birds.

He spoke of the second birth of man, and of the opening of the gates of the heavens; and of angels descending and bringing peace and good cheer to all men, and of angels ascending to the throne bearing the longings of men to the Lord God.

Then He looked into my eyes and gazed into the depths of my heart. And He said, "I have chosen you and your brother, and you must needs come with me. You have laboured and you have been heavy-laden. Now I shall give you rest. Take up my yoke and learn of me, for in my heart is peace, and your soul shall find abundance and a home-coming."

When He spoke thus I and my brother stood up before Him, and I said to Him, "Master, we will follow you to the ends of the earth. And if our burden were as heavy as the mountain we would bear it with you in gladness. And should we fall by the wayside we shall know that we have fallen on the way to heaven, and we shall be satisfied."

And my brother Andrew spoke and said, "Master, we would be threads between your hands and your loom. Weave us into the cloth if you will, for we would be in the raiment of the Most High."

And my wife raised her face, and the tears were upon her cheeks and she spoke with joy, and she said, "Blessed are you who come in the name of the Lord. Blessed is the womb that carried you, and the breast that gave you milk."

And my daughter, who was but twelve years old, sat at His feet and she nestled close to Him.

And the mother of my wife, who sat at the threshold, said no word. She only wept in silence and her shawl was wet with her tears.

Then Jesus walked over to her and He raised her face to His face and He said to her, "You are the mother of all these. You weep for joy, and I will keep your tears in my memory."

And now the old moon rose above the horizon. And Jesus gazed upon it for a moment, and then He turned to us and said, "It is late. Seek your beds, and may God visit your repose. I will be here in this arbour until dawn. I have cast my net this day and I have caught two men; I am satisfied, and now I bid you good-night."

Then my wife's mother said, "But we have laid your bed in the house, I pray you enter and rest."

And He answered her saying, "I would indeed rest, but not under a roof. Suffer me to lie this night under the canopy of the grapes and the stars."

And she made haste and brought out the mattress and the pillows and the coverings. And He smiled at her and He said, "Behold, I shall lie down upon a bed twice made."

Then we left Him and entered into the house, and my daughter was the last one to enter. And her eyes were upon Him until I had closed the door.

Thus for the first time I knew my Lord and Master.

And though it was many years ago, it still seems but of today.

CAIAPHAS, THE HIGH PRIEST

In speaking of that man Jesus and of His death let us consider two salient facts: the Torah must needs be held in safety by us, and this kingdom must needs be protected by Rome.

Now that man was defiant to us and to Rome. He poisoned the mind of the simple people, and He led them as if by magic against us and against Caesar.

My own slaves, both men and women, after hearing him speak in the market-place, turned sullen and rebellious. Some of them left my house and escaped to the desert whence they came.

Forget not that the Torah is our foundation and our tower of strength. No man shall undermine us while we have this power to restrain his hand, and no man shall overthrow Jerusalem so long as its walls stand upon the ancient stone that David laid.

If the seed of Abraham is indeed to live and thrive this soil must remain undefiled.

And that man Jesus was a defiler and a corrupter. We slew Him with a conscience both deliberate and clean. And we shall slay all those who would debase the laws of Moses or seek to befoul our sacred heritage.

We and Pontius Pilatus knew the danger in that man, and that it was wise to bring Him to an end.

I shall see that His followers come to the same end, and the echo of His words to the same silence.

If Judea is to live all men who oppose her must be brought down to the dust. And ere Judea shall die I will cover my grey head with ashes even as did Samuel the prophet, and I will tear off this garment of Aaron and clothe me in sackcloth until I go hence for ever.

JOANNA,
THE WIFE OF HEROD'S STEWARD

On Children

Jesus was never married but He was a friend of women, and He knew them as they would be known in sweet comradeship.

And He loved children as they would be loved in faith and understanding.

In the light of His eyes there was a father and a brother and a son.

He would hold a child upon His knees and say, "Of such is your might and your freedom; and of such is the kingdom of the spirit."

They say that Jesus heeded not the law of Moses, and that He was over-forgiving to the prostitutes of Jerusalem and the country side.

I myself at that time was deemed a prostitute, for I loved a man who was not my husband, and he was a Sadducee.

And on a day the Sadducees came upon me in my house when my lover was with me, and they seized me and held me, and my lover walked away and left me.

Then they led me to the market-place where Jesus was teaching.

it was their desire to hold me up before Him as a test and a trap for Him.

But Jesus judged me not. He laid shame upon those who would have had me shamed, and He reproached them.

And He bade me go my way.

And after that all the tasteless fruit of life turned sweet to my mouth, and the scentless blossoms breathed fragrance into my nostrils. I became a woman without a tainted memory, and I was free, and my head was no longer bowed down.

RAFCA,
The Bride of Cana

This happened before He was known to the people.

I was in my mother's garden tending the rose-bushes, when He stopped at our gate.

And He said, "I am thirsty. Will you give me water from your well?"

And I ran and brought the silver cup, and filled it with water; and I poured into it a few drops from the jasmine vial.

And He drank deep and was pleased.

Then He looked into my eyes and said, "My blessing shall be upon you."

When He said that I felt as it were a gust of wind rushing through my body. And I was no longer shy; and I said, "Sir, I am betrothed to a man of Cana in Galilee. And I shall be married on the fourth day of the coming week. Will you not come to my wedding and grace my marriage with your presence?"

And He answered, "I will come, my child."

Mind you, He said, "My child," yet He was but a youth, and I was nearly twenty.

Then He walked on down the road.

And I stood at the gate of our garden until my mother called me into the house.

On the fourth day of the following week I was taken to the house of my bridegroom and given in marriage.

And Jesus came, and with Him His mother and His brother James.

And they sat around the wedding-board with our guests whilst my maiden comrades sang the wedding-songs of Solomon the King. And Jesus ate our food and drank our wine and smiled upon me and upon the others.

And He heeded all the songs of the lover bringing his beloved into his tent; and of the young vineyard-keeper who loved the daughter of the lord of the vineyard and led her to his mother's house; and of the prince who met the beggar maiden and bore her to his realm and crowned her with the crown of his fathers.

And it seemed as if He were listening to yet other songs also, which I could not hear.

At sundown the father of my bridegroom came to the mother of Jesus and whispered saying, "We have no more wine for our guests. And the day is not yet over."

And Jesus heard the whispering, and He said, "The cup bearer knows that there is still more wine."

And so it was indeed – and as long as the guests remained there was fine wine for all who would drink.

Presently Jesus began to speak with us. He spoke of the wonders of earth and heaven; of sky flowers that bloom when night is upon the earth, and of earth flowers that blossom when the day hides the stars.

And He told us stories and parables, and His voice enchanted us so that we gazed upon Him as if seeing visions, and we forgot the cup and the plate.

And as I listened to Him it seemed as if I were in a land distant and unknown.

After a while one of the guests said to the father of my bridegroom, "You have kept the best wine till the end of the feast. Other hosts do not so."

And all believed that Jesus had wrought a miracle, that they should have more wine and better at the end of the wedding-feast than at the beginning.

I too thought that Jesus had poured the wine, but I was not astonished; for in His voice I had already listened to miracles.

And afterwards indeed, His voice remained close to my heart, even until I had been delivered of my first-born child.

And now even to this day in our village and in the villages near by, the word of our guest is still remembered. And they say, "The spirit of Jesus of Nazareth is the best and the oldest wine."

A PERSIAN PHILOSOPHER IN DAMASCUS

Of Ancient Gods and New

I cannot tell the fate of this man, nor can I say what shall befall His disciples.

A seed hidden in the heart of an apple is an orchard invisible. Yet should that seed fall upon a rock, it will come to naught.

But this I say: The ancient God of Israel is harsh and relentless. Israel should have another God; one who is gentle and forgiving, who would look down upon them with pity; one who would descend with the rays of the sun and walk on the path of their limitations, rather than sit for ever in the judgment seat to weigh their faults and measure their wrong-doings.

Israel should bring forth a God whose heart is not a jealous heart, and whose memory of their shortcomings is brief; one who would not avenge Himself upon them even to the third and the fourth generation.

Man here in Syria is like man in all lands. He would look into the mirror of his own understanding and therein find his deity. He would fashion the gods after his own likeness, and worship that which reflects his own image.

In truth man prays to his deeper longing, that it may rise and fulfil the sum of his desires.

There is no depth beyond the soul of man, and the soul is the deep that calls unto itself; for there is no other voice to speak and there are no other ears to hear.

Even we in Persia would see our faces in the disc of the sun and our bodies dancing in the fire that we kindle upon the altars.

Now the God of Jesus, whom He called Father, would not be a stranger unto the people of Jesus, and He would fulfil their desires.

The gods of Egypt have cast off their burden of stones and fled to the Nubian desert, to be free among those who are still free from knowing.

The gods of Greece and Rome are vanishing into their own sunset. They were too much like men to live in the ecstasy of men. The groves in which their magic was born have been cut down by the axes of the Athenians and the Alexandrians.

And in this land also the high places are made low by the lawyers of Beirut and the young hermits of Antioch.

Only the old women and the weary men seek the temples of their forefathers; only the exhausted at the end of the road seek its beginning.

But this man Jesus, this Nazarene, He has spoken of a God too vast to be unlike the soul of any man, too knowing to punish, too loving to remember the sins of His creatures. And this God of the Nazarene shall pass over the threshold of the children of the earth, and He shall sit at their hearth, and He shall be a blessing within their walls and a light upon their path.

But my God is the God of Zoroaster, the God who is the sun in the sky and fire upon the earth and light in the bosom of man. And I am content. I need no other God.

DAVID, ONE OF HIS FOLLOWERS

Jesus the Practical

I did not know the meaning of His discourses or His parables until He was no longer among us. Nay, I did not understand until His words took living forms before my eyes and fashioned themselves into bodies that walk in the procession of my own day.

Let me tell you this: On a night as I sat in my house pondering, and remembering His words and His deeds that I might inscribe them in a book, three thieves entered my house. And though I knew they came to rob me of my goods, I was too mindful of what I was doing to meet them with the sword, or even to say, "What do you here?"

But I continued writing my remembrances of the Master.

And when the thieves had gone then I remembered His saying, "He who would take your cloak, let him take your other cloak also."

And I understood.

As I sat recording His words no man could have stopped me even were he to have carried away all my possessions.

For though I would guard my possessions and also my person, I know there lies the greater treasure.

LUKE

On Hypocrites

Jesus despised and scorned the hypocrites, and His wrath was like a tempest that scourged them. His voice was thunder in their ears and He cowed them.

In their fear of Him they sought His death; and like moles in the dark earth they worked to undermine His footsteps. But He fell not into their snares.

He laughed at them, for well He knew that the spirit shall not be mocked, nor shall it be taken in the pitfall.

He held a mirror in His hand and therein He saw the sluggard and the limping and those who stagger and fall by the roadside on the way to the summit.

And He pitied them all. He would even have raised them to His stature and He would have carried their burden. Nay, He would have bid their weakness lean on His strength.

He did not utterly condemn the liar or the thief or the murderer, but He did utterly condemn the hypocrite whose face is masked and whose hand is gloved.

Often I have pondered on the heart that shelters all who come from the wasteland to its sanctuary, yet against the hypocrite is closed and sealed.

On a day as we rested with Him in the Garden of Pomegranates, I said to Him, "Master, you forgive and console the sinner and all the weak and the infirm save only the hypocrite alone."

And He said, "You have chosen your words well when you called the sinners weak and infirm. I do forgive them their weakness of body and their infirmity of spirit. For their failings have been laid upon them by their forefathers, or by the greed of their neighbours.

"But I tolerate not the hypocrite, because he himself lays a yoke upon the guileless and the yielding.

"Weaklings, whom you call sinners, are like the featherless young that fall from the nest. The hypocrite is the vulture waiting upon a rock for the death of the prey.

"Weaklings are men lost in a desert. But the hypocrite is not lost. He knows the way yet he laughs between the sand and the wind.

"For this cause I do not receive him."

Thus our Master spoke, and I did not understand. But I understand now.

Then the hypocrites of the land laid hands upon Him and they judged Him; and in so doing they deemed themselves justified. For they cited the law of Moses in the Sanhedrim in witness and evidence against Him.

And they who break the law at the rise of every dawn and break it again at sunset, brought about His death.

MATTHEW

The Sermon on the Mount

One harvest day Jesus called us and His other friends to the hills. The earth was fragrant, and like the daughter of a king at her wedding-feast, she wore all her jewels. And the sky was her bridegroom.

When we reached the heights Jesus stood still in the grove of the laurels, and He said, "Rest here, quiet your mind and tune your heart, for I have much to tell you."

Then we reclined on the grass, and the summer flowers were all about us, and Jesus sat in our midst.

And Jesus said:

"Blessed are the serene in spirit.

"Blessed are they who are not held by possessions, for they shall be free.

"Blessed are they who remember their pain, and in their pain await their joy.

"Blessed are they who hunger after truth and beauty, for their hunger shall bring bread, and their thirst cool water.

"Blessed are the kindly, for they shall be consoled by their own kindliness.

"Blessed are the pure in heart, for they shall be one with God.

"Blessed are the merciful, for mercy shall be in their portion.

"Blessed are the peacemakers, for their spirit shall dwell above the battle, and they shall turn the potter's field into a garden.

"Blessed are they who are hunted, for they shall be swift of foot and they shall be winged.

"Rejoice and be joyful, for you have found the kingdom of heaven within you. The singers of old were persecuted when they sang of that kingdom. You too shall be persecuted, and therein lies your honour, therein your reward.

"You are the salt of the earth; should the salt lose its savour wherewith shall the food of man's heart be salted?

"You are the light of the world. Put not that light under a bushel. Let it shine rather from the summit, to those who seek the City of God.

"Think not I came to destroy the laws of the scribes and the Pharisees; for my days among you are numbered and my words are counted, and I have but hours in which to fulfil another law and reveal a new covenant.

"You have been told that you shall not kill, but I say unto you, you shall not be angry without a cause.

"You have been charged by the ancients to bring your calf and your lamb and your dove to the temple, and to slay them upon the altar, that the nostrils of God may feed upon the odour of their fat, and that you may be forgiven your failings.

"But I say unto you, would you give God that which was His own from the beginning; and would you appease Him whose throne is above the silent deep and whose arms encircle space?

"Rather, seek out your brother and be reconciled unto him ere you seek the temple; and be a loving giver unto your neighbour. For in the soul of these God has builded a temple that shall not be destroyed, and in their heart He has raised an altar that shall never perish.

"You have been told, an eye for an eye and a tooth for a tooth. But I say unto you: Resist not evil, for resistance is food unto evil and makes it strong. And only the weak would revenge themselves. The strong of soul forgive, and it is honour in the injured to forgive.

"Only the fruitful tree is shaken or stoned for food.

"Be not heedful of the morrow, but rather gaze upon today, for sufficient for today is the miracle thereof.

"Be not over-mindful of yourself when you give but be mindful of the necessity. For every giver himself receives from the Father, and that much more abundantly.

"And give to each according to his need; for the Father gives not salt to the thirsty, nor a stone to the hungry, nor milk to the weaned.

"And give not that which is holy to dogs; nor cast your pearls before swine. For with such gifts you mock them; and they also shall mock your gift, and in their hate would fain destroy you.

"Lay not up for yourselves treasures that corrupt or that thieves may steal away. Lay up rather treasure which shall not corrupt or be stolen, and whose loveliness increases when many eyes behold it. For where your treasure is, your heart is also.

"You have been told that the murderer shall be put to the sword, that the thief shall be crucified, and the harlot stoned. But I say unto you that you are not free from wrongdoing of the murderer and the thief and the harlot, and when they are punished in the body your own spirit is darkened.

"Verily no crime is committed by one man or one woman. All crimes are committed by all. And he who pays the penalty may be breaking a link in the chain that hangs upon your own ankles. Perhaps he is paying with his sorrow the price for your passing joy."

Thus spake Jesus, and it was in my desire to kneel down and worship Him, yet in my shyness I could not move nor speak a word.

But at last I spoke; and I said, "I would pray this moment, yet my tongue is heavy. Teach me to pray."

And Jesus said, "When you would pray, let your longing pronounce the words. It is in my longing now to pray thus:

"Our Father in earth and heaven, sacred is Thy name.

Thy will be done with us, even as in space.

Give us of Thy bread sufficient for the day.

In Thy compassion forgive us and enlarge us to forgive one another.

Guide us towards Thee and stretch down Thy hand to us in darkness.

For Thine is the kingdom, and in Thee is our power and our fulfilment."

And it was now evening, and Jesus walked down from the hills, and all of us followed Him. And as I followed I was repeating His prayer, and remembering all that He had said; for I knew that the words that had fallen like flakes that day must set and grow firm like crystals, and that wings that had fluttered above our heads were to beat the earth like iron hoofs.

JOHN,
THE SON OF ZEBEDEE

On the Various Appellations of Jesus

You have remarked that some of us call Jesus the Christ, and some the Word, and others call Him the Nazarene, and still others the Son of Man.

I will try to make these names clear in the light that is given me.

The Christ, He who was in the ancient of days, is the flame of God that dwells in the spirit of man. He is the breath of life that visits us, and takes unto Himself a body like our bodies.

He is the will of the Lord.

He is the first Word, which would speak with our voice and live in our ear that we may heed and understand.

And the Word of the Lord our God built a house of flesh and bones, and was man like unto you and myself.

For we could not hear the song of the bodiless wind nor see our greater self walking in the mist.

Many times the Christ has come to the world, and He has walked many lands. And always He has been deemed a stranger and a madman.

Yet the sound of His voice descended never to emptiness, for the memory of man keeps that which his mind takes no care to keep.

This is the Christ, the innermost and the height, who walks with man towards eternity.

Have you not heard of Him at the cross-roads of India? And in the land of the Magi, and upon the sands of Egypt?

And here in your North Country your bards of old sang of Prometheus, the fire-bringer, he who was the desire of man fulfilled, the caged hope made free; and Orpheus, who came with a voice and a lyre to quicken the spirit in beast and man.

And know you not of Mithra the king, and of Zoroaster the prophet of the Persians, who woke from man's ancient sleep and stood at the bed of our dreaming?

We ourselves become man anointed when we meet in the Temple Invisible, once every thousand years. Then comes one forth embodied, and at His coming our silence turns to singing.

Yet our ears turn not always to listening nor our eyes to seeing.

Jesus the Nazarene was born and reared like ourselves; His mother and father were like our parents, and He was a man.

But the Christ, the Word, who was in the beginning, the Spirit who would have us live our fuller life, came unto Jesus and was with Him.

And the Spirit was the versed hand of the Lord, and Jesus was the harp.

The Spirit was the psalm, and Jesus was the turn thereof.

And Jesus, the Man of Nazareth, was the host and the mouthpiece of the Christ, who walked with us in the sun and who called us His friends.

In those days the hills of Galilee and her valleys heard but His voice. And I was a youth then, and trod in His path and pursued His footprints.

I pursued His footprints and trod in His path, to hear the words of the Christ from the lips of Jesus of Galilee.

Now you would know why some of us call Him the Son of Man.

He Himself desired to be called by that name, for He knew the hunger and the thirst of man, and He beheld man seeking after His greater self.

The Son of Man was Christ the Gracious, who would be with us all.

He was Jesus the Nazarene who would lead His brothers to the Anointed One, even to the Word which was in the beginning with God.

In my heart dwells Jesus of Galilee, the Man above men, the Poet who makes poets of us all, the Spirit who knocks at our door that we may wake and rise and walk out to meet truth naked and unencumbered.

A YOUNG PRIEST OF CAPERNAUM

Of Jesus the Magician

He was a magician, warp and woof, and a sorcerer, a man who bewildered the simple by charms and incantations. And He juggled with the words of our prophets and with the sanctities of our forefathers.

Aye, He even bade the dead be His witnesses, and the voiceless graves His forerunners and authority.

He sought the women of Jerusalem and the women of the countryside with the cunning of the spider that seeks the fly; and they were caught in His web.

For women are weak and empty-headed, and they follow the man who would comfort their unspent passion with soft and tender words. Were it not for these women, infirm and possessed by His evil spirit, His name would have been erased from the memory of man.

And who were the men who followed Him?

They were of the horde that are yoked and trodden down. In their ignorance and fear they would never have rebelled against their rightful masters. But when He promised them high stations in His kingdom of mirage, they yielded to His fantasy as clay to the potter.

Know you not, the slave in his dreaming would always be master; and the weakling would be a lion?

The Galilean was a conjuror and a deceiver, a man who forgave the sins of all sinners that He might hear Hail and Hosanna from their unclean mouths; and who fed the faint heart of the hopeless and the wretched that He might have ears for His voice and a retinue at His command.

He broke the Sabbath with those who break that He might gain the support of the lawless; and He spoke ill of our high priests that He might win attention in Sanhedrim, and by opposition increase His fame.

I have said often that I hated that man. Ay, I hate Him more than I hate the Romans who govern our country. Even His coming was from Nazareth, a town cursed by our prophets, a dunghill of the Gentiles, from which no good shall ever proceed.

A RICH LEVI,
IN THE NEIGHBOURHOOD OF NAZARETH

Jesus the Good Carpenter

He was a good carpenter. The doors He fashioned were never unlocked by thieves, and the windows he made were always ready to open to the east wind and to the west.

And He made chests of cedar wood, polished and enduring, and ploughs and pitchforks strong and yielding to the hand.

And He carved lecterns for our synagogues. He carved them out of the golden mulberry; and on both sides of the support, where the sacred book lies, He chiselled wings outspreading; and under the support, heads of bulls and doves, and large-eyed deer.

All this He wrought in the manner of the Chaldeans and the Greeks. But there was that in His skill which was neither Chaldean nor Greek.

Now this my house was builded by many hands thirty years ago. I sought builders and carpenters in all the towns of Galilee. They had each the skill and the art of building, and I was pleased and satisfied with all that they did.

But come now, and behold two doors and a window that were fashioned by Jesus of Nazareth. They in their stability mock at all else in my house.

See you not that these two doors are different from all other doors? And this window opening to the east, is it not different from other windows?

All my doors and windows are yielding to the years save these which He made. They alone stand strong against the elements.

And see those cross-beams, how he placed them; and these nails, how they are driven from one side of the board, and then caught and fastened so firmly upon the other side.

And what is passing strange is that that labourer who was worthy the wages of two men received but the wage of one man; and that same labourer now is deemed a prophet in Israel.

Had I known then that this youth with saw and plane was a prophet, I would have begged Him to speak rather than work, and then I would have overpaid Him for his words.

And now I still have many men working in my house and fields. How shall I know the man whose own hand is upon his tool, from the man upon whose hand God lays His hand?

Yea, how shall I know God's hand?

A SHEPHERD IN SOUTH LEBANON

A Parable

It was late summer when He and three other men first walked upon that road yonder. It was evening, and He stopped and stood there at the end of the pasture.

I was playing upon my flute, and my flock was grazing all around me. When He stopped I rose and walked over and stood before Him.

And He asked me, "Where is the grave of Elijah? Is it not somewhere near this place?"

And I answered Him, "It is there, Sir, underneath that great heap of stones. Even unto this day every passer-by brings a stone and places it upon the heap."

And He thanked me and walked away, and His friends walked behind Him.

And after three days Ganaliel who was also a shepherd, said to me that the man who had passed by was a prophet in Judea; but I did not believe him. Yet I thought of that man for many a moon.

When spring came Jesus passed once more by this pasture, and this time He was alone.

I was not playing on my flute that day for I had lost a sheep and I was bereaved, and my heart was downcast within me.

And I walked towards Him and stood still before Him, for I desired to be comforted.

And He looked at me and said, "You do not play upon your flute this day. Whence is the sorrow in your eyes?" ý

And I answered, "A sheep from among my sheep is lost. I have sought her everywhere but I find her not. And I know not what to do."

And He was silent for a moment. Then He smiled upon me and said, "Wait here awhile and I will find your sheep." And He walked away and disappeared among the hills.

After an hour He returned, and my sheep was close behind Him. And as He stood before me, the sheep looked up into His face even as I was looking. Then I embraced her inn gladness.

And He put His hand upon my shoulder and said, "From this day you shall love this sheep more than any other in your flock, for she was lost and now she is found."

And again I embraced my sheep in gladness, and she came close to me, and I was silent.

But when I raised my head to thank Jesus, He was already walking afar off, and I had not the courage to follow Him.

JOHN THE BAPTIST

He Speaks in Prison to His Disciples

I am not silent in this foul hole while the voice of Jesus is heard on the battlefield. I am not to be held nor confined while He is free.

They tell me the vipers are coiling round His loins, but I answer: The vipers shall awaken His strength, and He shall crush them with His heel.

I am only the thunder of His lightning. Though I spoke first, His was the word and the purpose.

They caught me unwarned. Perhaps they will lay hands on Him also. Yet not before He has pronounced His word in full. And He shall overcome them.

His chariot shall pass over them, and the hoofs of His horses shall trample them, and He shall be triumphant.

They shall go forth with lance and sword, but He shall meet them with the power of the Spirit.

His blood shall run upon the earth, but they themselves shall know the wounds and the pain thereof, and they shall be baptized in their tears until they are cleansed of their sins.

Their legions shall march towards His cities with rams of iron, but on their way they shall be drowned in the River Jordan.

And His walls and His towers shall rise higher, and the shields of His warriors shall shine brighter in the sun.

They say I am in league with Him, and that our design is to urge the people to rise and revolt against the kingdom of Judea.

I answer, and would that I had flames for words: if they deem this pit of iniquity a kingdom, let it fall into destruction and be no more. Let it go the way Sodom and Gomorrah, and let this race be forgotten by God, and this land be turned to ashes.

Aye, behind these prison walls I am indeed an ally to Jesus of Nazareth, and He shall lead my armies, horse and foot. And I myself, though a captain, am not worthy to loose the strings of His sandals.

Go to Him and repeat my words, and then in my name beg Him for comfort and blessing.

I shall not be here long. At night 'twixt waking and waking I feel slow feet with measured steps treading above this body. And when I hearken, I hear the rain falling upon my grave.

Go to Jesus, and say that John of Kedron whose soul is filled with shadows and then emptied again, prays for Him, while the grave-digger stands close by, and the swordman outstretches his hand for his wages.

JOSEPH OF ARIMATHEA

On the Primal Aims of Jesus

You would know the primal aim of Jesus, and I would fain tell you. But none can touch with fingers the life of the blessed wine, nor see the sap that feeds the branches.

And though I have eaten of the grapes and have tasted the new vintage at the winepress, I cannot tell you all.

I can only relate what I know of Him.

Our Master and our Beloved lived but three prophet's seasons. They were the spring of His song, the summer of His ecstasy, and the autumn of His passion; and each season was a thousand years.

The spring of His song was spent in Galilee. It was there that He gathered His lovers about Him, and it was on the shores of the blue lake that He first spoke of the Father, and of our release and our freedom.

By the Lake of Galilee we lost ourselves to find our way to the Father; and oh, the little loss that turned to such gain.

It was there the angels sang in our ears and bade us leave the arid land for the garden of heart's desire.

He spoke of fields and green pastures; of the slopes of Lebanon where the white lilies are heedless of the caravans passing in the dust of the valley.

He spoke of the wild brier that smiles in the sun and yields its incense to the passing breeze.

And He would say, "The lilies and the brier live but a day, yet that day is eternity spent in freedom."

And one evening as we sat beside the stream He said, "Behold the brook and listen to its music. Forever shall it seek the sea, and though it is for ever seeking, it sings its mystery from noon to noon.

"Would that you seek the Father as the brook seeks the sea."

Then came the summer of His ecstasy, and the June of His love was upon us. He spoke of naught then but the other man – the neighbour, the road-fellow, the stranger, and our childhood's playmates.

He spoke of the traveller journeying from the east to Egypt, of the ploughman coming home with his oxen at eventide, of the chance guest led by dusk to our door.

And He would say, "Your neighbour is your unknown self made visible. His face shall be reflected in your still waters, and if you gaze therein you shall behold your own countenance.

"Should you listen in the night, you shall hear him speak, and his words shall be the throbbing of your own heart.

"Be unto him that which you would have him be unto you.

"This is my law, and I shall say it unto you, and unto your children, and they unto their children until time is spent and generations are no more."

And on another day He said, "You shall not be yourself alone. You are in the deeds of other men, and they though unknowing are with you all your days.

"They shall not commit a crime and your hand not be with their hand.

"They shall not fall down but that you shall also fall down; and they shall not rise but that you shall rise with them.

"Their road to the sanctuary is your road, and when they seek the wasteland you too seek with them.

"You and your neighbour are two seeds sown in the field. Together you grow and together you shall sway in the wind. And neither of you shall claim the field. For a seed on its way to growth claims not even its own ecstasy.

"Today I am with you. Tomorrow I go westward; but ere I go, I say unto you that your neighbour is your unknown self made visible. Seek him in love that you may know yourself, for only in that knowledge shall you become my brothers."

Then came the autumn of His passion.

And He spoke to us of freedom, even as He had spoken in Galilee in the spring of His song; but now His words sought our deeper understanding.

He spoke of leaves that sing only when blown upon the wind; and of man as a cup filled by the ministering angel of the day to quench the thirst of another angel. Yet whether that cup is full or empty it shall stand crystalline upon the board of the Most High.

He said, "You are the cup and you are the wine. Drink yourselves to the dregs; or else remember me and you shall be quenched."

And on our way to the southward He said, "Jerusalem, which stands in pride upon the height, shall descend to the depth of Jahannum the dark valley, and in the midst of her desolation I shall stand alone.

"The temple shall fall to dust, and around the portico you shall hear the cry of widows and orphans; and men in their haste to escape shall not know the faces of their brothers, for fear shall be upon them all.

"But even there, if two of you shall meet and utter my name and look to the west, you shall see me, and these my words shall again visit your ears."

And when we reached the hill of Bethany, He said, "Let us go to Jerusalem. The city awaits us. I will enter the gate riding upon a colt, and I will speak to the multitude.

"Many are there who would chain me, and many who would put out my flame, but in my death you shall find life and you shall be free.

"They shall seek the breath that hovers betwixt heart and mind as the swallow hovers between the field and his nest. But my breath has already escaped them, and they shall not overcome me.

"The walls that my Father has built around me shall not fall down, and the acre He has made holy shall not be profaned.

"When the dawn shall come, the sun will crown my head and I shall be with you to face the day. And that day shall be long, and the world shall not see its eventide.

"The scribes and the Pharisees say the earth is thirsty for my blood. I would quench the thirst of the earth with my blood. But the drops shall rise oak trees and maple, and the east shall carry the acorns to other lands."

And then He said, "Judea would have a king, and she would march against the legions of Rome.

"I shall not be her king. The diadems of Zion were fashioned for lesser brows. And the ring of Solomon is small for this finger.

"Behold my hand. See you not that it is over-strong to hold a sceptre, and over-sinewed to wield a common sword?

"Nay, I shall not command Syrian flesh against Roman. But you with my words shall wake that city, and my spirit shall speak to her second dawn.

"My words shall be an invisible army with horses and chariots, and without axe or spear I shall conquer the priests of Jerusalem, and the Caesars.

"I shall not sit upon a throne where slaves have sat and ruled other slaves. Nor will I rebel against the sons of Italy.

"But I shall be a tempest in their sky, and a song in their soul.

"And I shall be remembered.

"They shall call me Jesus the Anointed."

These things He said outside the walls of Jerusalem before He entered the city.

And His words are graven as with chisels.

NATHANIEL

Jesus was not Meek

They say that Jesus of Nazareth was humble and meek.

They say that though He was a just man and righteous, He was a weakling, and was often confounded by the strong and the powerful; and that when He stood before men of authority He was but a lamb among lions.

But I say Jesus had authority over men, and that He knew His power and proclaimed it among the hills of Galilee, and in the cities of Judea and Phoenicia.

What man yielding and soft would say, "I am life, and I am the way to truth"?

What man meek and lowly would say, "I am in God, our Father; and our God, the Father, is in me"?

What man unmindful of His own strength would say, "He who believes not in me believes not in this life nor in the life everlasting"?

What man uncertain of tomorrow would proclaim, "Your world shall pass away and be naught but scattered ashes ere my words shall pass away"?

Was He doubtful of Himself when He said to those who would confound Him with a harlot, "He who is without sin, let him cast a stone"?

Did He fear authority when He drove the money-changers from the court of the temple, though they were licensed by the priests?

Were His wings shorn when He cried aloud, "My kingdom is above your earthly kingdoms"?

Was He seeking shelter in words when He repeated again and yet again, "Destroy this temple and I will rebuild it in three days"?

Was it a coward who shook His hand in the face of the authorities and pronounced them "liars, low, filthy, and degenerate"?

Shall a man bold enough to say these things to those who ruled Judea be deemed meek and humble?

Nay. The eagle builds not his nest in the weeping willow. And the lion seeks not his den among the ferns.

I am sickened and the bowels within me stir and rise when I hear the faint-hearted call Jesus humble and meek, that they may justify their own faint-heartedness; and when the downtrodden, for comfort and companionship, speak of Jesus as a worm shining by their side.

Yea, my heart is sickened by such men. It is the mighty hunter I would preach, and the mountainous spirit unconquerable.

SABA OF ANTIOCH

On Saul of Tarsus

This day I heard Saul of Tarsus preaching the Christ unto the Jews of this city.

He calls himself Paul now, the apostle to the Gentiles.

I knew him in my youth, and in those days he persecuted the friends of the Nazarene. Well do I remember his satisfaction when his fellows stoned the radiant youth called Stephen.

This Paul is indeed a strange man. His souls is not the soul of a free man.

At times he seems like an animal in the forest, hunted and wounded, seeking a cave wherein he would hide his pain from the world.

He speaks not of Jesus, nor does he repeat His words. He preaches the Messiah whom the prophets of old had foretold.

And though he himself is a learned Jew he addresses his fellow Jews in Greek; and his Greek is halting, and he ill chooses his words.

But he is a man of hidden powers and his presence is affirmed by those who gather around him. And at times he assures them of what he himself is not assured.

We who knew Jesus and heard his discourses say that He taught man how to break the chains of his bondage that he might be free from his yesterdays.

But Paul is forging chains for the man of tomorrow. He would strike with his own hammer upon the anvil in the name of one whom he does not know.

The Nazarene would have us live the hour in passion and ecstasy.

The man of Tarsus would have us be mindful of laws recorded in the ancient books.

Jesus gave His breath to the breathless dead. And in my lone nights I believe and I understand.

When He sat at the board, He told stories that gave happiness to the feasters, and spiced with His joy the meat and the wine.

But Paul would prescribe our loaf and our cup.

Suffer me not to turn my eyes the other way.

SALOME TO A WOMAN FRIEND

A Desire Unfulfilled
He was like poplars shimmering in the sun;
And like a lake among the lonely hills,
Shining in the sun;
And like snow upon the mountain heights,
White, white in the sun.
Yea, He was like unto all these,
And I loved Him.
Yet I feared His presence.
And my feet would not carry my burden of love
That I might girdle His feet with my arms.
I would have said to Him,
"I have slain your friend in an hour of passion.
Will you forgive me my sin?
And will you not in mercy release my youth
From its blind deed,
That it may walk in your light?"
I know He would have forgiven my dancing
For the saintly head of His friend.
I know He would have seen in me
An object of His own teaching.
For there was no valley of hunger He could not bridge,
And no desert of thirst He could not cross.
Yea, He was even as the poplars,
And as the lakes among the hills,
And like snow upon Lebanon.
And I would have cooled my lips in the folds of His garment.

But He was far from me,
And I was ashamed.
And my mother held me back
When the desire to seek Him was upon me.
Whenever He passed by, my heart ached for his loveliness,
But my mother frowned at Him in contempt,
And would hasten me from the window
To my bedchamber.
And she would cry aloud saying,
"Who is He but another locust-eater from the desert?
What is He but a scoffer and a renegade,
A seditious riot-monger, who would rob us of sceptre and crown,
And bid the foxes and the jackals of His accursed land
Howl in our halls and sit upon our throne?
Go hide your face from this day,
And await the day when His head shall fall down,
But not upon your platter."
These things my mother said.
But my heart would not keep her words.
I loved Him in secret,
And my sleep was girdled with flames.
He is gone now.
And something that was in me is gone also.
Perhaps it was my youth
That would not tarry here,
Since the God of youth was slain.

RACHAEL, A WOMAN DISCIPLE

On Jesus the Vision and the Man

I often wonder whether Jesus was a man of flesh and blood like ourselves, or a thought without a body, in the mind, or an idea that visits the vision of man.

Often it seems to me that He was but a dream dreamed by the countless men and women at the same time in a sleep deeper than sleep and a dawn more serene than all dawns.

And it seems that in relating the dream, the one to the other, we began to deem it a reality that had indeed come to pass; and in giving it body of our fancy and a voice of our longing we made it a substance of our own substance.

But in truth He was not a dream. We knew Him for three years and beheld Him with our open eyes in the high tide of noon.

We touched His hands, and we followed Him from one place to another. We heard His discourses and witnessed His deeds. Think you that we were a thought seeking after more thought, or a dream in the region of dreams?

Great events always seem alien to our daily lives, though their nature may be rooted in our nature. But though they appear sudden in their coming and sudden in their passing, their true span is for years and for generations.

Jesus of Nazareth was Himself the Great Event. That man whose father and mother and brothers we know, was Himself a miracle wrought in Judea. Yea, all His own miracles, if placed at His feet, would not rise to the height of His ankles.

And all the rivers of all the years shall not carry away our remembrance of Him.

He was a mountain burning in the night, yet He was a soft glow beyond the hills. He was a tempest in the sky, yet He was a murmur in the mist of daybreak.

He was a torrent pouring from the heights to the plains to destroy all things in its path. And He was like the laughter of children.

Every year I had waited for spring to visit this valley. I had waited for the lilies and the cyclamen, and then every year my soul had been saddened within me; for ever I longed to rejoice with the spring, yet I could not.

But when Jesus came to my seasons He was indeed a spring, and in Him was the promise of all the years to come. He filled my heart with joy; and like the violets I grew, a shy thing, in the light of His coming.

And now the changing seasons of worlds not yet ours shall not erase His loveliness from this our world.

Nay, Jesus was not a phantom, nor a conception of the poets. He was man like yourself and myself. But only to sight and touch and hearing; in all other ways He was unlike us.

He was a man of joy; and it was upon the path of joy that He met the sorrows of all men. And it was from the high roofs of His sorrows that He beheld the joy of all men.

He saw visions that we did not see, and heard voices that we did not hear; and He spoke as if to invisible multitudes, and ofttimes He spoke through us to races yet unborn.

And Jesus was often alone. He was among us yet not one with us. He was upon the earth, yet He was of the sky. And only in our aloneness may we visit the land of His aloneness.

He loved us with tender love. His heart was a winepress. You and I could approach with a cup and drink therefrom.

One thing I did not use to understand in Jesus: He would make merry with His listeners; He would tell jests and play upon words, and laugh with all the fullness of His heart, even when there were distances in His eyes and sadness in His voice. But I understand now.

I often think of the earth as a woman heavy with her first child. When Jesus was born, He was the first child. And when He died, He was the first man to die.

For did it not appear to you that the earth was stilled on that dark Friday, and the heavens were at war with the heavens?

And felt you not when His face disappeared from our sight as if we were naught but memories in the mist?

CLEOPAS OF BETHROUNE

On the Law and the Prophets

When Jesus spoke the whole world was hushed to listen. His words were not for our ears but rather for the elements of which God made this earth.

He spoke to the sea, our vast mother, that gave us birth. He spoke to the mountain, our elder brother whose summit is a promise.

And He spoke to the angels beyond the sea and the mountain to whom we entrusted our dreams ere the clay in us was made hard in the sun.

And still His speech slumbers within our breast like a love-song half forgotten, and sometimes it burns itself through to our memory.

His speech was simple and joyous, and the sound of His voice was like cool water in a land of drought.

Once He raised His hand against the sky, and His fingers were like the branches of a sycamore tree; and He said with a great voice:

"The prophets of old have spoken to you, and your ears are filled with their speech. But I say unto you, empty your ears of what you have heard."

And these words of Jesus, "But I say unto you," were not uttered by a man of our race nor of our world; but rather by a host of seraphim marching across the sky of Judea.

Again and yet again He would quote the law and the prophets, and then he would say, "But I say unto you."

Oh, what burning words, what waves of seas unknown to the shores of our mind, "But I say unto you."

What stars seeking the darkness of the soul, and what sleepless souls awaiting the dawn.

To tell of the speech of Jesus one must needs have His speech or the echo thereof.

I have neither the speech nor the echo.

I beg you to forgive me for beginning a story that I cannot end. But the end is not yet upon my lips. It is still a love song in the wind.

NAAMAN OF THE GADARENES

On the Death of Stephen

His disciples are dispersed. He gave them the legacy of pain ere He Himself was put to death. They are hunted like the deer, and the foxes of the fields, and the quiver of the hunter is yet full of arrows.

But when they are caught and led to death, they are joyous, and their faces shine like the face of the bridegroom at the wedding-feast. For He gave them also the legacy of joy.

I had a friend from the North Country, and his name was Stephen; and because he proclaimed Jesus as the Son of God, he was led to the market-place and stoned.

And when Stephen fell to earth he outstretched his arms as if he would die as his Master had died. His arms were spread like wings ready for flight. And when the last gleam of light was fading in his eyes, with my own eyes I saw a smile upon his lips. It was a smile like the breath that comes before the end of winter for a pledge and a promise of spring.

How shall I describe it?

It seemed that Stephen was saying, "If I should go to another world, and other men should lead me to another market-place to stone me, even then I would proclaim Him for the truth which was in Him, and for that same truth which is in me now."

And I noticed that there was a man standing near, and looking with pleasure upon the stoning of Stephen.

His name is Saul of Tarsus, and it was he who had yielded Stephen to the priests and the Romans and the crowd, for stoning.

Saul was bald of head and short of stature. His shoulders were crooked and his features ill-sorted; and I liked him not.

I have been told that he is now preaching Jesus from the house tops. It is hard to believe.

But the grave halts not Jesus' walking to the enemies' camp to tame and take captive those who had opposed Him.

Still I do not like that man of Tarsus, though I have been told that after Stephen's death he was tamed and conquered on the road to Damascus. But his head is too large for his heart to be that of a true disciple.

And yet perhaps I am mistaken. I am often mistaken.

THOMAS

On the Forefathers of His Doubts

My grandfather who was a lawyer once said, "Let us observe truth, but only when truth is made manifest unto us."

When Jesus called me I heeded Him, for His command was more potent than my will; yet I kept my counsel.

When He spoke and the others were swayed like branches in the wind, I listened immovable. Yet I loved Him.

Three years ago He left us, a scattered company to sing His name, and to be His witnesses unto the nations.

At that time I was called Thomas the Doubter. The shadow of my grandfather was still upon me, and always I would have truth made manifest.

I would even put my hand in my own wound to feel the blood ere I would believe in my pain.

Now a man who loves with his heart yet holds a doubt in his mind, is but a slave in a galley who sleeps at his oar and dreams of his freedom, till the lash of the master wakes him.

I myself was that slave, and I dreamed of freedom, but the sleep of my grandfather was upon me. My flesh needed the whip of my own day.

Even in the presence of the Nazarene I had closed my eyes to see my hands chained to the oar.

Doubt is a pain too lonely to know that faith is his twin brother.

Doubt is a foundling unhappy and astray, and though his own mother who gave him birth should find him and enfold him, he would withdraw in caution and in fear.

For Doubt will not know truth till his wounds are healed and restored.

I doubted Jesus until He made Himself manifest to me, and thrust my own hand into His very wounds.

Then indeed I believed, and after that I was rid of my yesterday and the yesterdays of my forefathers.

The dead in me buried their dead; and the living shall live for the Anointed King, even for Him who was the Son of Man.

Yesterday they told me that I must go and utter His name among the Persians and the Hindus.

I shall go. And from this day to my last day, at dawn and at eventide, I shall see my Lord rising in majesty and I shall hear Him speak.

ELMADAM THE LOGICIAN

Jesus the Outcast

You bid me speak of Jesus the Nazarene, and much have I to tell, but the time has not come. Yet whatever I say of Him now is the truth; for all speech is worthless save when it discloses the truth.

Behold a man disorderly, against all order; a mendicant, opposed to all possessions; a drunkard who would only make merry with rogues and castaways.

He was not the proud son of the State, nor was He the protected citizen of the Empire; therefore He had contempt for both State and Empire.

He would live as free and dutiless as the fowls of the air, and for this the hunters brought Him to earth with arrows.

No one shall open the flood gates of his ancestors without drowning. It is the law. And because the Nazarene broke the law, He and His witless followers were brought to naught.

And there lived many others like Him, men who would change the course of our destiny.

They themselves were changed, and they were the losers.

There is a grapeless vine that grows by the city walls. It creeps upward and clings to the stones. Should that vine say in her heart, "With my might and my weight I shall destroy these walls," what would other plants say? Surely they would laugh at her foolishness.

Now sir, I cannot but laugh at this man and His ill-advised disciples.

ONE OF THE MARYS

On His Sadness and His Smile

His head was always high, and the flame of God was in His eyes.

He was often sad, but His sadness was tenderness shown to those in pain, and comradeship given to the lonely.

When He smiled His smile was as the hunger of those who long after the unknown. It was like the dust of stars falling upon the eyelids of children. And it was like a morsel of bread in the throat.

He was sad, yet it was a sadness that would rise to the lips and become a smile.

It was like a golden veil in the forest when autumn is upon the world. And sometimes it seemed like moonlight upon the shores of the lake.

He smiled as if His lips would sing at the wedding-feast.

Yet He was sad with the sadness of the winged who will not soar above his comrade.

RUMANOUS, A GREEK POET

Jesus the Poet

He was a poet. He saw for our eyes and heard for our ears, and our silent words were upon His lips; and His fingers touched what we could not feel.

Out of His heart there flew countless singing birds to the north and to the south, and the little flowers on the hill-sides stayed His steps towards the heavens.

Oftentimes I have seen Him bending down to touch the blades of grass. And in my heart I have heard Him say: "Little green things, you shall be with me in my kingdom, even as the oaks of Besan, and the cedars of Lebanon."

He loved all things of loveliness, the shy faces of children, and the myrrh and frankincense from the south.

He loved a pomegranate or a cup of wine given Him in kindness; it mattered not whether it was offered by a stranger in the inn or by a rich host.

And He loved the almond blossoms. I have seen Him gathering them into His hands and covering His face with the petals, as though He would embrace with His love all the trees in the world.

He knew the sea and the heavens; and He spoke of pearls which have light that is not of this light, and of stars that are beyond our night.

He knew the mountains as eagles know them, and the valleys as they are known by the brooks and the streams. And there was a desert in His silence and a garden in His speech.

Aye, He was a poet whose heart dwelt in a bower beyond the heights, and His songs though sung for our ears, were sung for other ears also, and to men in another land where life is for ever young and time is always dawn.

Once I too deemed myself a poet, but when I stood before Him in Bethany, I knew what it is to hold an instrument with but a single string before one who commands all instruments. For in His voice there was the laughter of thunder and the tears of rain, and the joyous dancing of trees in the wind.

And since I have known that my lyre has but one string, and that my voice weaves neither the memories of yesterday nor the hopes of tomorrow, I have put aside my lyre and I shall keep silence. But always at twilight I shall hearken, and I shall listen to the Poet who is the sovereign of all poets.

LEVI,
A DISCIPLE

On Those who would Confound Jesus

Upon an eventide He passed by my house, and my soul was quickened within me.

He spoke to me and said, "Come, Levi, and follow me."

And I followed Him that day.

And at eventide of the next day I begged Him to enter my house and be my guest. And He and His friends crossed my threshold and blessed me and my wife and my children.

And I had other guests. They were publicans and men of learning, but they were against Him in their hearts.

And when we were sitting about the board, one of the publicans questioned Jesus, saying, "Is it true that you and your disciples break the law, and make fire on the Sabbath day?"

And Jesus answered him saying, "We do indeed make fire on the Sabbath day. We would inflame the Sabbath day, and we would burn with our touch the dry stubble of all days."

And another publican said, "It was brought to us that you drink wine with the unclean at the inn."

And Jesus answered, "Aye, these also we would comfort. Came we here except to share the loaf and the cup with the uncrowned and the unshod amongst you?

"Few, aye too few are the featherless who dare the wind, and many are the winged and full-fledged yet in the nest.

"And we would feed them all with our beak, both the sluggish and the swift."

And another publican said, "Have I not been told that you would protect the harlots of Jerusalem?"

Then in the face of Jesus I saw, as it were, the rocky heights of Lebanon, and He said, "It is true.

"On the day of reckoning these women shall rise before the throne of my Father, and they shall be made pure by their own tears. But you shall be held down by the chains of your own judgment.

"Babylon was not put to waste by her prostitutes; Babylon fell to ashes that the eyes of her hypocrites might no longer see the light of day."

And other publicans would have questioned Him, but I made a sign and bade them be silent, for I knew He would confound them; and they too were my guests, and I would not have them put to shame.

When it was midnight the publicans left my house, and their souls were limping.

Then I closed my eyes and I saw, as if in a vision, seven women in white raiment standing about Jesus. Their arms were crossed upon their bosoms, and their heads were bent down, and I looked deep into the mist of my dream and beheld the face of one of the seven women, and it shone in my darkness.

It was the face of a harlot who lived in Jerusalem.

Then I opened my eyes and looked at Him, and He was smiling at me and at the others who had not left the board.

And I closed my eyes again, and I saw in a light seven men in white garments standing around Him. And I beheld the face of one of them.

It was the face of the thief who was crucified afterward at His right hand.

And later Jesus and His comrades left my house for the road.

A WIDOW IN GALILEE

Jesus the Cruel

My son was my first and my only born. He laboured in our field and he was contented until he heard the man called Jesus speaking to the multitude.

Then my son suddenly became different, as if a new spirit, foreign and unwholesome, had embraced his spirit.

He abandoned the field and the garden; and he abandoned me also. He became worthless, a creature of the highways.

That man Jesus of Nazareth was evil, for what good man would separate a son from his mother?

The last thing my child said to me was this: "I am going with one of His disciples to the North Country. My life is established upon the Nazarene. You have given me birth, and for that I am grateful to you. But I needs must go. Am I not leaving with you our rich land, and all our silver and gold? I shall take naught but this garment and this staff."

Thus my son spoke, and departed.

And now the Romans and the priests have laid hold upon Jesus and crucified Him; and they have done well.

A man who would part mother and son could not be godly.

The man who sends our children to the cities of the Gentiles cannot be our friend.

I know my son will not return to me. I saw it in his eyes. And for this I hate Jesus of Nazareth who caused me to be alone in this unploughed field and this withered garden.

And I hate all those who praise Him.

Not many days ago they told me that Jesus once said, "My father and my mother and my brethren are those who hear my word and follow me."

But why should sons leave their mothers to follow His footsteps?

And why should the milk of my breast be forgotten for a fountain not yet tasted? And the warmth of my arms be forsaken for the Northland, cold and unfriendly?

Aye, I hate the Nazarene, and I shall hate Him to the end of my days, for He has robbed me of my first-born, my only son.

JUDAS,
THE COUSIN OF JESUS

On the Death of John the Baptist

Upon a night in the month of August we were with the Master on a heath not far from the lake. The heath was called by the ancients the Meadow of Skulls.

And Jesus was reclining on the grass and gazing at the stars.

And of a sudden two men came rushing towards us breathless. They were as if in agony, and they fell prostrate at the feet of Jesus.

And Jesus stood up and He said, "Whence came you?"

And one of the men answered, "From Machaereus."

And Jesus looked upon him and was troubled, and He said, "What of John?"

And the man said, "He was slain this day. He was beheaded in his prison cell."

Then Jesus lifted up His head. And then He walked a little way from us. After a while He stood again in our midst.

And He said, "The king could have slain the prophet ere this day. Verily the king has tried the pleasure of His subjects. Kings of yore were not so slow in giving the head of a prophet to the head-hunters.

"I grieve not for John, but rather for Herod, who let fall the sword. Poor king, like an animal caught and led with a ring and a rope.

"Poor petty tetrarchs lost in their own darkness, they stumble and fall down. And what could you of the stagnant sea but dead fishes?"

"I hate not kings. Let them rule men, but only when they are wiser than men."

And the Master looked at the two sorrowful faces and then He looked at us, and He spoke again and said, "John was born wounded, and the blood of his wounds streamed forth with his words. He was freedom not yet free from itself, and patient only with the straight and the just.

"In truth he was a voice crying in the land of the deaf; and I loved him in his pain and his aloneness.

"And I loved his pride that would give its head to the sword ere it would yield it to the dust.

"Verily I say unto you that John, the son of Zachariah, was the last of his race, and like his forefathers he was slain between the threshold of the temple and the altar."

And again Jesus walked away from us.

Then He returned and He said, "Forever it has been that those who rule for an hour would slay the rulers of years. And forever they would hold a trial and pronounce condemnation upon a man not yet born, and decree his death ere he commits the crime.

"The son of Zachariah shall live with me in my kingdom and his day shall be long."

Then He turned to the disciples of John and said, "Every deed has its morrow. I myself may be the morrow of this deed. Go back to my friend's friends, and tell them I shall be with them."

And the two men walked away from us, and they seemed less heavy-hearted.

Then Jesus laid Himself down again upon the grass and outstretched His arms, and again He gazed at the stars.

Now it was late. And I lay not far from Him, and I would fain have rested, but there was a hand knocking upon the gate of my sleep, and I lay awake until Jesus and the dawn called me again to the road.

THE MAN FROM THE DESERT

On the Money-Changers

I was a stranger in Jerusalem. I had come to the Holy City to behold the great temple, and to sacrifice upon the altar, for my wife had given twin sons to my tribe.

And after I had made my offering, I stood in the portico of them temple looking down upon the money-changers and those who sold doves for sacrifice, and listening to the great noise in the court.

And as I stood there came of a sudden a man into the midst of the money-changers and those who sold doves.

He was a man of majesty, and He came swiftly.

In His hand He held a rope of goat's hide; and He began to overturn the tables of the money-changers and to beat the pedlars of birds with the rope.

And I heard Him saying with a loud voice, "Render these birds unto the sky which is their nest."

Men and women fled from before His face, and He moved amongst them as the whirling wind moves on the sad-hills.

All this came to pass in but a moment, and then the court of the Temple was emptied of the money-changers. Only the man stood there alone, and His followers stood at a distance.

Then I turned my face and I saw another man in the portico of the temple. And I walked towards him and said, "Sir, who is this man who stands alone, even like another temple?" And he answered me, "This is Jesus of Nazareth, a prophet who has appeared of late in Galilee. Here in Jerusalem all men hate Him."

And I said, "My heart was strong enough to be with His whip, and yielding enough to be at His feet."

And Jesus turned towards His followers who were awaiting Him. But before He reached them, three of the temple doves flew back, and one alighted upon His left shoulder and the other two at His feet. And he touched each one tenderly. Then He walked on, and there were leagues in every step of His steps.

Now tell me, what power had He to attack and disperse hundreds of men and women without opposition? I was told that they all hate Him, yet no one stood before Him on that day. Had He plucked out the fangs of hate on His way to the court of the temple?

PETER

On the Morrow of His Followers

Once at sundown Jesus led us into the village of Beithsaida. We were a tired company, and the dust of the road was upon us. And we came to a great house in the midst of a garden, and the owner stood at the gate.

And Jesus said to him, "These men are weary and footsore. Let them sleep in your house. The night is cold and they are in need of warmth and rest."

And the rich man said, "They shall not sleep in my house."

And Jesus said, "Suffer them then to sleep in your garden."

And the man answered, "Nay, they shall not sleep in my garden."

Then Jesus turned to us and said, "This is what your tomorrow will be, and this present is like your future. All doors shall be closed in your face, and not even the gardens that lie under the stars may be your couch.

"Should your feet indeed be patient with the road and follow me, it may be you will find a basin and a bed, and perhaps bread and wine also. But if it should be that you find none of those things, forget not then that you have crossed one of my deserts.

"Come, let us go forth."

And the rich man was disturbed, and his face was changed, and he muttered to himself words that I did not hear; and he shrank away from us and turned into his garden.

And we followed Jesus upon the road.

MELACHI OF BABYLON, AN ASTRONOMER

The Miracles of Jesus

You question me concerning the miracles of Jesus.

Every thousand thousand years the sun and the moon and this earth and all her sister planets meet in a straight line, and they confer for a moment together.

Then they slowly disperse and await the passing of another thousand thousand years.

There are no miracles beyond the seasons, yet you and I do not know all the seasons. And what if a season shall be made manifest in the shape of a man?

In Jesus the elements of our bodies and our dreams came together according to law. All that was timeless before Him became timeful in Him.

They say He gave sight to the blind and walking to the paralysed, and that He drove devils out of madmen.

Perchance blindness is but a dark thought that can be overcome by a burning thought. Perchance a withered limb is but idleness that can be quickened by energy. And perhaps the devils, these restless elements in our life, are driven out by the angels of peace and serenity.

They say He raised the dead to life. If you can tell me what is death, then I will tell you what is life.

In a field I have watched an acorn, a thing so still and seemingly useless. And in the spring I have seen that acorn take roots and rise, the beginning of an oak tree, towards the sun.

Surely you would deem this a miracle, yet that miracle is wrought a thousand thousand times in the drowsiness of every autumn and the passion of every spring.

Why shall it not be wrought in the heart of man? Shall not the seasons meet in the hand or upon the lips of a Man Anointed?

If our God has given to earth the art to nestle seed whilst the seed is seemingly dead, why shall He not give to the heart of man to breathe life into another heart, even a heart seemingly dead?

I have spoken of these miracles which I deem but little beside the greater miracle, which is the man Himself, the Wayfarer, the man who turned my dross into gold, who taught me how to love those who hate me, and in so doing brought me comfort and gave sweet dreams to my sleep.

This is the miracle in my own life.

My soul was blind, my soul was lame. I was possessed by restless spirits, and I was dead.

But now I see clearly, and I walk erect. I am at peace, and I live to witness and proclaim my own being every hour of the day.

And I am not one of His followers. I am but an old astronomer who visits the fields of space once a season, and who would be heedful of the law and the miracles thereof.

And I am at the twilight of my time, but whenever I would seek its dawning, I seek the youth of Jesus.

And for ever shall age seek youth. In me now it is knowledge that is seeking vision.

A PHILOSOPHER

On Wonder and Beauty

When he was with us He gazed at us and at our world with eyes of wonder, for His eyes were not veiled with the veil of years, and all that He saw was clear in the light of His youth.

Though He knew the depth of beauty, He was for ever surprised by its peace and its majesty; and He stood before the earth as the first man had stood before the first day.

We whose senses have been dulled, we gaze in full daylight and yet we do not see. We would cup our ears, but we do not hear; and stretch forth our hands, but we do not touch. And though all the incense of Arabia is burned, we go our way and do not smell.

We see not the ploughman returning from his field at eventide; nor hear the shepherd's flute when he leads his flock to the fold, nor do we stretch our arms to touch the sunset; and our nostrils hunger no longer for the roses of Sharon.

Nay, we honour no kings without kingdoms; nor hear the sound of harps save when the strings are plucked by hands; nor do we see a child playing in our olive grove as if he were a young olive tree. And all words must needs rise from lips of flesh, or else we deem each other dumb and deaf.

In truth we gaze but do not see, and hearken but do not hear; we eat and drink but do not taste. And there lies the difference between Jesus of Nazareth and ourselves.

His senses were all continually made new, and the world to Him was always a new world.

To Him the lisping of a babe was not less than the cry of all mankind, while to us it is only lisping.

To Him the root of a buttercup was a longing towards God, while to us it is naught but a root.

URIAH,
AN OLD MAN OF NAZARETH

He was a Stranger in our Midst

He was a stranger in our midst, and His life was hidden with dark veils.

He walked not the path of our God, but followed the course of the foul and the infamous.

His childhood revolted, and rejected the sweet milk of our nature.

His youth was inflamed like dry grass that burns in the night.

And when He became a man, He took arms against us all.

Such men are conceived in the ebb tide of human kindness, and born in unholy tempests. And in tempests they live a day and the perish forever.

Do you not remember Him, a boy overweening, who would argue with our learned elders, and laugh at their dignity?

And remember you not His youth, when He lived by the saw and the chisel? He would not accompany our sons and daughters on their holidays. He would walk alone.

And He would not return the salutation of those who hailed Him, as though He were above us.

I myself met Him once in the field and greeted Him, and He only smiled, and in His smile I beheld arrogance and insult.

Not long afterward my daughter went with her companions to the vineyards to gather the grapes, and she spoke to Him and He did not answer her.

He spoke only to the whole company of grape-gatherers, as if my daughter had not been among them.

When He abandoned His people and turned vagabond He became naught but a babbler. His voice was like a claw in our flesh, and the sound of His voice is still a pain in our memory.

He would utter only evil of us and of our fathers and forefathers. And His tongue sought our bosoms like a poisoned arrow.

Such was Jesus.

If He had been my son, I would have committed Him with the Roman legions to Arabia, and I would have begged the captain to place Him in the forefront of the battle, so that the archer of the foe might mark Him, and free me of His insolence.

But I have no son. And mayhap I should be grateful. For what if my son had been an enemy of his own people, and my grey hairs were now seeking the dust with shame, my white beard humbled?

NICODEMUS THE POET

On Fools and Jugglers

Many are the fools who say that Jesus stood in His own path and opposed Himself; that He knew not His own mind, and in the absence of that knowledge confounded Himself.

Many indeed are the owls who know no song unlike their own hooting.

You and I know the jugglers of words who would honour only a greater juggler, men who carry their heads in baskets to the market-place and sell them to the first bidder.

We know the pygmies who abuse the sky-man. And we know what the weed would say of the oak tree and the cedar.

I pity them that they cannot rise to the heights.

I pity the shrivelling thorn envying the elm that dares the seasons.

But pity, though enfolded by the regret of all the angels, can bring them no light.

I know the scarecrow whose rotting garments flutter in the corn, yet he himself is dead to the corn and to the singing wind.

I know the wingless spider that weaves a net for all who fly.

I know the crafty, the blowers of horns and the beaters of drums, who in the abundance of their own noise cannot hear the skylark nor the east wind in the forest.

I know him who paddles against all streams, but never finds the source, who runs with all rivers, but never dares to the sea.

I know him who offers his unskilled hands to the builder of the temple, and when his unskilled hands are rejected, says in the darkness of his heart, "I will destroy all that shall be builded."

I know all these. They are the men who object that Jesus said on a certain day, "I bring peace unto you," and on another day, "I bring a sword."

They cannot understand that in truth He said, "I bring peace unto men of goodwill, and I lay a sword between him who would peace and him who would a sword."

They wonder that He who said, "My kingdom is not of this earth," said also, "Render unto Caesar that which is Caesar's"; and know not that if they would indeed be free to enter the kingdom of their passion, they must not resist the gate-keeper of their necessities. It behooves them gladly to pay that dole to enter into that city.

There are the men who say, "He preached tenderness and kindliness and filial love, yet He would not heed His mother and His brothers when they sought Him in the streets of Jerusalem."

They do not know that His mother and brothers in their loving fear would have had Him return to the bench of the carpenter, whereas He was opening our eyes to the dawn of a new day.

His mother and His brothers would have had Him live in the shadow of death, but He Himself was challenging death upon yonder hill that He might live in our sleepless memory.

I know these moles that dig paths to nowhere. Are they not the ones who accuse Jesus of glorifying Himself in that He said to the multitude, "I am the path and the gate to salvation," and even called Himself the life and the resurrection.

But Jesus was not claiming more than the month of May claims in her high tide.

Was He not to tell the shining truth because it was so shining?

He indeed said that He was the way and the life and the resurrection of the heart; and I myself as a testimony to His truth.

Do you not remember me, Nicodemus, who believed in naught but the laws and decrees and was in continual subjection to observances?

And behold me now, a man who walks with life and laughs with the sun from the first moment it smiles upon the mountain until it yields itself to bed behind the hills.

Why do you halt before the word salvation? I myself through Him have attained my salvation.

I care not for what shall befall me tomorrow, for I know that Jesus quickened my sleep and made my distant dreams my companions and my road-fellows.

Am I less man because I believe in a greater man?

The barriers of flesh and bone fell down when the Poet of Galilee spoke to me; and I was held by a spirit, and was lifted to the heights, and in midair my wings gathered the song of passion.

And when I dismounted from the wind and in the Sanhedrim my pinions were shorn, even then my ribs, my featherless wings, kept and guarded the song. And all the poverties of the lowlands cannot rob me of my treasure.

I have said enough. Let the deaf bury the humming of life in their dead ears. I am content with the sound of His lyre, which He held and struck while the hands of His body were nailed and bleeding.

JOSEPH OF ARIMETHEA

The Two Streams in Jesus' Heart

There were two streams running in the heart of the Nazarene: the stream of kinship to God whom He called Father, and the stream of rapture which He called the kingdom of the Above-world.

And in my solitude I thought of Him and I followed these two streams in His heart. Upon the banks of the one I met my own soul; and sometimes my soul was a beggar and a wanderer, and sometimes it was a princess in her garden.

Then I followed the other stream in His heart, and on my way I met one who had been beaten and robbed of his gold, and he was smiling. And farther on I saw the robber who had robbed him, and there were unshed tears upon his face.

Then I heard the murmur of these two streams in my own bosom also, and I was gladdened.

When I visited Jesus the day before Pontius Pilatus and the elders laid hands on Him, we talked long, and I asked Him many questions, and He answered my questionings with graciousness; and when I left Him I knew He was the Lord and Master of this our earth.

It is long since our cedar tree has fallen, but its fragrance endures, and will forever seek the four corners of the earth.

GEORGUS OF BEIRUT

On Strangers

He and his friends were in the grove of pines beyond my hedge, and He was talking to them.

I stood near the hedge and listened. And I knew who He was, for His fame had reached these shores ere He Himself visited them.

When He ceased speaking I approached Him, and I said, "Sir, come with these men and honour me and my roof."

And He smiled upon me and said, "Not this day, my friend. Not this day."

And there was a blessing in His words, and His voice enfolded me like a garment on a cold night.

Then He turned to His friends and said, "Behold a man who deems us not strangers, and though He has not seen us ere this day, he bids us to His threshold.

"Verily in my kingdom there are no strangers. Our life is but the life of all other men, given us that we may know all men, and in that knowledge love them.

"The deeds of all men are but our deeds, both the hidden and the revealed.

"I charge you not to be one self but rather many selves, the householder and the homeless, the ploughman and the sparrow that picks the grain ere it slumber in the earth, the giver who gives in gratitude, and the receiver who receives in pride and recognition.

"The beauty of the day is not only in what you see, but in what other men see.

"For this I have chosen you from among the many who have chosen me."

Then He turned to me again and smiled and said, "I say these things to you also, and you also shall remember them."

Then I entreated Him and said, "Master, will you not visit in my house?"

And He answered, "I know your heart, and I have visited your larger house."

And as He walked away with His disciples He said, "Good-night, and may your house be large enough to shelter all the wanderers of the land."

MARY MAGDALENE

His Mouth was like the Heart of a Pomegranate

His mouth was like the heart of a pomegranate, and the shadows in His eyes were deep.

And He was gentle, like a man mindful of his own strength.

In my dreams I beheld the kings of the earth standing in awe in His presence.

I would speak of His face, but how shall I?

It was like night without darkness, and like day without the noise of day.

It was a sad face, and it was a joyous face.

And well I remember how once He raised His hand towards the sky, and His parted fingers were like the branches of an elm.

And I remember Him pacing the evening. He was not walking. He Himself was a road above the road; even as a cloud above the earth that would descend to refresh the earth.

But when I stood before Him and spoke to him, He was a man, and His face was powerful to behold. And He said to me, "What would you, Miriam?"

I would not answer Him, but my wings enfolded my secret, and I was made warm.

And because I could bear His light no more, I turned and walked away, but not in shame. I was only shy, and I would be alone, with His fingers upon the strings of my heart.

JOTHAM OF NAZARETH, TO A ROMAN

On Living and Being

My friend, you like all other Romans would conceive life rather than live it. You would rule lands rather than be ruled by the spirit.

You would conquer races and be cursed by them rather than stay in Rome and be blest and happy.

You think but of armies marching and of ships launched into the sea.

How shall you then understand Jesus of Nazareth, a man simple and alone, who came without armies or ships, to establish a kingdom in the heart and an empire in the free spaces of the soul?

How shall you understand the man who was not a warrior, but who came with the power of the mighty ether?

He was not a god, He was a man like unto ourselves; but in Him the myrrh of the earth rose to meet the frankincense of the sky; and in His words our lisping embraced the whispering of the unseen; and in His voice we heard a song unfathomable.

Aye, Jesus was a man and not a god, and therein lies our wonder and our surprise.

But you Romans wonder not save at the gods, and no man shall surprise you. Therefore you understand not the Nazarene.

He belonged to the youth of the mind and you belong to its old age.

You govern us today; but let us wait another day.

Who knows that this man with neither armies nor ships shall govern tomorrow?

We who follow the spirit shall sweat blood while journeying after Him. But Rome shall lie a white skeleton in the sun.

We shall suffer much, yet we shall endure and we shall live. But Rome must needs fall into the dust.

Yet if Rome, when humbled and made low, shall pronounce His name, He will heed her voice. And He will breathe new life into her bones that she may rise again, a city among the cities of the earth.

But this He shall do without legions, nor with slaves to oar His galleys. He will be alone.

EPHRAIM OF JERICHO

The Other Wedding-Feast

When he came again to Jericho I sought Him out and said to Him, "Master, on the morrow my son will take a wife. I beg you come to the wedding-feast and do us honour, even as you honoured the wedding at Cana of Galilee."

And He answered, "It is true that I was once a guest at a wedding-feast, but I shall not be a guest again. I am myself now the Bridegroom."

And I said, "I entreat you, Master, come to the wedding-feast of my son."

And He smiled as though He would rebuke me, and said, "Why do you entreat me? Have you not wine enough?"

And I said, "My jugs are full, Master; yet I beseech you, come to my son's wedding-feast."

Then He said, "Who knows? I may come, I may surely come, if your heart is an altar in your temple."

Upon the morrow my son was married, but Jesus came not to the wedding-feast. And though we had many guests, I felt that no one had come.

In very truth, I myself who welcomed the guests, was not there.

Perhaps my heart had not been an altar when I invited Him. Perhaps I desired another miracle.

BARCA,
A MERCHANT OF TYRE

On Buying and Selling

I believe that neither the Romans nor the Jews understood Jesus of Nazareth, nor did His disciples who now preach His name.

The Romans slew Him and that was a blunder. The Galileans would make a god of Him and that is a mistake.

Jesus was the heart of man.

I have sailed the Seven Seas with my ships, and bartered with kings and princes and with cheats and the wily in the market-places of distant cities; but never have I seen a man who understood merchants as He did.

I heard Him once tell this parable:

"A merchant left his country for a foreign land. He had two servants, and he gave each a handful of gold, saying: 'Even as I go abroad, you also shall go forth and seek profit. Make just exchange, and see that you serve in giving and taking.'

"And after a year the merchant returned.

"And he asked his two servants what they had done with his gold.

"The first servant said, 'Behold, Master, I have bought and sold, and I have gained.'

"And the merchant answered, 'The gain shall be yours, for you have done well, and have been faithful to me and to yourself.'

"Then the other servant stood forth and said, 'Sir, I feared the loss of your money; and I did not buy nor sell. Behold, it is all here in this purse.'

"And the merchant took the gold, and said, 'Little is your faith. To barter and lose is better than not to go forth. For even as the wind scatters her seed and waits for the fruit, so must all merchants. It were fitter for you henceforth to serve others.' "

When Jesus spoke thus, though He was no merchant, He disclosed the secret of commerce.

Moreover, His parables often brought to my mind lands more distant than my journeys, and yet nearer than my house and my goods.

But the young Nazarene was not a god; and it is a pity His followers seek to make a god of such a sage.

PHUMIAH, THE HIGH PRIESTESS OF SIDON

An Invocation

Take your harps and let me sing.

Beat your strings, the silver and the gold;

For I would sing the dauntless Man

Who slew the dragon of the valley,

Then gazed down with pity

Upon the thing He had slain.

Take your harps and sing with me

The lofty Oak upon the height,

The sky-hearted and the ocean-handed Man,

Who kissed the pallid lips of death,

Yet quivers now upon the mouth of life.

Take your harps and let us sing

The fearless Hunter on the hill,

Who marked the beast, and shot His viewless arrow,

And brought the horn and tusk

Down to the earth.

Take your harps and sing with me

The valiant Youth who conquered the mountain cities,

And the cities of the plain that coiled like serpents in the sand.

He fought not against pygmies but against gods

Who hungered for our flesh and thirsted for our blood.
And like the first Golden Hawk
He would rival only eagles;
For His wings were vast and proud
And would not outwing the less winged.
Take your harps and sing with me
The joyous song of sea and cliff.
The gods are dead,
And they are lying still
In the forgotten isle of a forgotten sea.
And He who slew them sits upon His throne.
He was but a youth.
Spring had not yet given Him full beard,
And His summer was still young in His field.
Take your harps and sing with me
The tempest in the forest
That breaks the dry branch and the leafless twig,
Yet sends the living root to nestle deeper at the breast of earth.
Take your harps and sing with me
The deathless song of our Beloved.
Nay, my maidens, stay your hands.
Lay by your harps.
We cannot sing Him now.
The faint whisper of our song cannot reach His tempest,
Nor pierce the majesty of His silence.
Lay by your harps and gather close around me,
I would repeat His words to you,
And I would tell you of His deeds,
For the echo of His voice is deeper than our passion.

BENJAMIN THE SCRIBE

Let the Dead Bury Their Dead
It has been said that Jesus was the enemy of Rome and Judea.

But I say that Jesus was the enemy of no man and no race.

I have heard Him say, "The birds of the air and the mountain tops are not mindful of the serpents in their dark holes.

"Let the dead bury their dead. Be you yourself among the living, and soar high."

I was not one of His disciples. I was but one of the many who went after Him to gaze upon His face.

He looked upon Rome and upon us who are the slaves of Rome, as a father looks upon his children playing with toys and fighting among themselves for the larger toy. And He laughed from His height.

He was greater than State and race; He was greater than revolution.

He was single and alone, and He was an awakening.

He wept all our unshed tears and smiled all our revolts.

We knew it was in His power to be born with all who are not yet born, and to bid them see, not with their eyes but with His vision.

Jesus was the beginning of a new kingdom upon the earth, and that kingdom shall remain.

He was the son and the grandson of all the kings who builded the kingdom of the spirit.

And only the kings of spirit have ruled our world.

ZACCHAEUS

On the Fate of Jesus

You believe in what you hear said. Believe in the unsaid, for the silence of men is nearer the truth than their words.

You ask if Jesus could have escaped His shameful death and saved His followers from persecution.

I answer, He could indeed have escaped had He chosen, but He did not seek safety nor was He mindful of protecting His flock from wolves of the night.

He knew His fate and the morrow of His constant lovers. He foretold and prophesied what should befall every one of us. He sought not His death; but He accepted death as a husband-man shrouding his corn with earth, accepts the winter, and then awaits the spring and harvest; and as a builder lays the largest stone in the foundation.

We were men of Galilee and from the slopes of Lebanon. Our Master could have led us back to our country, to live with His youth in our gardens until old age should come and whisper us back into the years.

Was anything barring His path back to the temples of our villages where others were reading the prophets and then disclosing their hearts?

Could He not have said, "Now I go east with the west wind," and so saying dismiss us with a smile upon His lips?

Aye, He could have said, "Go back to your kin. The world is not ready for me. I shall return a thousand years hence. Teach your children to await my return."

He could have done this had He so chosen.

But He knew that to build the temple invisible He must needs lay Himself the corner-stone, and lay us around as little pebbles cemented close to Himself.

He knew that the sap of His tree must rise from its roots, and He poured His blood upon its roots; and to Him it was not sacrifice but rather gain.

Death is the revealer. The death of Jesus revealed His life.

Had He escaped you and His enemies, you would have been the conquerors of the world. Therefore He did not escape.

Only He who desires all shall give all.

Aye, Jesus could have escaped His enemies and lived to old age. But He knew the passing of the seasons, and He would sing His song.

What man facing the armed world would not be conquered for the moment that he might overcome the ages?

And now you ask who, in very truth, slew Jesus, the Romans or the priests of Jerusalem?

Neither the Romans slew Him, nor the priests. The whole world stood to honour Him upon that hill.

JONATHAN

Among the Water-Lilies

Upon a day my beloved and I were rowing upon the lake of sweet waters. And the hills of Lebanon were about us.

We moved beside the weeping willows, and the reflections of the willows were deep around us.

And while I steered the boat with an oar, my beloved took her lute and sang thus:

What flower save the lotus knows the waters and the sun?
What heart save the lotus heart shall know both earth and sky?
Behold my love, the golden flower that floats 'twixt deep and high
Even as you and I float betwixt a love that has for ever been
And shall for ever be.
Dip your oar, my love,
And let me touch my strings.
Let us follow the willows, and let us leave not the water-lilies.
In Nazareth there lives a Poet, and His heart is like the lotus.
He has visited the soul of woman,
He knows her thirst is growing out of the waters,
And her hunger for the sun, though all her lips are fed.
They say He walks in Galilee.
I say He is rowing with us.
Can you not see His face, my love?
Can you not see, where the willow bough and its reflection meet,
He is moving as we move?
Beloved, it is good to know the youth of life.
It is good to know its singing joy.
Would that you might always have the oar,
And I my stringed lute,
Where the lotus laughs in the sun,
And the willow is dipping to the waters,
And His voice is upon my strings.
Dip your oar, my beloved,

And let me touch my strings.

There is a Poet in Nazareth

Who knows and loves us both.

Dip your oar, my lover,

And let me touch my strings.

HANNAH OF BETHSAIDA

She Speaks of her Father's Sister

The sister of my father had left us in her youth to dwell in a hut beside her father's ancient vineyard.

She lived alone, and the people of the countryside sought her in their maladies, and she healed them with green herbs, and with roots and flowers dried in the sun.

And they deemed her a seeress; but there were those also who called her witch and sorceress.

One day my father said to me, "Take these loaves of wheaten bread to my sister, and take this jug of wine and this basket of raisins."

And it was all put upon the back of a colt, and I followed the road until I reached the vineyard, and the hut of my father's sister. And she was gladdened.

Now as we sat together in the cool of the day, a man came by upon the road, and He greeted the sister of my father, saying, "Good-even to you, and the blessing of the night be upon you."

Then she rose up; and she stood as in awe before Him and said, "Good-even to you, master of all good spirits, and conqueror of all evil spirits."

The man looked at her with tender eyes, and then He passed on by.

But I laughed in my heart. Methought my father's sister was mad. But now I know that she was not mad. It was I who did not understand.

She knew of my laughter, though it was hidden.

And she spoke, but not in anger. She said, "Listen, my daughter, and hearken and keep my word in remembrance: the man who but now passed by, like the shadow of a bird flying between the sun and the earth, shall prevail against the Caesars and the empire of the Caesars. He shall wrestle with the crowned bull of Chaldea, and the man-headed lion of Egypt, and He shall overcome them; and He shall rule the world.

"But this land that now He walks shall come to naught; and Jerusalem, which sits proudly upon the hill, shall drift away in smoke upon the wind of desolation."

When she spoke thus, my laughter turned to stillness and I was quiet. Then I said, "Who is this man, and of what country and tribe does He come? And how shall He conquer the great kings and the empires of the great kings?"

And she answered, "He is one born here in this land, but we have conceived Him in our longing from the beginning of years. He is of all tribes and yet of none. He shall conquer by the word of His mouth and by the flame of His spirit."

Then suddenly she rose and stood up like a pinnacle of rock; and she said, "May the angel of the Lord forgive me for pronouncing this word also: He shall be slain, and His youth shall be shrouded, and He shall be laid in silence beside the tongue-less heart of the earth. And the maidens of Judea shall weep for Him."

Then she lifted her hand skyward and spoke again, and she said, "But He shall be slain only in the body.

"In the spirit He shall rise and go forth leading His host from this land where the sun is born, to the land where the sun is slain at eventide.

"And His name shall be first among men."

She was an aged seeress when she said these things, and I was but a girl, a field unploughed, a stone not yet in a wall.

But all that she beheld in the mirror of her mind has come to pass even in my day.

Jesus of Nazareth rose from the dead and led men and women unto the people of the sunset. The city that yielded Him to judgment was given unto destruction; and in the Judgment Hall where He was tried and sentenced, the owl hoots a dirge while the night weeps the dew of her heart upon the fallen marble.

And I am an old woman, and the years bend me down. My people are no more and my race is vanished.

I saw Him but once again after that day, and once again heard His voice. It was upon a hill-top when He was talking to His friends and followers.

And now I am old and alone, yet still He visits my dreams.

He comes like a white angel with pinions; and with His grace He hushes my dread of darkness. And He uplifts me to dreams yet more distant.

I am still a field unploughed, a ripe fruit that would not fall. The most that I possess is the warmth of the sun, and the memory of that man.

I know that among my people these shall not rise again king nor prophet nor priest, even as the sister of my father foretold.

We shall pass with the flowing of the rivers, and we shall be nameless.

But those who crossed Him in mid-stream shall be remembered for crossing Him in mid-stream.

MANASSEH

On the Speech and Gesture of Jesus

Yes, I used to hear Him speak. There was always a ready word upon His lips.

But I admired Him as a man rather than as a leader. He preached something beyond my liking, perhaps beyond my reason. And I would have no man preach to me.

I was taken by His voice and His gestures, not by the substance of His speech. He charmed me but never convinced me; for He was too vague, too distant and obscure to reach my mind.

I have known other men like Him. They are never constant nor are they consistent. It is with eloquence not with principles that they hold your ear and your passing thought, but never the core of your heart.

What a pity that His enemies confronted Him and forced the issue. It was not necessary. I believe their hostility will add to His stature and turn His mildness to power.

For is it not strange that in opposing a man you give Him courage? And in staying His feet you give Him wings?

I know not His enemies, yet I am certain that in their fear of a harmless man they have lent Him strength and made Him dangerous.

JEPHTHA OF CAESAREA

A Man Weary of Jesus

This man who fills your day and haunts your night is repellent to me. Yet you would tire my eyes with His sayings and my mind with His deeds.

I am weary of His words, and all that He did. His very name offends me, and the name of His countryside. I will none of Him.

Why make you a prophet of a man who was but a shadow? Why see a tower in this sand-dune, or imagine a lake in the raindrops gathered together in this hoof-print?

I scorn not the echo of caves in valleys nor the long shadows of the sunset; but I would not listen to the deceptions that hum in your head, nor study the reflections in your eyes.

What word did Jesus utter that Halliel had not spoken? What wisdom did He reveal that was not of Gamaliel? What are His lispings to the voice of Philo? What cymbals did He beat that were not beaten ere ever He lived?

I hearken to the echo from the caves into the silent valleys, and I gaze upon the long shadows of sunset; but I would not have this man's heart echo the sound of another heart, nor would I have a shadow of the seers call himself a prophet.

What man shall speak since Isaiah has spoken? Who dares sing since David? And shall wisdom be born now, after Solomon has been gathered to his fathers?

And what of our prophets, whose tongues were swords and their lips flames?

Left they a straw behind for this gleaner of Galilee? Or a fallen fruit for the beggar from the North Country? There was naught for Him save to break the loaf already baked by our ancestors, and to pour the wine which their holy feet had already passed from the grapes of old.

It is the potter's hand I honour not the man who buys the ware.

I honour those who sit at the loom rather than the boor who wears the cloth.

Who was this Jesus of Nazareth, and what is He? A man who dared not live His mind. Therefore He faded into oblivion and that is His end.

I beg you, charge not my ears with His words or His deeds. My heart is overfull with the prophets of old, and that is enough.

JOHN THE BELOVED DISCIPLE

On Jesus the Word

You would have me speak of Jesus, but how can I lure the passion-song of the world into a hollowed reed?

In every aspect of the day Jesus was aware of the Father. He beheld Him in the clouds and in the shadows of the clouds that pass over the earth. He saw the Father's face reflected in the quiet pools, and the faint print of His feet upon the sand; and He often closed His eyes to gaze into the Holy Eyes.

The night spoke to Him with the voice of the Father, and in solitude He heard the angel of the Lord calling to Him. And when He stilled Himself to sleep He heard the whispering of the heavens in His dreams.

He was often happy with us, and He would call us brothers.

Behold, He who was the first Word called us brothers, though we were but syllables uttered yesterday.

You ask why I call Him the first Word.

Listen, and I will answer:

In the beginning God moved in space, and out of His measureless stirring the earth was born and the seasons thereof.

Then God moved again, and life streamed forth, and the longing of life sought the height and the depth and would have more of itself.

Then God spoke thus, and His words were man, and man was a spirit begotten by God's Spirit.

And when God spoke thus, the Christ was His first Word and that Word was perfect; and when Jesus of Nazareth came to the world the first Word was uttered unto us and the sound was made flesh and blood.

Jesus the Anointed was the first Word of God uttered unto man, even as if an apple tree in an orchard should bud and blossom a day before the other trees. And in God's orchard that day was an aeon.

We are all sons and daughters of the Most High, but the Anointed One was His first-born, who dwelt in the body of Jesus of Nazareth, and He walked among us and we beheld Him.

All this I say that you may understand not only in the mind but rather in the spirit. The mind weighs and measures but it is the spirit that reaches the heart of life and embraces the secret; and the seed of the spirit is deathless.

The wind may blow and then cease, and the sea shall swell and then weary, but the heart of life is a sphere quiet and serene, and the star that shines therein is fixed for evermore.

MANNUS THE POMPEIIAN, TO A GREEK

On the Semitic Deity

The Jews, like their neighbours the Phoenicians and the Arabs, will not suffer their gods to rest for a moment upon the wind.

They are over-thoughtful of their deity, and over-observant of one another's prayer and worship and sacrifice.

While we Romans build marble temples to our gods, these people would discuss their god's nature. When we are in ecstasy we sing and dance round the altars of Jupiter and Juno, of Mars and Venus; but they in their rapture wear sackcloth and cover their heads with ashes – and even lament the day that gave them birth.

And Jesus, the man who revealed God as a being of joy, they tortured Him, and then put Him to death.

These people would not be happy with a happy god. They know only the gods of their pain.

Even Jesus' friends and disciples who knew His mirth and heard His laughter, make an image of His sorrow, and they worship that image.

And in such worship they rise not to their deity; they only bring their deity down to themselves.

I believe however that this philosopher, Jesus, who was not unlike Socrates, will have power over His race and mayhap over other races.

For we are all creatures of sadness and of small doubts. And when a man says to us, "Let us be joyous with the gods," we cannot but heed his voice. Strange that the pain of this man has been fashioned into a rite.

These people would discover another Adonis, a god slain in the forest, and they would celebrate his slaying. It is a pity they heed not His laughter.

But let us confess, as Roman to Greek. Do even we ourselves hear the laughter of Socrates in the streets of Athens? Is it ever in us to forget the cup of hemlock, even at the theatre of Dionysus?

Do not rather our fathers still stop at the street corners to chat of troubles and to have a happy moment remembering the doleful end of all our great men?

PONTIUS PILATUS

Of Eastern Rites and Cults

My wife spoke of Him many times ere He was brought before me, but I was not concerned.

My wife is a dreamer, and she is given, like so many Roman women of her rank, to Eastern cults and rituals. And these cults are dangerous to the Empire; and when they find a path to the hearts of our women they become destructive.

Egypt came to an end when the Hyskos of Arabia brought to her the one God of their desert. And Greece was overcome and fell to dust when Ashtarte and her seven maidens came from the Syrian shores.

As for Jesus, I never saw the man before He was delivered up to me as a malefactor, as an enemy of His own nation and also of Rome.

He was brought into the Hall of Judgment with His arms bound to His body with ropes.

I was sitting upon the dais, and He walked towards me with long, firm steps; then He stood erect and His head was held high.

And I cannot fathom what came over me at that moment; but it was suddenly my desire, though not my will, to rise and go down from the dais and fall before Him.

I felt as if Caesar had entered the Hall, a man greater than even Rome herself.

But this lasted only a moment. And then I saw simply a man who was accused of treason by His own people. And I was His governor and His judge.

I questioned Him but he would not answer. He only looked at me. And in His look was pity, as if it were He who was my governor and my judge.

Then there rose from without the cries of the people. But He remained silent, and still He was looking at me with pity in His eyes.

And I went out upon the steps of the palace, and when the people saw me they ceased to cry out. And I said, "What would you with this man?"

And they shouted as if with one throat, "We would crucify Him. He is our enemy and the enemy of Rome."

And some called out, "Did He not say He would destroy the temple? And was it not He who claimed the kingdom? We will have no king but Caesar."

Then I left them and went back into the Judgment Hall again, and I saw Him still standing there alone, and His head was still high.

And I remembered what I had read that a Greek philosopher said, "The lonely man is the strongest man." At that moment the Nazarene was greater than His race.

And I did not feel clement towards Him. He was beyond my clemency.

I asked Him then, "Are you the King of the Jews?"

And He said not a word.

And I asked Him again, "Have you not said that you are the King of the Jews?"

And He looked upon me.

Then He answered with a quiet voice, "You yourself proclaimed me king. Perhaps to this end I was born, and for this cause came to bear witness unto truth."

Behold a man speaking of truth at such a moment.

In my impatience I said aloud, to myself as much as to Him, "What is truth? And what is truth to the guiltless when the hand of the executioner is already upon him?"

Then Jesus said with power, "None shall rule the world save with the Spirit and truth."

And I asked Him saying, "Are you of the Spirit?"

He answered, "So are you also, though you know it not."

And what was the Spirit and what was truth, when I, for the sake of the State, and they from jealousy for their ancient rites, delivered an innocent man unto His death?

No man, no race, no empire would halt before a truth on its way towards self-fulfilment.

And I said again, "Are you the King of the Jews?"

And He answered, "You yourself say this. I have conquered the world ere this hour."

And this alone of all that He said was unseemly, inasmuch as only Rome has conquered the world.

But now the voices of the people rose again, and the noise was greater than before.

And I descended from my seat and said to Him, "Follow me."

And again I appeared upon the steps of the palace, and He stood there beside me.

When the people saw Him they roared like the roaring thunder. And in their clamour I heard naught save "Crucify Him, crucify Him."

Then I yielded Him to the priests who had yielded Him to me and I said to them, "Do what you will with this just man. And if it is your desire, take with you soldiers of Rome to guard Him."

Then they took Him, and I decreed that there be written upon the cross above His head, "Jesus of Nazareth, King of the Jews." I should have said instead, "Jesus of Nazareth, a King."

And the man was stripped and flogged and crucified.

It would have been within my power to save Him, but saving Him would have caused a revolution; and it is always wise for the governor of a Roman province not to be intolerant of the religious scruples of a conquered race.

I believe unto this hour that the man was more than an agitator. What I decreed was not my will, but rather for the sake of Rome.

Not long after, we left Syria, and from that day my wife has been a woman of sorrow. Sometimes even here in this garden I see a tragedy in her face.

I am told she talks much of Jesus to other women of Rome.

Behold, the man whose death I decreed returns from the world of shadows and enters into my own house.

And within myself I ask again and again,

What is truth and what is not truth?

Can it be that the Syrian is conquering us in the quiet hours of the night?

It should not indeed be so.

For Rome must needs prevail against the nightmares of our wives.

BARTHOLOMEW IN EPHESUS

On Slaves and Outcasts

The enemies of Jesus say that He addressed His appeal to slaves and outcasts, and would have incited them against their lords. They say that because He was of the lowly He invoked His own kind, yet that He sought to conceal His own origin.

But let us consider the followers of Jesus, and His leadership.

In the beginning He chose for companions few men from the North Country, and they were freemen. They were strong of body and bold of spirit, and in these past two-score years they have had the courage to face death with willingness and defiance.

Think you that these men were slaves or outcasts?

And think you that the proud princes of Lebanon and Armenia have forgotten their station in accepting Jesus as a prophet of God?

Or think you the high-born men and women of Antioch and Byzantium and Athens and Rome could be held by the voice of a leader of slaves?

Nay, the Nazarene was not with the servant against his master; neither was He with the master against his servant. He was with no man against another man.

He was a man above men, and the streams that ran in His sinews sang together with passion and with might.

If nobility lies in being protective, He was the noblest of all men. If freedom is in thought and word and action, He was the freest of all men. If high birth is in pride that yields only to love and in aloofness that is ever gentle and gracious, then He was of all men the highest born.

Forget not that only the strong and the swift shall win the race and the laurels, and that Jesus was crowned by those who loved Him, and also by His enemies though they knew it not.

Even now He is crowned every day by the priestesses of Artemis in the secret places of her temple.

MATTHEW

On Jesus by a Prison Wall

Upon an evening Jesus passed by a prison that was in the Tower of David. And we were walking after Him.

Of a sudden He tarried and laid His cheek against the stones of the prison wall. And thus He spoke:

"Brothers of my ancient day, my heart beats with your hearts behind the bars. Would that you could be free in my freedom and walk with me and my comrades.

"You are confined, but not alone. Many are the prisoners who walk the open streets. Their wings are not shorn, but like the peacock they flutter yet cannot fly.

"Brothers of my second day, I shall soon visit you in your cells and yield my shoulder to your burden. For the innocent and the guilty are not parted, and like the two bones of the forearm they shall never be cleaved.

"Brothers of this day, which is my day, you swam against the current of their reasoning and you were caught. They say I too shall swim against that current. Perhaps I shall soon be with you, a law-breaker among the law-breakers.

"Brothers of a day not yet come, these walls shall fall down, and out of the stones other shapes shall be fashioned by Him whose mallet is light, and whose chisel is the wind, and you shall stand free in the freedom of my new day."

Thus spoke Jesus and He walked on, and His hand was upon the prison wall until He passed by the Tower of David.

ANDREW

On Prostitutes

The bitterness of death is less bitter than life without Him. The days were hushed and made still when he was silenced. Only the echo in my memory repeats His words. But not His voice.

Once I heard Him say: "Go forth in your longing to the fields, and sit by the lilies, and you shall hear them humming in the sun. They weave not cloth for raiment, nor do they raise wood or stone for shelter; yet they sing.

"He who works in the night fulfils their needs and the dew of His grace is upon their petals.

"And are not you also His care who never wearies nor rests?"

And once I heard Him say, "The birds of the sky are counted and enrolled by Your Father even as the hairs of your head are numbered. Not a bird shall lie at the archer's feet, neither shall a hair of your head turn grey or fall into the emptiness of age without His will."

And once again He said, "I have heard you murmur in your hearts: 'Our God shall be more merciful unto us, children of Abraham, than unto those who knew Him not in the beginning.'

"But I say unto you that the owner of the vineyard who calls a labourer in the morning to reap, and calls another at sundown, and yet renders wages to the last even as to the first, that man is indeed justified. Does he not pay out of his own purse and with his own will?

"So shall my Father open the gate of His mansion at the knocking of the Gentiles even as at your knocking. For His ear heeds the new melody with the same love that it feels for the oft-heard song. And with a special welcome because it is the youngest string of His heart."

And once again I heard Him say, "Remember this: a thief is a man in need, a liar is a man in fear; the hunter who is hunted by the watchman of your night is also hunted by the watchman of his own darkness.

"I would have you pity them all.

"Should they seek your house, see that you open your door and bid them sit at your board. If you do not accept them you shall not be free from whatever they have committed."

And on a day I followed Him to the market-place of Jerusalem as the others followed Him. And He told us the parable of the prodigal son, and the parable of the merchant who sold all his possessions that he might buy a pearl.

But as He was speaking the Pharisees brought into the midst of the crowd a woman whom they called a harlot. And they confronted Jesus and said to Him, "She defiled her marriage vow, and she was taken in the act."

And He gazed at her; and He placed His hand upon her forehead and looked deep into her eyes.

Then he turned to the men who had brought her to Him, and He looked long at them; and He leaned down and with His finger He began to write upon the earth.

He wrote the name of every man, and beside the name He wrote the sin that every man had committed.

And as He wrote they escaped in shame into the streets.

And ere He had finished writing only that woman and ourselves stood before Him.

And again He looked into her eyes, and He said, "You have loved overmuch. They who brought you here loved but little. But they brought you as a snare for my ensnaring.

"And now go in peace.

"None of them is here to judge you. And if it is in your desire to be wise even as you are loving, then seek me; for the Son of Man will not judge you."

And I wondered then whether He said this to her because He Himself was not without sin.

But since that day I have pondered long, and I know now that only the pure of heart forgive the thirst that leads to dead waters.

And only the sure of foot can give a hand to him who stumbles.

And again and yet again I say, the bitterness of death is less bitter than life without Him.

A RICH MAN

On Possessions

He spoke ill of rich men. And upon a day I questioned Him saying, "Sir, what shall I do to attain the peace of the spirit?"

And He bade me give my possessions to the poor and follow Him.

But He possessed nothing; therefore He knew not the assurance and the freedom of possessions, nor the dignity and the self-respect that lie within.

In my household there are seven-score slaves and stewards; some labour in my groves and vineyards, and some direct my ships to distant isles.

Now had I heeded Him and given my possessions to the poor, what would have befallen my slaves and my servants and their wives and children? They too would have become beggars at the gate of the city or the portico of the temple.

Nay that good man did not fathom the secret of possessions. Because He and His followers lived on the bounty of others He thought all men should live likewise.

Behold a contradiction and a riddle: Should rich men bestow their riches upon the poor, and must the poor have the cup and the loaf of the rich man ere they welcome him to their board?

And must needs the holder of the tower be host to his tenants ere he calls himself lord of his own land?

The ant that stores food for the winter is wiser than a grasshopper that sings one day and hungers another.

Last Sabbath one of His followers said in the market-place, "At the threshold of heaven where Jesus may leave His sandals, no other man is worthy to lay his head."

But I ask, at the threshold of whose house that honest vagabond could have left His sandals? He Himself never had a house nor a threshold; and often He went without sandals.

JOHN AT PATMOS

Jesus the Gracious

Once more I would speak of Him.

God gave me the voice and the burning lips though not the speech.

And unworthy am I for the fuller word, yet I would summon my heart to my lips.

Jesus loved me and I knew not why.

And I loved Him because He quickened my spirit to heights beyond my stature, and to depths beyond my sounding.

Love is a sacred mystery.

To those who love, it remains forever wordless;

But to those who do not love, it may be but a heartless jest.

Jesus called me and my brother when we were labouring in the field.

I was young then and only the voice of dawn had visited my ears.

But His voice and the trumpet of His voice was the end of my labour and the beginning of my passion.

And there were naught for me then but to walk in the sun and worship the loveliness of the hour.

Could you conceive a majesty too kind to be majestic? And a beauty too radiant to seem beautiful?

Could you hear in your dreams a voice shy of its own rapture?

He called me and I followed Him.

That evening I returned to my father's house to get my other cloak.

And I said to my mother, "Jesus of Nazareth would have me in His company."

And she said, "Go His way my son, even like your brother."

And I accompanied Him.

His fragrance called me and commanded me, but only to release me.

Love is a gracious host to his guests though to the unbidden his house is a mirage and a mockery.

Now you would have me explain the miracles of Jesus.

We are all the miraculous gesture of the moment; our Lord and Master was the centre of that moment.

Yet it was not in His desire that His gestures be known.

I have heard Him say to the lame, "Rise and go home, but say not to the priest that I have made you whole."

And Jesus' mind was not with the cripple; it was rather with the strong and the upright.

His mind sought and held other minds and His complete spirit visited other spirits.

And is so doing His spirit changed these minds and these spirits.

It seemed miraculous, but with our Lord and Master it was simply like breathing the air of every day.

And now let me speak of other things.

On a day when He and I were alone walking in a field, we were both hungry, and we came to a wild apple tree.

There were only two apples hanging on the bough.

And He held the trunk of the tree with His arm and shook it, and the two apples fell down.

He picked them both up and gave one to me. The other He held in His hand.

In my hunger I ate the apple, and I ate it fast.

Then I looked at Him and I saw that He still held the other apple in His hand.

And He gave it to me saying, "Eat this also."

And I took the apple, and in my shameless hunger I ate it.

And as we walked on I looked upon His face.

But how shall I tell you of what I saw?

> A night where candles burn in space,
>
> A dream beyond our reaching;
>
> A noon where all shepherds are at peace and happy that their flock are grazing;
>
> An eventide, and a stillness, and a homecoming;
>
> Then a sleep and a dream.
>
> All these things I saw in His face.

He had given me the two apples. And I knew He was hungry even as I was hungry.

But I now know that in giving them to me He had been satisfied. He Himself ate of other fruit from another tree.

I would tell you more of Him, but how shall I?

When love becomes vast love becomes wordless.

And when memory is overladen it seeks the silent deep.

PETER

On the Neighbour

Once in Capernaum my Lord and Master spoke thus:

"Your neighbour is your other self dwelling behind a wall. In understanding, all walls shall fall down.

"Who knows but that your neighbour is your better self wearing another body? See that you love him as you would love yourself.

"He too is a manifestation of the Most High, whom you do not know.

"Your neighbour is a field where the springs of your hope walk in their green garments, and where the winters of your desire dream of snowy heights.

"Your neighbour is a mirror wherein you shall behold your countenance made beautiful by a joy which you yourself if not know, and by a sorrow you yourself did not share.

"I would have you love your neighbour even as I have loved you."

Then I asked Him saying, "How can I love a neighbour who loves me not, and who covets my property? One who would steal my possessions?"

And He answered, "When you are ploughing and your manservant is sowing the seed behind you, would you stop and look backward and put to flight a sparrow feeding upon a few of your seeds? Should you do this, you were not worthy of the riches of your harvest."

When Jesus had said this, I was ashamed and I was silent. But I was not in fear, for He smiled upon me.

A COBBLER IN JERUSALEM

A Neutral

I loved him not, yet I did not hate Him. I listened to Him not to hear His words but rather he sound of His voice; for His voice pleased me.

All that He said was vague to my mind, but the music thereof was clear to my ear.

Indeed were it not for what others have said to me of His teaching, I should not have known even so much as whether He was with Judea or against it.

SUZANNAH OF NAZARETH

Of the Youth and Manhood of Jesus

I knew Mary the mother of Jesus, before she became the wife of Joseph the carpenter, when we were both still unwedded.

In those days Mary would behold visions and hear voices, and she would speak of heavenly ministers who visited her dreams.

And the people of Nazareth were mindful of her, and they observed her going and her coming. And they gazed upon her brows and spaces in her steps.

But some said she was possessed. They said this because she would go only upon her own errands.

I deemed her old while she was young, for there was a harvest in her blossoming and ripe fruit in her spring.

She was born and reared amongst us yet she was like an alien from the North Country. In her eyes there was always the astonishment of one not yet familiar with our faces.

And she was as haughty as Miriam of old who marched with her brothers form the Nile to the wilderness.

Then Mary was betrothed to Joseph the carpenter.

When Mary was big with Jesus she would walk among the hills and return at eventide with loveliness and pain in her eyes.

And when Jesus was born I was told that Mary said to her mother, "I am but a tree unpruned. See you to this fruit." Martha the midwife heard her.

After three days I visited her. And there was wonder in her eyes, and her breasts heaved, and her arm was around her first-born like the shell that holds the pearl.

We all loved Mary's babe and we watched Him, for there was warmth in His being and He throbbed with the pace of His life.

The seasons passed, and He became a boy full of laughter and little wanderings. None of us knew what He would do for He seemed always outside of our race. But He was never rebuked though He was venturous and over-daring.

He played with the other children rather than they with Him.

When He was twelve years old, one day He led a blind man across the brook to the safety of the open road.

And in gratitude the blind man asked Him, "Little boy, who are you?"

And He answered, "I am not a little boy. I am Jesus."

And the blind man said, "Who is your father?"

And He answered, "God is my father."

And the blind man laughed and replied, "Well said, my little boy. But who is your mother?"

And Jesus answered, "I am not your little boy. And my mother is the earth."

And the blind man said, "Then behold, I was led by the Son of God and the earth across the stream."

And Jesus answered, "I will lead you wherever you would go, and my eyes will accompany your feet."

And He grew like a precious palm tree in our gardens.

When He was nineteen He was as comely as a hart, and His eyes were like honey and full of the surprise of day.

And upon His mouth there was the thirst of the desert flock for the lake.

He would walk the fields alone and our eyes would follow Him, and the eyes of all the maidens of Nazareth. But we were shy of Him.

Love is forever shy of beauty, yet beauty shall forever be pursued by love.

Then the years bade Him speak in the temple and in the gardens of Galilee.

And at times Mary followed Him to listen to His words and to hear the sound of her own heart. But when He and those who loved Him went down to Jerusalem she would not go.

For we at the North Country are often mocked in the streets of Jerusalem, even when we go carrying our offerings to the temple.

And Mary was too proud to yield to the South Country.

And Jesus visited other lands in the east and in the west. We knew not what lands He visited, yet our hearts followed Him.

But Mary awaited Him upon her threshold and every eventide her eyes sought the road for His home-coming.

Yet upon His return she would say to us, "He is too vast to be my Son, too eloquent for my silent heart. How shall I claim Him?"

It seemed to us that Mary could not believe that the plain had given birth to the mountain; in the whiteness of her heart she did not see that the ridge is a pathway to the summit.

She knew the man, but because He was her Son she dared not know Him.

And on a day when Jesus went to the lake to be with the fishermen she said to me, "What is man but this restless being that would rise from the earth, and who is man but a longing that desires the stars?

"My son is a longing. He is all of us longing for the stars.

"Did I say my son? May God forgive me. Yet in my heart I would be His mother."

Now, it is hard to tell more of Mary and her Son, but though there shall be husks in my throat, and my words shall reach you like cripples on crutches, I must needs relate what I have seen and heard.

It was in the youth of the year when the red anemones were upon the hills that Jesus called His disciples saying to them, "Come with me to Jerusalem and witness the slaying of the lamb for the Passover."

Upon the selfsame day Mary came to my door and said, "He is seeking the Holy City. Will you come and follow Him with me and the other women?"

And we walked the long road behind Mary and her son till we reached Jerusalem. And there a company of men and women hailed us at the gate, for His coming had been heralded to those who loved Him.

But upon that very night Jesus left the city with His men.

We were told that He had gone to Bethany.

And Mary stayed with us in the inn, awaiting His return.

Upon the eve of the following Thursday He was caught without the walls, and was held prisoner.

And when we heard He was a prisoner, Mary uttered not a word, but there appeared in her eyes the fulfilment of that promised pain and joy which we had beheld when she was but a bride in Nazareth.

She did not weep. She only moved among us like the ghost of a mother who would not bewail the ghost of her son.

We sat low upon the floor but she was erect, walking up and down the room.

She would stand beside the window and gaze eastward, and then with the fingers of her two hands brush back her hair.

At dawn she was still standing among us, like a lone banner in the wilderness wherein there are no hosts.

We wept because we knew the morrow of her son; but she did not weep for she knew also what would befall Him.

Her bones were of bronze and her sinews of the ancient elms, and her eyes were like the sky, wide and daring.

Have you heard a thrush sing while its nest burns in the wind?

Have you seen a woman whose sorrow is too much for tears, or a wounded heart that would rise beyond its own pain?

You have not seen such a woman, for you have not stood in the presence of Mary; and you have not been enfolded by the Mother Invisible.

In that still moment when the muffled hoofs of silence beat upon the breasts of the sleepless, John the young son of Zebedee, came and said: "Mary Mother, Jesus is going forth. Come, let us follow Him."

And Mary laid her hand upon John's shoulder and they went out, and we followed them.

When we came to the Tower of David we saw Jesus carrying His cross. And there was a great crowd about Him.

And two other men were also carrying their crosses.

And Mary's head was held high, and she walked with us after her son. And her step was firm.

And behind her walked Zion and Rome, ay, the whole world, to revenge itself upon one free Man.

When we reached the hill, He was raised high upon the cross.

And I looked at Mary. And her face was not the face of a woman bereaved. It was the countenance of the fertile earth, forever giving birth, forever burying her children.

Then to her eyes came the remembrance of His childhood, and she said aloud, "My son, who is not my son; man who once visited my womb, I glory in your power. I know that every drop of blood that runs down from your hands shall be the well-stream of a nation.

"You die in this tempest even as my heart once died in the sunset, and I shall now sorrow."

At that moment I desired to cover my face with my cloak and run away to the North Country. But of a sudden I heard Mary say, "My son, who is not my son, what have you said to the man at your right hand that has made him happy in his agony? The shadow of death is light upon his face, and he cannot turn his eyes from you.

"Now you smile upon me, and because you smile I know you have conquered."

And Jesus looked upon His mother and said, "Mary, from this hour be you the mother of John."

And to John He said, "Be a loving son unto this woman. Go to her house and let your shadow cross the threshold where I once stood. Do this in remembrance of me."

And Mary raised her right hand towards Him, and she was like a tree with one branch. And again she cried, "My son, who is not my son, if this be of God may God give us patience and the knowledge thereof. And if it be of man may God forgive him forevermore.

"If it be of God, the snow of Lebanon shall be your shroud; and if it be only of the priests and soldiers, then I have this garment for your nakedness.

"My son, who is not my son, that which God builds here shall not perish; and that which man would destroy shall remain builded, but not in his sight."

And at that moment the heavens yielded Him to the earth, a cry and a breath.

And Mary yielded Him also unto man, a wound and a balsam.

And Mary said, "Now behold, He is gone. The battle is over. The star has shone forth. The ship has reached the harbour. He who once lay against my heart is throbbing in space."

And we came close to her, and she said to us, "Even in death He smiles. He has conquered. I would indeed be the mother of a conqueror."

And Mary returned to Jerusalem leaning upon John the young disciple.

And she was a woman fulfilled.

And when we reached the gate of the city, I gazed upon her face and I was astonished, for on that day the head of Jesus was the highest among men, and yet Mary's head was not less high.

All this came to pass in the spring of the year.

And now it is autumn. And Mary the mother of Jesus has come again to her dwelling-place, and she is alone.

Two Sabbaths ago my heart was as a stone in my breast, for my son had left me for a ship in Tyre. He would be a sailor.

And he said he would return no more.

And upon an evening I sought Mary.

When I entered her house she was sitting at her loom, but she was not weaving. She was looking into the sky beyond Nazareth.

And I said to her, "Hail, Mary."

And she stretched out her arm to me, and said, "Come and sit beside me, and let us watch the sun pour its blood upon the hills."

And I sat beside her on the bench and we gazed into the west through the window.

And after a moment Mary said, "I wonder who is crucifying the sun this eventide."

Then I said, "I came to you for comfort. My son has left me for the sea and I am alone in the house across the way."

Then Mary said, "I would comfort you but how shall I?"

And I said, "If you will only speak of your son I shall be comforted."

And Mary smiled upon me, and she laid her hand about my shoulder and she said, "I will speak of Him. That which will console you will give me consolation."

Then she spoke of Jesus, and she spoke long of all that was in the beginning.

And it seemed to me that in her speech she would have no difference between her son and mine.

For she said to me, "My son is also a seafarer. Why would you not trust your son to the waves even as I have trusted Him?

"Woman shall be forever the womb and the cradle but never the tomb. We die that we may give life unto life even as our fingers spin the thread for the raiment that we shall never wear.

"And we cast the net for the fish that we shall never taste.

"And for this we sorrow, yet in all this is our joy."

Thus spoke Mary to me.

And I left her and came to my house, and though the light of the day was spent I sat at my loom to weave more of the cloth.

JOSEPH SURNAMED JUSTUS

Jesus the Wayfarer

They say he was vulgar, the common offspring of common seed, a man uncouth and violent.

They say that only the wind combed His hair, and only the rain brought His clothes and His body together.

They deem Him mad, and they attribute His words to demons.

Yet behold, the Man despised sounded a challenge and the sound thereof shall never cease.

He sang a song and none shall arrest that melody. It shall hover from generation to generation and it shall rise from sphere to sphere remembering the lips that gave it birth and the ears that cradled it.

He was a stranger. Aye, He was a stranger, a wayfarer on His way to a shrine, a visitor who knocked at our door, a guest from a far country.

And because He found not a gracious host, He has returned to His own place.

PHILIP

And When He Died All Mankind Died

When our beloved died, all mankind died and all things for a space were still and grey. Then the east was darkened, and a tempest rushed out of it and swept the land. The eyes of the sky opened and shut, and the rain came down in torrents and carried away the blood that streamed from His hands and His feet.

I too died. But in the depth of my oblivion I heard Him speak and say, "Father forgive them, for they know not what they do."

And His voice sought my drowned spirit and I was brought back to the shore.

And I opened my eyes and I saw His white body hanging against the cloud, and His words that I had heard took the shape within me and became a new man. And I sorrowed no more.

Who would sorrow for a sea that is unveiling its face, or for a mountain that laughs in the sun?

Was it ever in the heart of man, when that heart was pierced, to say such words?

What other judge of men has released His judges? And did ever love challenge hate with power more certain of itself?

Was ever such a trumpet heard 'twixt heaven and earth?

Was it known before that the murdered had compassion on his murderers? Or that the meteor stayed his footsteps for the mole?

The seasons shall tire and the years grow old, ere they exhaust these words: "Father forgive them, for they know not what they do."

And you and I, though born again and again, shall keep them.

And now I would go into my house, and stand an exalted beggar, at His door.

BIRBARAH OF YAMMOUNI

On Jesus the Impatient

Jesus was patient with the dullard and the stupid, even as the winter awaits the spring.

He was patient like a mountain in the wind.

He answered with kindliness the harsh questionings of His foes.

He could even be silent to cavil and dispute, for He was strong and the strong can be forbearing.

But Jesus was also impatient.

He spared not the hypocrite.

He yielded not to men of cunning nor to the jugglers of words.

And He would not be governed.

He was impatient with those who believed not in light because they themselves dwelt in shadow; and with those who sought after signs in the sky rather than in their own hearts.

He was impatient with those who weighed and measured the day and the night before they would trust their dreams to dawn or eventide.

Jesus was patient.

Yet He was the most impatient of men.

He would have you weave the cloth though you spend years between the loom and the linen.

But He would have none tear an inch off the woven fabric.

PILATE'S WIFE TO A ROMAN LADY

I was walking with my maidens in the groves outside of Jerusalem when I saw Him with a few men and women sitting about Him; and He was speaking to them in a language which I only half understood.

But one needs not a language to perceive a pillar of light or a mountain of crystal. The heart knows what the tongue may never utter and the ears may never hear.

He was speaking to His friends of love and strength. I know He spoke of love because there was melody in His voice; and I know He spoke of strength because there were armies in His gestures. And He was tender, though even my husband could not have spoken with such authority.

When He saw me passing by He stopped speaking for a moment and looked kindly upon me. And I was humbled; and in my soul I knew I had passed by a god.

After that day His image visited my privacy when I would not be visited by man or woman; and His eyes searched my soul when my own eyes were closed. And His voice governs the stillness of my nights.

I am held fast forevermore; and there is peace in my pain, and freedom in my tears.

Belovèd friend, you have never seen that man, and you will never see Him.

He is gone beyond our senses, but of all men He is now the nearest to me.

A MAN OUTSIDE OF JERUSALEM

Of Judas

Judas came to my house that Friday, upon the eve of the Passover; and he knocked at my door with force.

When he entered I looked at him, and his face was ashen. His hands trembled like dry twigs in the wind, and his clothes were as wet as if he had stepped out from a river; for on that evening there were great tempests.

He looked at me, and the sockets of his eyes were like dark caves and his eyes were blood-sodden.

And he said, "I have delivered Jesus of Nazareth to His enemies and to my enemies."

Then Judas wrung his hands and he said, "Jesus declared that He would overcome all His foes and the foes of our people. And I believed and I followed Him.

"When first He called us to Him He promised us a kingdom mighty and vast, and in our faith we sought His favour that we might have honourable stations in His court.

"We beheld ourselves princes dealing with these Romans as they have dealt with us. And Jesus said much about His kingdom, and I thought He had chosen me a captain of His chariots, and a chief man of his warriors. And I followed His footsteps willingly.

"But I found it was not a kingdom that Jesus sought, nor was it from the Romans He would have had us free. His kingdom was but the kingdom of the heart. I heard Him talk of love and charity and forgiveness, and the wayside women listened gladly, but my heart grew bitter and I was hardened.

"My promised king of Judea seemed suddenly to have turned flute-player, to soothe the mind of wanderers and vagabonds.

"I had loved Him as others of my tribe had loved Him. I had beheld Him a hope and a deliverance from the yoke of the aliens. But when He would not utter a word or move a hand to free us from that yoke, and when He would even have rendered unto Caesar that which is Caesar's, then despair filled me and my hopes died. And I said, 'He who murders my hopes shall be murdered, for my hopes and expectations are more precious than the life of any man'."

Then Judas gnashed his teeth; and he bent down his head. And when he spoke again, he said, "I have delivered Him up. And He was crucified this day. . . . Yet when He died upon the cross, He died a king. He died in the tempest as deliverers die, like vast men who live beyond the shroud and the stone.

"And all the while He was dying, He was gracious, and He was kindly; and His heart was full of pity. He felt pity even for me who had delivered Him up."

And I said, "Judas, you have committed a grave wrong."

And Judas answered, "But He died a king. Why did He not live a king?"

And I said again, "You have committed a grave crime."

And he sat down there, upon that bench, and he was as still as a stone.

But I walked to and fro in the room, and once more I said, "You have committed a great sin."

But Judas said not a word. He remained as silent as the earth.

And after a while he stood up and faced me and he seemed taller, and when he spoke his voice was like the sound of a cracked vessel; and he said, "Sin was not in my heart. This very night I shall seek His kingdom, and I shall stand in His presence and beg His forgiveness.

"He died a king, and I shall die a felon. But in my heart I know He will forgive me."

After saying these words he folded his wet cloak around him and he said, "It was good that I came to you this night even though I have brought you trouble. Will you also forgive me?

"Say to your sons and to your sons' sons: 'Judas Iscariot delivered Jesus of Nazareth to His enemies because he believed Jesus was an enemy to His own race.'

"And say also that Judas upon the selfsame day of his great error followed the King to the steps of His throne to deliver up his own soul and to be judged.

"I shall tell Him that my blood also was impatient for the sod, and my crippled spirit would be free."

Then Judas leaned his head back against the wall and he cried out, "O God whose dreaded name no man shall utter ere his lips are touched by the fingers of death, why did you burn me with a fire that had no light?

"Why did you give the Galilean a passion for a land unknown and burden me with desire that would not escape kin or hearth? And who is this man Judas, whose hands are dipped in blood?

"Lend me a hand to cast him off, an old garment and a tattered harness.

"Help me to do this tonight.

"And let me stand again outside of these walls.

"I am weary of this wingless liberty. I would a larger dungeon.

"I would flow a stream of tears to the bitter sea. I would be a man of your mercy rather than one knocking at the gate of his own heart."

Thus Judas spoke, and thereupon he opened the door and went out again into the tempest.

Three days afterwards I visited Jerusalem and heard of all that had come to pass. And I also heard that Judas had flung himself from the summit of the High Rock.

I have pondered long since that day, and I understand Judas. He fulfilled his little life, which hovered like a mist on this land and enslaved by the Romans, while the great prophet was ascending the heights.

One man longed for a kingdom in which he was to be a prince.

Another man desired a kingdom in which all men shall be princes.

SARKIS,
AN OLD GREEK SHEPHERD, CALLED THE MADMAN

Jesus and Pan

In a dream I saw Jesus and My God Pan sitting together in the heart of the forest.

They laughed at each other's speech, with the brook that ran near them, and the laughter of Jesus was the merrier. And they conversed long.

Pan spoke of earth and her secrets, and of his hoofed brothers and his horned sisters; and of dreams. And he spoke of roots and their nestlings, and of the sap that wakes and rises and sings to summer.

And Jesus told of the young shoots in the forest, and of flowers and fruit, and the seed that they shall bear in a season not yet come.

He spoke of birds in space and their singing in the upper world.

And He told of white harts in the desert wherein God shepherds them.

And Pan was pleased with the speech of the new God, and his nostrils quivered.

And in the same dream I beheld Pan and Jesus grow quiet and still in the stillness of the green shadows.

And then Pan took his reeds and played to Jesus.

The trees were shaken and the ferns trembled, and there was a fear upon me.

And Jesus said, "Good brother, you have the glade and the rocky height in your reeds."

Then Pan gave the reeds to Jesus and said, "You play now. It is your turn."

And Jesus said, "These reeds are too many for my mouth. I have this flute."

And He took His flute and He played.

And I heard the sound of rain in the leaves, and the singing of streams among the hills, and the falling of snow on the mountain-top.

The pulse of my heart, that had once beaten with the wind, was restored again to the wind, and all the waves of my yesterdays were upon my shore, and I was again Sarkis the shepherd, and the flute of Jesus became the pipes of countless shepherds calling to countless flocks.

Then Pan said to Jesus, "Your youth is more kin to the reed than my years. And long ere this in my stillness I have heard your song and the murmur of your name.

"Your name has a goodly sound; well shall it rise with the sap to the branches, and well shall it run with the hoofs among the hills.

And it is not strange to me, though my father called me not by that name. It was your flute that brought it back to my memory.

"And now let us play our reeds together."

And they played together.

And their music smote heaven and earth, and a terror struck all living things.

I heard the bellow of beasts and the hunger of the forest. And I heard the cry of lonely men, and the plaint of those who long for what they know not.

I heard the sighing of the maiden for her lover, and the panting of the luckless hunter for his prey.

And then there came peace into their music, and the heavens and the earth sang together.

All this I saw in my dream, and all this I heard.

ANNAS THE HIGH PRIEST

On Jesus the Rabble

He was of the rabble, a brigand, a mountebank and a self-trumpeter. He appealed only to the unclean and the disinherited, and for this He had to go the way of all the tainted and the defiled.

He made sport of us and of our laws; He mocked at our honour and jeered at our dignity. He even said He would destroy the temple and desecrate the holy places. He was shameless, and for this He had to die a shameful death.

He was a man from Galilee of the Gentiles, an alien, from the North Country where Adonis and Ashtarte still claim power against Israel and the God of Israel.

He whose tongue halted when He spoke the speech of our prophets was loud and ear-splitting when he spoke the bastard language of the low-born and the vulgar.

What else was there for me but to decree His death?

Am I not a guardian of the temple? Am I not a keeper of the law? Could I have turned my back on Him, saying in all tranquillity: "He is a madman among madmen. Let Him alone to exhaust Himself raving; for the mad and the crazed and those possessed with devils shall be naught in the path of Israel" ?

Could I have been deaf unto Him when he called us liars. hypocrites, wolves, vipers, and the sons of vipers?

Nay I could not be deaf to Him, for He was not a madman. He was self-possessed; and in His big-sounding sanity He denounced and challenged us all.

For this I had Him crucified, and His crucifixion was a signal and warning unto the others who are stamped with the same damned seal.

I know well I have been blamed for this, even by some of the elders in the Sanhedrim. But I was mindful then as I am mindful now, that one man should die for the people rather than the people be led astray by one man.

Jesus was conquered by an enemy from without. I shall see that Judea is not conquered again, by an enemy from within.

No man from the cursed North shall reach our Holy of Holies nor lay His shadow across the Ark of the Covenant.

A WOMAN,
ONE OF MARY'S NEIGHBOURS

A Lamentation

On the fortieth day after His death, all the women neighbours came to the house of Mary to console her and to sing threnodies.

And one of the women sang this song:

Whereto my Spring, whereto?

And to what other space your perfume ascending?

In what other fields shall you walk?

And to what sky shall you lift up your head to speak your heart?

These valleys shall be barren,

And we shall have naught but dried fields and arid.

All green things will parch in the sun,

And our orchards will bring forth sour apples,

And our vineyards bitter grapes.

We shall thirst for your wine,

And our nostrils will long for your fragrance.

Whereto Flower of our first spring., whereto?

And will you return no more?

Will not your jasmine visit us again,

And your cyclamen stand by our wayside

To tell us that we too have our roots deep in earth,

And that our ceaseless breath would forever climb the sky?

Whereto Jesus, whereto,

Son of my neighbour Mary,

And comrade to my son?

Whither, our first Spring, and to what other fields?

Will you return to us again?

Will you in your love-tide visit the barren shores of our dreams?

AHAZ THE PORTLY

The Keeper of the Inn

Well do I remember the last time I saw Jesus the Nazarene. Judas had come to me at the noon hour of that Thursday, and bidden me prepare supper for Jesus and His friends.

He gave me two silver pieces and said, "Buy all that you deem needful for the meal."

And after He was gone my wife said to me, "This is indeed a distinction." For Jesus had become a prophet and He had wrought many miracles.

At twilight He came and His followers, and they sat in the upper chamber around the board, but they were silent and quiet.

Last year also and the year before they had come and then they had been joyous. They broke the bread and drank the wine and sang our ancient strains; and Jesus would talk to them till midnight.

After that they would leave Him alone in the upper chamber and go to sleep in other rooms; for after midnight it was His desire to be alone.

And He would remain awake; I would hear His steps as I lay upon my bed.

But this last time He and His friends were not happy.

My wife had prepared fishes from the Lake of Galilee, and pheasants from Houran stuffed with rice and pomegranate seeds, and I had carried them a jug of my cypress wine.

And then I had left them for I felt that they wished to be alone.

They stayed until it was full dark, and then they all descended together from the upper chamber, but at the foot of the stairs Jesus tarried awhile. And He looked at me and my wife, and He placed His hand upon the head of my daughter and He said, "Good night to you all. We shall come back again to your upper chamber, but we shall not leave you at this early hour. We shall stay until the sun rises above the horizon.

"In a little while we shall return and ask for more bread and more wine. You and your wife have been good hosts to us, and we shall remember you when we come to our mansion and sit at our own board."

And I said, "Sir, it was an honour to serve you. The other innkeepers envy me because of your visits, and in my pride I smile at them in the market-place. Sometimes I even make a grimace."

And He said, "All innkeepers should be proud in serving. For he who gives bread and wine is the brother of him who reaps and gathers the sheaves for the threshing-floor, and of him who crushes the grapes at the winepress. And you are all kindly. You give of your bounty even to those who come with naught but hunger and thirst."

Then He turned to Judas Iscariot who kept the purse of the company, and He said, "Give me two shekels."

And Judas gave Him two shekels saying: "These are the last silver pieces in my purse."

Jesus looked at him and said, "Soon, oversoon, your purse shall be filled with silver."

Then He put the two pieces into my hand and said, "With these buy a silken girdle for your daughter, and bid her wear it on the day of the Passover, in remembrance of me."

And looking again into the face of my daughter, He leaned down and kissed her brow. And then He said once more, "Good-night to you all."

And He walked away.

I have been told that what He said to us has been recorded upon a parchment by one of His friends, but I repeat it to you even as I heard it from His own lips.

Never shall I forget the sound of His voice as He said those words, "Good night to you all."

If you would know more of Him, ask my daughter. She is a woman now, but she cherishes the memory of her girlhood. And her words are more ready than mine.

BARABBAS

The Last Words of Jesus

They released me and chose Him. Then He rose and I fell down.

And they held Him a victim and a sacrifice for the Passover.

I was freed from my chains, and walked with the throng behind Him, but I was a living man going to my own grave.

I should have fled to the desert where shame is burned out by the sun.

Yet I walked with those who had chosen Him to bear my crime.

When they nailed Him on His cross I stood there.

I saw and I heard but I seemed outside of my body.

The thief who was crucified on His right said to Him, "Are you bleeding with me, even you, Jesus of Nazareth?"

And Jesus answered and said, "Were it not for this nail that stays my hand I would reach forth and clasp your hand.

"We are crucified together. Would they had raised your cross nearer to mine."

Then He looked down and gazed upon His mother and a young man who stood beside her.

He said, "Mother, behold your son standing beside you.

"Woman, behold a man who shall carry these drops of my blood to the North Country."

And when he heard the wailing of the women of Galilee He said, "Behold, they weep and I thirst.

"I am held too high to reach their tears.

"I will not take vinegar and gall to quench this thirst."

Then His eyes opened wide to the sky, and He said, "Father, why hast Thou forsaken us?"

And then He said in compassion, "Father, forgive them, for they know not what they do."

When He uttered those words methought I saw all men prostrated before God beseeching forgiveness for the crucifixion of this one man.

Then again He said with a great voice: "Father, into Thy hand I yield back my spirit."

And at last He lifted up His head and said, "Now it is finished, but only upon this hill."

And He closed His eyes.

Then lightning cracked the dark skies, and there was a great thunder.

I know now that those who slew Him in my stead achieved my endless torment.

His crucifixion endured but for an hour.

But I shall be crucified unto the end of my years.

CLAUDIUS, A ROMAN SENTINEL

Jesus the Stoic

After he was taken, they entrusted Him to me. And I was ordered by Pontius Pilatus to keep Him in custody until the following morning.

My soldiers led Him prisoner, and He was obedient to them.

At midnight I left my wife and children and visited the arsenal. It was my habit to go about and see all that was well with my battalions in Jerusalem; and that night I visited the arsenal where He was held.

My soldiers and some of the young Jews were making sport of Him. They had stripped Him of His garment, and they had put a crown of last year's brier-thorns upon His head.

They had seated Him against a pillar, and they were dancing and shouting before Him.

And they had given Him a reed to hold in His hand.

As I entered someone shouted, "Behold, O Captain, the King of the Jews."

I stood before Him and looked at Him, and I was ashamed. I knew not why.

I had fought in Gallia and in Spain, and with my men I had faced death. Yet never had I been in fear, nor been a coward. But when I stood before that man and He looked at me I lost heart. It seemed as though my lips were sealed, and I could not utter no word.

And straightway I left the arsenal.

This chanced thirty years ago. My sons who were babes then are men now. And they are serving Caesar and Rome.

But often in counselling them I have spoken of Him, a man facing death with the sap of life upon His lips, and with compassion for His slayers in His eyes.

And now I am old. I have lived the years fully. And I think truly that neither Pompey nor Caesar was so great a commander as that Man of Galilee.

For since His unresisting death an army has risen out of the earth to fight for Him. . . . And He is better served by them, though dead, than ever Pompey or Caesar was served, though living.

JAMES,
THE BROTHER OF THE LORD

The Last Supper

A thousand times I have been visited by the memory of that night. And I know now that I shall be visited a thousand times again.

The earth shall forget the furrows ploughed upon her breast, and a woman the pain and joy of childbirth, ere I shall forget that night.

In the afternoon we had been outside the walls of Jerusalem, and Jesus had said, "Let us go into the city now and take supper at the inn."

It was dark when we reached the inn, and we were hungry. The innkeeper greeted us and led us to an upper chamber.

And Jesus bade us sit around the board, but He himself remained standing, and His eyes rested upon us.

And He spoke to the keeper of the inn and said, "Bring me a basin and a pitcher full of water, and a towel."

And He looked at us again and said gently, "Cast off your sandals."

We did not understand, but at His command we cast them off.

Then the keeper of the inn brought the basin and the pitcher; and Jesus said, "Now I will wash your feet. For I must needs free your feet from the dust of the ancient road, and give them the freedom of the new way."

And we were all abashed and shy.

Then Simon Peter stood up and said: "How shall I suffer my Master and my Lord to wash my feet?"

And Jesus answered, "I will wash your feet that you may remember that he who serves men shall be the greatest among men."

Then He looked at each one of us and He said: "The Son of Man who has chosen you for His brethren, He whose feet were anointed yesterday with myrrh of Arabia and dried with a women's hair, desires now to wash your feet."

And He took the basin and the pitcher and kneeled down and washed our feet, beginning with Judas Iscariot.

Then He sat down with us at the board; and His face was like the dawn rising upon a battlefield after a night of strife and blood-shedding.

And the keeper of the inn came with his wife, bringing food and wine.

And though I had been hungry before Jesus knelt at my feet, now I had no stomach for food. And there was a flame in my throat which I would not quench with wine.

Then Jesus took a loaf of bread and gave to us, saying, "Perhaps we shall not break bread again. Let us eat this morsel in remembrance of our days in Galilee."

And He poured wine from the jug into a cup and He drank, and gave to us, and He said, "Drink this in remembrance of a thirst we have known together. And drink it also in hope for the new vintage. When I am enfolded and am no more among you, and when you meet here or elsewhere, break the bread and pour the wine, and eat and drink even as you are doing now. Then look about you; and perchance you may see me sitting with you at the board."

After saying this He began to distribute among us morsels of fish and pheasant, like a bird feeding its fledglings.

We ate little yet we were filled; and we drank but a drop, for we felt that the cup was like a space between this land and another land.

Then Jesus said, "Ere we leave this board let us rise and sing the joyous hymns of Galilee."

And we rose and sang together, and His voice was above our voices, and there was a ringing in every word of His words.

And He looked at our faces, each and every one, and He said, "Now I bid you farewell. Let us go beyond these walls. Let us go unto Gethsemane."

And John the Son of Zebedee said, "Master, why do you say farewell to us this night?"

And Jesus said, "Let not your heart be troubled. I only leave you to prepare a place for you in my Father's house. But if you shall be in need of me, I will come back to you. Where you call me, there I shall hear you, and wherever your spirit shall seek me, there I will be.

"Forget not that thirst leads to the winepress, and hunger to the wedding-feast.

"It is in your longing that you shall find the Son of Man. For longing is the fountain-head of ecstasy, and it is the path to the Father."

And John spoke again and said, "If you would indeed leave us, how shall we be of good cheer? And why speak you of separation?"

And Jesus said, "The hunted stag knows the arrow of the hunter before it feels it in his breast; and the river is aware of the sea ere it comes to her shore. And the Son of Man has travelled the ways of men.

Before another almond tree renders her blossoms to the sun, my roots shall be reaching into the heart of another field."

Then Simon Peter said: "Master, leave us not now, and deny us not the joy of your presence. Where you go we too will go; and wherever you abide there we will be also."

And Jesus put His hand upon Simon Peter's shoulder, and smiled upon him, and He said, "Who knows but that you may deny me before this night is over, and leave me before I leave you?"

Then of a sudden He said, "Now let us go hence."

And He left the inn and we followed Him. But when we reached the gate of the city, Judas of Iscariot was no longer with us. And we crossed the Valley of Jahannam. Jesus walked far ahead of us, and we walked close to one another.

When He reached an olive grove he stopped and turned towards us saying, "Rest here for an hour."

The evening was cool, though it was full spring with the mulberries unfolding their shoots and the apple trees in bloom. And the gardens were sweet.

Each one of us sought the trunk of a tree, and we lay down. I myself gathered my cloak around me and lay under a pine tree.

But Jesus left us and walked by Himself in the olive grove. And I watched Him while the others slept.

He would suddenly stand still, and again He would walk up and down. This He did many times.

Then I saw Him lift His face towards the sky and outstretch His arms to east and west.

Once He had said, "Heaven and earth, and hell too, are of man." And now I remembered His saying, and I knew that He who was pacing the olive grove was heaven made man; and I bethought me that the womb of the earth is not a beginning nor an end, but rather a chariot, a pause; and a moment of wonder and surprise; and hell I saw also, in the valley called Jahannam, which lay between Him and the Holy City.

And as He stood there and I lay wrapped in my garment, I heard His voice speaking. But He was not speaking to us. Thrice I heard Him pronounce the word Father . And that was all I heard.

After a while His arms dropped down, and He stood still like a cypress tree between my eyes and the sky.

At last He came over among us again, and He said to us, "Wake and rise. My hour has come. The world is already upon us, armed for battle."

And then He said, "A moment ago I heard the voice of my Father. If I see you not again, remember that the conqueror shall not have peace until he is conquered."

And when we had risen and come close to Him, His face was like the starry heaven above the desert.

Then He kissed each one of us upon the cheek. And when His lips touched my cheek, they were hot, like the hand of a child in fever.

Suddenly we heard a great noise in the distance, as of numbers, and when it came near it was a company of men approaching with lanterns and slaves. And they came in haste.

As they reached the hedge of the grove Jesus left us and went forth and met them. And Judas of Iscariot was leading them.

There were Roman soldiers with swords and spears, and men of Jerusalem with clubs and pickaxes.

And Judas came up to Jesus and kissed Him. And then he said to the armed men, "This is the Man."

And Jesus said to Judas, "Judas, you were patient with me. This could have been yesterday."

Then He turned to the armed men and said: "Take me now. But see that your cage is large enough for these wings."

Then they fell upon Him and held Him, and they were all shouting.

But we in our fear ran away and sought to escape. I ran alone through the olive groves, nor had I power to be mindful, nor did any voice speak in me except my fear.

Through the two or three hours that remained of that night I was fleeing and hiding, and at dawn I found myself in a village near Jericho.

Why had I left Him? I do not know. But to my sorrow I did leave Him. I was a coward and I fled from the face of His enemies.

Then I was sick and ashamed at heart, and I returned to Jerusalem, but He was a prisoner, and no friend could have speech with Him.

He was crucified, and His blood has made new clay of the earth.

And I am living still; I am living upon the honeycomb of His sweet life.

SIMON THE CYRENE

He who Carried the Cross

I was on my way to the fields when I saw Him carrying His cross; and multitudes were following Him.

Then I too walked beside Him.

His burden stopped Him many a time, for His body was exhausted.

Then a Roman soldier approached me, saying, "Come, you are strong and firm built; carry the cross of this man."

When I heard these words my heart swelled within me and I was grateful.

And I carried His cross.

It was heavy, for it was made of poplar soaked through with the rains of winter.

And Jesus looked at me. And the sweat of His forehead was running down upon His beard.

Again He looked at me and He said, "Do you too drink this cup? You shall indeed sip its rim with me to the end of time."

So saying He placed His hand upon my free shoulder. And we walked together towards the Hill of the Skull.

But now I felt not the weight of the cross. I felt only His hand. And it was like the wing of a bird upon my shoulder.

Then we reached the hill top, and there they were to crucify Him.

And then I felt the weight of the tree.

He uttered no word when they drove the nails into His hands and feet, nor made He any sound.

And His limbs did not quiver under the hammer.

It seemed as if His hands and feet had died and would only live again when bathed in blood. Yet it seemed also as if He sought the nails as the prince would seek the sceptre; and that He craved to be raised to the heights.

And my heart did not think to pity Him, for I was too filled to wonder.

Now, the man whose cross I carried has become my cross.

Should they say to me again, "Carry the cross of this man," I would carry it till my road ended at the grave.

But I would beg Him to place His hand upon my shoulder.

This happened many years ago; and still whenever I follow the furrow in the field, and in that drowsy moment before sleep, I think always of that Beloved Man.

And I feel His winged hand, here, on my left shoulder.

CYBOREA

The Mother of Judas

My son was a good man and upright. He was tender and kind to me, and he loved his kin and his countrymen. And he hated our enemies, the cursed Romans, who wear purple cloth though they spin no thread nor sit at any loom; and who reap and gather where they have not ploughed nor sowed the seed.

My son was but seventeen when he was caught shooting arrows at the Roman legion passing through our vineyard.

Even at that age he would speak to the other youths of the glory of Israel, and he would utter many strange things that I did not understand.

He was my son, my only son.

He drank life from these breasts now dry, and he took his first steps in this garden, grasping these fingers that are now like trembling reeds.

With these selfsame hands, young and fresh then like the grapes of Lebanon, I put away his first sandals in a linen kerchief that my mother had given me. I still keep them there in that chest, beside the window.

He was my first-born, and when he took his first step, I too took my first step. For women travel not save when led by their children.

And now they tell me he is dead by his own hand; that he flung himself from the High Rock in remorse because he had betrayed his friend Jesus of Nazareth.

I know my son is dead. But I know he betrayed no one; for he loved his kin and hated none but the Romans.

My son sought the glory of Israel, and naught but that glory was upon his lips and in his deeds.

When he met Jesus on the highway he left me to follow Him. And in my heart I knew that he was wrong to follow any man.

When he bade me farewell I told him that he was wrong, but he listened not.

Our children do not heed us; like the high tide of today, they take no counsel with the high tide of yesterday.

I beg you question me no further about my son.

I loved him and I shall love him forevermore.

If love were in the flesh I would burn it out with hot irons and be at peace. But it is in the soul, unreachable.

And now I would speak no more. Go question another woman more honoured than the mother of Judas.

Go to the mother of Jesus. The sword is in her heart also; she will tell you of me, and you will understand.

THE WOMAN OF BYBLOS

A Lamentation

Weep with me, ye daughters of Ashtarte, and all ye lovers of Tamouz,

Bid your heart melt and rise and run blood-tears,

For He who was made of gold and ivory is no more.

In the dark forest the boar overcame Him,

And the tusks of the boar pierced His flesh.

Now He lies stained with the leaves of yesteryear,

And no longer shall His footsteps wake the seeds that sleep in the bosom of the spring.

His voice will not come with the dawn to my window,

And I shall be forever alone.

Weep with me, ye daughters of Ashtarte, and all ye lovers of Tamouz,

For my Beloved has escaped me;

He who spoke as the rivers speak;

He whose voice and time were twins;

He whose mouth was a red pain made sweet;

He on whose lips gall would turn to honey.

Weep with me, daughters of Ashtarte, and ye lovers of Tamouz.

Weep with me around His bier as the stars weep,

And as the moon-petals fall upon His wounded body.

Wet with your tears the silken covers of my bed,

Where my Beloved once lay in my dream,

And was gone away in my awakening.

I charge ye, daughters of Ashtarte, and all ye lovers of Tamouz,

Bare your breasts and weep and comfort me,

For Jesus of Nazareth is dead.

MARY MAGDALEN, THIRTY YEARS LATER

On the Resurrection of the Spirit

Once again I say that with death Jesus conquered death, and rose from the grave a spirit and a power. And He walked in our solitude and visited the gardens of our passion.

He lies not there in that cleft rock behind the stone.

We who love Him beheld Him with these our eyes which He made to see; and we touched Him with these our hands which He taught to reach forth.

I know you who believe not in Him. I was one of you, and you are many; but your number shall be diminished.

Must your break your harp and your lyre to find the music therein?

Or must you fell a tree ere you can believe it bears fruit?

You hate Jesus because someone from the North Country said He was the Son of God. But you hate one another because each of you deems himself too great to be the brother of the next man.

You hate Him because someone said He was born of a virgin, and not of man's seed.

But you know not the mothers who go to the tomb in virginity, nor the men who go down to the grave choked with their own thirst.

You know not that the earth was given in marriage to the sun, and that earth it is who sends us forth to the mountain and the desert.

There is a gulf that yawns between those who love Him and those who hate Him, between those who believe and those who do not believe.

But when the years have bridged that gulf you shall know that He who lived in us is deathless, that He was the Son of God even as we are the children of God; that He was born of a virgin even as we are born of the husbandless earth.

It is passing strange that the earth gives not to the unbelievers the roots that would suck at her breast, nor the wings wherewith to fly high and drink, and be filled with the dews of her space.

But I know what I know, and it is enough.

A MAN FROM LEBANON

Nineteen Centuries Afterward

Master, master singer,

Master of words unspoken,

Seven times was I born, and seven times have I died

Since your last hasty visit and our brief welcome.

And behold I live again,

Remembering a day and a night among the hills,

When your tide lifted us up.

Thereafter many lands and many seas did I cross,

And wherever I was led by saddle or sail

Your name was prayer or argument.

Men would bless you or curse you;

The curse, a protest against failure,

The blessing, a hymn of the hunter

Who comes back from the hills

With provision for his mate.

Your friends are yet with us for comfort and support,

And your enemies also, for strength and assurance.

Your mother is with us;

I have beheld the sheen of her face in the countenance of all mothers;

Her hand rocks cradles with gentleness,

Her hand folds shrouds with tenderness.

And Mary Magdalene is yet in our midst,

She who drank the vinegar of life, and then its wine.
And Judas, the man of pain and small ambitions,
He too walks the earth;
Even now he preys upon himself when his hunger find naught else,
And seeks his larger self in self-destruction.
And John, he whose youth loved beauty, is here,
And he sings though unheeded.
And Simon Peter the impetuous, who denied you that he might live longer for you,
He too sits by our fire.
He may deny you again ere the dawn of another day,
Yet he would be crucified for your purpose, and deem himself unworthy
of the honour.
And Caiaphas and Annas still live their day,
And judge the guilty and the innocent.
They sleep upon their feathered bed
Whilst he whom they have judged is whipped with the rods.
And the woman who was taken in adultery,
She too walks the streets of our cities,
And hungers for bread not yet baked,
And she is alone in an empty house.
And Pontius Pilatus is here also:
He stands in awe before you,
And still questions you,
But he dares not risk his station or defy an alien race;
And he is still washing his hands.
Even now Jerusalem holds the basin and Rome the ewer,
And betwixt the two thousand thousand hands would be washed to whiteness.
Master, Master Poet,
Master of words sung and spoken,
They have builded temples to house your name,

And upon every height they have raised your cross,
A sign and a symbol to guide their wayward feet,
But not unto your joy.
Your joy is a hill beyond their vision,
And it does not comfort them.
They would honour the man unknown to them.
And what consolation is there in a man like themselves, a man whose kindliness is like their own kindliness,
A god whose love is like their own love,
And whose mercy is in their own mercy?
They honour not the man, the living man,
The first man who opened His eyes and gazed at the sun
With eyelids unquivering.
Nay, they do not know Him, and they would not be like Him.

*

They would be unknown, walking in the procession of the unknown.
They would bear sorrow, their sorrow,
And they would not find comfort in your joy.
Their aching heart seeks not consolation in your words and the song thereof.
And their pain, silent and unshapen,
Makes them creatures lonely and unvisited.
Though hemmed about my kin and kind,
They live in fear, uncomraded;
Yet they would not be alone.
They would bend eastward when the west wind blows.
They call you king,
And they would be in your court.
They pronounce you the Messiah,
And they would themselves be anointed with the holy oil.
Yea, they would live upon your life.
Master, Master Singer,

Your tears were like the showers of May,
And your laughter like the waves of the white sea.
When you spoke your words were the far-off whisper of their lips when those lips should be kindled with fire;
You laughed for the marrow in their bones that was not yet ready for laughter;
And you wept for their eyes that yet were dry.
Your voice fathered their thoughts and their understanding.
Your voice mothered their words and their breath.
Seven times was I born and seven times have I died,
And now I live again, and I behold you,
The fighter among fighters,
The poet of poets
King above all kings,
A man half-naked with your road-fellows.
Every day the bishop bends down his head
When he pronounces your name.
And every day the beggars say:
"For Jesus' sake
Give us a penny to buy bread."
We call upon each other,
But in truth we call upon you,
Like the flood tide in the spring of our want and desire,
And when our autumn comes, like the ebb tide.
High or low, your name is upon our lips,
The Master of infinite compassion.
Master, Master of our lonely hours,
Here and there, betwixt the cradle and the coffin, I meet your silent brothers,
The free men, unshackled,
Sons of your mother earth and space.
They are like the birds of the sky,

And like the lilies of the field.
They live your life and think your thoughts,
And they echo your song.
But they are empty-handed,
And they are not crucified with the great crucifixion,
And therein is their pain.
The world crucifies them every day,
But only in little ways.
The sky is not shaken,
And the earth travails not with her dead.
They are crucified and there is none to witness their agony.
They turn their face to right and left
And find not one to promise them a station in his kingdom.
Yet they would be crucified again and yet again,
That your God may be their God,
And your Father their Father.
Master, Master Lover,
The Princess awaits your coming in her fragrant chamber,
And the married unmarried woman in her cage;
The harlot who seeks bread in the streets of her shame,
And the nun in her cloister who has no husband;
The childless woman too at her window,
Where frost designs the forest on the pane,
She finds you in that symmetry,
And she would mother you, and be comforted.
Master, Master Poet,
Master of our silent desires,
The heart of the world quivers with the throbbing of your heart,
But it burns not with your song.
The world sits listening to your voice in tranquil delight,
But it rises not from its seat
To scale the ridges of your hills.

Man would dream your dream but he would not wake to your dawn
Which is his greater dream.
He would see with your vision,
But he would not drag his heavy feet to your throne.
Yet many have been enthroned inn your name
And mitred with your power,
And have turned your golden visit
Into crowns for their head and sceptres for their hand.
Master, Master of Light,
Whose eye dwells in the seeking fingers of the blind,
You are still despised and mocked,
A man too weak and infirm to be God,
A God too much man to call forth adoration.
Their mass and their hymn,
Their sacrament and their rosary, are for their imprisoned self.
You are their yet distant self, their far-off cry, and their passion.
But Master, Sky-heart, Knight of our fairer dream,
You do still tread this day;
Nor bows nor spears shall stay your steps.
You walk through all our arrows.
You smile down upon us,
And though you are the youngest of us all
You father us all.
Poet, Singer, Great Heart,
May our God bless your name,
And the womb that held you, and the breasts that gave you milk.
And may God forgive us all.
THE END.

BOOK FOUR.
THE EARTH GODS

When the night of the twelfth aeon fell,
And silence, the high tide of night, swallowed the hills,
The three earth-born gods, the Master Titans of life,
Appeared upon the mountains.
Rivers ran about their feet;
The mist floated across their breasts,
And their heads rose in majesty above the world.
Then they spoke, and like distant thunder
Their voices rolled over the plains.

FIRST GOD

The wind blows eastward;
I would turn my face to the south,
For the wind crowds my nostrils with the odours of dead things.

SECOND GOD

It is the scent of burnt flesh, sweet and bountiful.
I would breathe it.

FIRST GOD

It is the odour of mortality parching upon its own faint flame.
Heavily does it hang upon the air,
And like foul breath of the pit
It offends my senses.
I would turn my face to the scentless north.

SECOND GOD

It is the inflamed fragrance of brooding life
This I would breathe now and forever.

Gods live upon sacrifice,
Their thirst quenched by blood,
Their hearts appeased with young souls,
Their sinews strengthened by the deathless sighs
Of those who dwell with death;
Their thrones are built upon the ashes of generations.

FIRST GOD

Weary is my spirit of all there is.
I would not move a hand to create a world
Nor to erase one.
I would not live could I but die,
For the weight of aeons is upon me,
And the ceaseless moan of the seas exhausts my sleep.
Could I but lose the primal aim
And vanish like a wasted sun;
Could I but strip my divinity of its purpose
And breathe my immortality into space,
And be no more;
Could I but be consumed and pass from time's memory
Into the emptiness of nowhere!

THIRD GOD

Listen my brothers, my ancient brothers.
A youth in yonder vale
Is singing his heart to the night.
His lyre is gold and ebony.
His voice is silver and gold.

SECOND GOD

I would not be so vain as to be no more.
I could not but choose the hardest way;

To follow the seasons and support the majesty of the years;
To sow the seed and to watch it thrust through the soil;
To call the flower from its hiding place
And give it strength to nestle its own life,
And then to pluck it when the storm laughs in the forest;
To raise man from secret darkness,
Yet keep his roots clinging to the earth;
To give him thirst for life, and make death his cupbearer;
To endow him with love that waxeth with pain,
And exalts with desire, and increases with longing,
And fadeth away with the first embrace;
To girdle his nights with dreams of higher days,
And infuse his days with visions of blissful nights,
And yet to confine his days and his nights
To their immutable resemblance;
To make his fancy like the eagle of the mountain,
And his thought as the tempests of the seas,
And yet to give him hands slow in decision,
And feet heavy with deliberation;
To give him gladness that he may sing before us,
And sorrow that he may call unto us,
And then to lay him low,
When the earth in her hunger cries for food;
To raise his soul high above the firmament
That he may foretaste our tomorrow,
And to keep his body grovelling in the mire
That he may not forget his yesterday.
Thus shall we rule man unto the end of time,
Governing the breath that began with his mother's crying,
And ends with the lamentation of his children.

FIRST GOD

My heart thirsts, yet I would not drink the faint blood of a feeble race,
For the cup is tainted, and the vintage therein is bitter to my mouth.
Like thee I have kneaded the clay and fashioned it to breathing forms
That crept out of my dripping fingers unto the marshes and the hills.
Like thee I have kindled the dark depths of beginning life
And watched it crawl from caves to rocky heights.
Like thee I have summoned spring and laid the beauty thereof
For a lure that seizes youth and binds it to generate and multiply.
Like thee I have led man from shrine to shrine,
And turned his mute fear of things unseen
To tremulous faith in us, the unvisited and the unknown.
Like thee I have ridden the wild tempest over his head
That he might bow before us,
And shaken the earth beneath him until he cried unto us;
And like thee, led the savage ocean against his nestled isle,
Till he hath died calling upon us.
All this have I done, and more.
And all that I have done is empty and vain.
Vain is the waking and empty is the sleep,
And thrice empty and vain is the dream.

THIRD GOD

Brothers, my august brothers,
Down in the myrtle grove
A girl is dancing to the moon,
A thousand dew-stars are in her hair,
About her feet a thousand wings.

SECOND GOD

We have planted man, our vine, and tilled the soil
In the purple mist of the first dawn.

We watched the lean branches grow,

And through the days of seasonless years

We nursed the infant leaves.

From the angry element we shielded the bud,

And against all dark spirits we guarded the flower.

And now that our vine hath yielded the grape

You will not take it to the winepress and fill the cup.

Whose mightier hand than yours shall reap the fruit?

And what nobler end than your thirst awaits the wine?

Man is food for the gods,

And the glory of man begins

When his aimless breath is sucked by gods' hallowed lips.

All that is human counts for naught if human it remain;

The innocence of childhood, and the sweet ecstasy of youth,

The passion of stern manhood, and the wisdom of old age;

The splendour of kings and the triumph of warriors,

The fame of poets and the honour of dreamers and saints;

All these and all that lieth therein is bred for gods.

And naught but bread ungraced shall it be

If the gods raise it not to their mouths.

And as the mute grain turns to love songs when swallowed by the nightingale,

Even so as bread of gods shall man taste godhead.

FIRST GOD

Aye, man is meat for gods!

And all that is man shall come upon the gods' eternal board!

The pain of child-bearing and the agony of childbirth,

The blind cry of the infant that pierces the naked night,

And the anguish of the mother wrestling with the sleep she craves,

To pour life exhausted from her breast;

The flaming breath of youth tormented,

And the burdened sobs of passion unspent;

The dripping brows of manhood tilling the barren land,
And the regret of pale old age when life against life's will
Calls to the grave.
Behold this is man!
A creature bred on hunger and made food for hungry gods.
A vine that creeps in dust beneath the feet of deathless death.
The flower that blooms in nights of evil shadows;
The grape of mournful days, and days of terror and shame.
And yet you would have me eat and drink.
You would bid me sit amongst shrouded faces
And draw my life from stony lips
And from withered hands receive my eternity.

THIRD GOD
Brothers, my dreaded brothers,
Thrice deep the youth is singing,
And thrice higher is his song.
His voice shakes the forest
And pierces the sky,
And scatters the slumbering of earth.

SECOND GOD (*Always unhearing*)
The bee hums harshly in your ears,
And foul is the honey to your lips.
Fain would I comfort you,
But how shall I?
Only the abyss listens when gods call unto gods,
For measureless is the gulf that lies between divinities,
And windless is the space.
Yet I would comfort you,
I would make serene your clouded sphere;
And though equal we are in power and judgement,

I would counsel you.

When out of chaos came the earth, and we, sons of the beginning, beheld each other in the lustless light, we breathed the first hushed, tremulous sound that quickened the currents of air and sea.

Then we walked, hand in hand, upon the grey infant world, and out of the echoes of our first drowsy steps time was born, a fourth divinity, that sets his feet upon our footprints, shadowing our thoughts and desires, and seeing only with our eyes.

And unto earth came life, and unto life came the spirit, the winged melody of the universe. And we ruled life and spirit, and none save us knew the measure of the years nor the weight of years' nebulous dreams, till we, at noontide of the seventh aeon, gave the sea in marriage to the sun.

And from the inner chamber of their nuptial ecstasy, we brought man, a creature who, though yielding and infirm, bears ever the marks of his parentage.

Through man who walks earth with eyes upon the stars, we find pathways to earth's distant regions; and of man, the humble reed growing beside dark waters, we make a flute through whose hollowed heart we pour our voice to the silence-bound world. From the sunless north to the sun-smitten sand of the south.

From the lotus land where days are born

To perilous isles where days are slain,

Man the faint hearted, overbold by our purpose,

Ventures with lyre and sword.

Ours is the will he heralds,

And ours the sovereignty he proclaims,

And his love trodden courses are rivers, to the sea of our desires.

We, upon the heights, in man's sleep dream our dreams.

We urge his days to part from the valley of twilights

And seek their fullness upon the hills.

Our hands direct the tempests that sweep the world

And summon man from sterile peace to fertile strife,

And on to triumph.

In our eyes is the vision that turns man's soul to flame,

And leads him to exalted loneliness and rebellious prophecy,

And on to crucifixion.

Man is born to bondage,

And in bondage is his honour and his reward.

In man we seek a mouthpiece,

And in his life our self fulfilment.

Whose heart shall echo our voice if the human heart is deafened with dust?

Who shall behold our shining if man's eye is blinded with night?

And what would you do with man, child of our earliest heart, our own self image?

THIRD GOD

Brothers, my mighty brothers,

The dancer's feet are drunk with songs.

They set the air a-throbbing,

And like doves her hands fly upward.

FIRST GOD

The lark calls to the lark,

But upward the eagle soars,

Nor tarries to hear the song.

You would teach me self love fulfilled in man's worship,

And content with man's servitude.

But my self love is limitless and without measure.

I would rise beyond my earthbound mortality

And throne me upon the heavens.

My arms wood girdle space and encompass the spheres.

I would take the starry way for a bow,

And the comets for arrows,

And with the infinite would I conquer the infinite.

But you would not do this, were it in your power.

For ever as man is to man,

So are gods to gods.

Nay, you would bring to my weary heart
Remembrance of cycles spent in mist,
When my soul sought itself among the mountains
And mine eyes pursued their own image in slumbering waters;
Though my yesterday died in child-birth
And only silence visits her womb,
And the wind strewn sand nestles at her breast.
Oh yesterday, dead yesterday,
Mother of my chained divinity,
What super-god caught you in your flight
And made you breed in the cage?
What giant sun warmed your bosom
To give me birth?
I bless you not, yet I would not curse you;
For even as you have burdened me with life
So I have burdened man
But less cruel have I been.
I, immortal, made man a passing shadow;
And you, dying, conceived me deathless.
Yesterday, dead yesterday,
Shall you return with distant tomorrow,
That I may bring you to judgment?
And will you wake with life's second dawn
That I may erase your earth-clinging memory from the earth?
Would that you might rise with all the dead of yore,
Till the land choke with its own bitter fruit,
And all the seas be stagnant with the slain,
And woe upon woe exhaust earth's vain fertility.

THIRD GOD

Brother, my sacred brothers,
The girl has heard the song.

And now she seeks the singer.
Like a fawn in glad surprise
She leaps over rocks and streams
And turns her to every side.
Oh, the joy in mortal intent,
The eye of purpose half-born;
The smile on lips that quiver
With foretaste of promised delight!
What flower has fallen from heaven,
What flame has risen from hell.
That startled the heart of silence
To this breathless joy and fear?
What dream dreamt we upon the height,
What thought gave we to the wind
That woke the drowsing valley
And made watchful the night?

SECOND GOD

The sacred loom is given you,
And the art to weave the fabric.
The loom and the art shall be yours for evermore,
And yours the dark thread and the light,
And yours the purple and the gold.
Yet you would grudge yourself a raiment.
Your hands have spun man's soul
From living air and fire,
Yet now you would break the thread,
And lend your versed fingers to an idle eternity.

FIRST GOD

Nay, unto eternity unmoulded I would give my hands,
And to untrodden fields assign my feet.

What joy is there in songs oft heard,
Whose tune the remembering ear arrests
Ere the breath yields it to the wind?
My heart longs for what my heart conceives not,
And unto the unknown where memory dwells not
I would command my spirit.
Oh, tempt me not with glory possessed,
And seek not to comfort me with your dream or mine,
For all that I am, and all that there is on earth,
And all that shall be, inviteth not my soul.
Oh my soul,
Silent is thy face,
And in Thine eyes the shadows of night are sleeping.
But terrible is thy silence,
And thou art terrible.

THIRD GOD

Brothers, my solemn brothers,
The girl has found the singer.
She sees his raptured face.
Panther-like she slips with subtle steps
Through rustling vine and fern.
And now amid his ardent cries
He gazes full on her.
Oh my brothers, my heedless brothers,
Is it some other god in passion
Who has woven this web of scarlet and white?
What unbridled star has gone astray?
Whose secret keepeth night from morning?
And whose hand is upon our world?

FIRST GOD

Oh my soul, my soul,
Thou burning sphere that girdles me,
How shall I guide thy course.
And unto what space direct thy eagerness?
Oh my mateless soul,
In thy hunger thou preyest upon thyself,
And with thine own tears thou wouldst quench thy thirst;
For night gathers not her dew into thy cup,
And the day brings thee no fruit.
Oh my soul, my soul,
Thou grounded ship laden with desire,
Whence shall come the wind to fill thy sail,
And what higher tide shall release thy rudder?
Weighed is thine anchor and thy wings would spread,
But the skies are silent above thee,
And the still sea mocks at thy immobility.
And what hope is there for thee and me?
What shifting of worlds, what new purpose in the heavens,
That shall claim thee?
Does the womb of the virgin infinite
Bear the seed of thy Redeemer,
One mightier than thy vision
Whose hand shall deliver thee from thy captivity?

SECOND GOD

Hold your importunate cry,
And the breath of your burning heart,
For deaf is the ear of the infinite,
And heedless is the sky.
We are the beyond and we are the Most High,
And between us and boundless eternity

Is naught save our unshaped passion
And the motive thereof.
You invoke the unknown,
And the unknown clad with moving mist
Dwells in your own soul.
Yea, in your own soul your Redeemer lies asleep,
And in sleep sees what your waking eye does not see.
And that is the secret of our being.
Would you leave the harvest ungathered,
In haste to sow again the dreaming furrow?
And wherefore spread you your cloud in trackless fields and desolate,
When your own flock is seeking you,
And would fain gather in your own shadow?
Forbear and look down upon the world.
Behold the unweaned children of your love.
The earth is your abode, and the earth is your throne;
And high beyond man's furtherest hope
Your hand upholds his destiny.
You would not abandon him
Who strives to reach you through gladness and through pain.
You would not turn away your face from the need in his eyes.

FIRST GOD

Does dawn hold the heart of night unto her heart?
Or shall the sea heed the bodies of her dead?
Like dawn my soul rises within me
Naked and unencumbered.
And like the unresting sea
My heart casts out a perishing wrack of man and earth.
I would not cling to that clings to me.
But unto that that rises beyond my reach I would arise.

THIRD GOD

Brothers, behold, my brothers,
They meet, two star-bound spirits in the sky encountering.
In silence they gaze the one upon the other.
He sings no more,
And yet his sunburnt throat throbs with the song;
And in her limbs the happy dance is stayed
But not asleep.
Brothers, my strange brothers,
The night waxeth deep,
And brighter is the moon,
And twixt the meadow and the sea
A voice in rapture calleth you and me.

SECOND GOD

To be, to rise, to burn before the burning sun,
To live, and to watch the nights of the living
As Orion watches us!
To face the four winds with a head crowned and high,
And to heal the ills of man with our tideless breath!
The tentmaker sits darkly at his loom,
And the potter turns his wheel unaware;
But we, the sleepless and the knowing,
We are released from guessing and from chance.
We pause not nor do we wait for thought.
We are beyond all restless questioning.
Be content and let the dreaming go.
Like rivers let us flow to ocean
Unwounded by the edges of the rocks;
And when we reach her heart and are merged,
No more shall we wrangle and reason of tomorrow.

FIRST GOD

Oh, this ache of ceaseless divining,
This vigil of guiding the day unto twilight,
And the night unto dawn;
This tide of ever remembering and forgetting;
This ever sowing destinies and reaping but hopes;
This changeless lifting of self from dust to mist,
Only to long for dust, and to fall down with longing unto dust,
And still with greater longing to seek the mist again.
And this timeless measuring of time.
Must my soul needs to be a sea whose currents forever confound one another,
Or the sky where the warring winds turn hurricane?
Were I man, a blind fragment,
I could have met it with patience.
Or if I were the Supreme Godhead,
Who fills the emptiness of man and of gods,
I would be fulfilled.
But you and I are neither human,
Nor the Supreme above us.
We are but twilights ever rising and ever fading
Between horizon and horizon.
We are but gods holding a world and held by it,
Fates that sound the trumpets
Whilst the breath and the music come from beyond.
And I rebel.
I would exhaust myself to emptiness.
I would dissolve myself afar from your vision,
And from the memory of this silent youth, our younger brother,
Who sits beside us gazing into yonder valley,
And though his lips move, utters not a word.

THIRD GOD

I speak, my unheeding brothers,

I do indeed speak,

But you hear only your own words.

I bid you see your glory and mine,

But you turn, and close your eyes,

And rock your thrones.

Ye sovereigns who would govern the above world and the world beneath,

God self-bent, whose yesterday is ever jealous of your tomorrow,

Self-weary, who would unleash your temper with speech

And lash our orb with thunderings!

Your feud is but the sounding of an Ancient Lyre

Whose strings have been half forgotten by His fingers

Who has Orion for a harp and the Pleiades for cymbals.

Even now, while you are muttering and rumbling,

His harp rings, His cymbals clash,

And I beseech you hear his song.

Behold, man and woman,

Flame to flame,

In white ecstasy.

Roots that suck at the breast of purple earth,

Flame flowers at the breasts of the sky.

And we are the purple breast,

And we are the enduring sky.

Our soul, even the soul of life, your soul and mine,

Dwells this night in a throat enflamed,

And garments the body of a girl with beating waves.

Your sceptre cannot sway this destiny,

Your weariness is but ambition.

This and all is wiped away

In the passion of a man and a maid.

SECOND GOD

Yea, what of this love of man and woman?

See how the east wind dances with her dancing feet,

And the west wind rises singing with his song.

Behold our sacred purpose now enthroned,

In the yielding of a spirit that sings to a body that dances.

FIRST GOD

I will not turn my eyes downward to the conceit of earth,

Nor to her children in their slow agony that you call love.

And what is love,

But the muffled drum and leads the long procession of sweet uncertainty

To another slow agony?

I will not look downward.

What is there to behold

Save a man and a woman in the forest that grew to trap them

That they might renounce self

And parent creatures for our unborn tomorrow?

THIRD GOD

Oh, the affliction of knowing,

The starless veil of prying and questioning

Which we have laid upon the world;

And the challenge to human forbearance!

We would lay under a stone a waxen shape

And say, It is a thing of clay,

And in clay let it find its end.

We would hold in our hands a white flame

And say in our heart,

It is a fragment of ourselves returning,

A breath of our breath that had escaped,

And now haunts our hands and lips for more fragrance.

Earth gods, my brothers,
High upon the mountain,
We are still earth-bound,
Through man desiring the golden hours of man's destiny.
Shall our wisdom ravish beauty from his eyes?
Shall our measures subdue his passion to stillness,
Or to our own passion?
What would your armies of reasoning
Where love encamps his host?
They who are conquered by love,
And upon whose bodies love's chariot ran
From sea to mountain
And again form mountain to the sea,
Stand even now in a shy half-embrace.
Petal unto petal they breathe the sacred perfume,
Soul to soul they find the soul of life,
And upon their eyelids lies a prayer
Unto you and unto me.
Love is a night bent down to a bower anointed,
A sky turned meadow, and all the stars to fireflies.
True it is, we are the beyond,
And we are the most high.
But love is beyond our questioning,
And love outsoars our song.

SECOND GOD
Seek you a distant orb,
And would not consider this star
Where your sinews are planted?
There is no centre in space
Save where self is wedded to self,
And beauty filling our hands to shame our lips.

The most distant is the most near.
And where beauty is, there are all things.
Oh, lofty dreaming brother,
Return to us from time's dim borderland!
Unlace your feet from no-where and no-when,
And dwell with us in this security
Which your hand intertwined with ours
Has builded stone upon stone.
Cast off your mantle of brooding,
And comrade us, masters of the young earth green and warm.

FIRST GOD
Eternal Altar! Wouldst thou indeed this night
A god for sacrifice?
Now then, I come, and coming I offer up
My passion and my pain.
Lo, there is the dancer, carved out of our ancient eagerness,
And the singer is crying mine own songs unto the wind.
And in that dancing and in that singing
A god is slain within me.
My god-heart within my human ribs
Shouts to my god-heart in mid-air.
The human pit that wearied me calls to divinity.
The beauty that we have sought from the beginning
Calls unto divinity.
I heed, and I have measured the call,
And now I yield.
Beauty is a path that leads to self self-slain.
Beat your strings
I will to walk the path.
It stretches ever to another dawn.

THIRD GOD

Love triumphs.

The white and green of love beside a lake,

And the proud majesty of love in tower or balcony;

Love in a garden or in the desert untrodden,

Love is our lord and master.

It is not a wanton decay of the flesh,

Nor the crumbling of desire

When desire and self are wrestling;

Nor is it flesh that takes arms against the spirit.

Love rebels not.

It only leaves the trodden way of ancient destinies for the sacred grove,

To sing and dance its secret to eternity.

Love is youth with chains broken,

Manhood made free from the sod,

And womanhood warmed by the flame

And shining with the light of heaven deeper than our heaven.

Love is a distant laughter in the spirit.

It is a wild assault that hushes you to your awakening.

It is a new dawn unto the earth,

A day not yet achieved in your eyes or mine,

But already achieved in its own greater heart.

Brothers, my brothers,

The bride comes from the heart of dawn,

And the bridegroom from the sunset.

There is a wedding in the valley.

A day too vast for recording.

SECOND GOD

Thus has it been since the first morn

Discharged the plains to hill and vale,

And thus shall it be to the last even-tide.

Our roots have brought forth the dancing branches in the valley,
And we are the flowering of the song-scent that rises to the heights.
Immortal and mortal, twin rivers calling to the sea.
There is no emptiness between call and call,
But only in the ear.
Time maketh our listening more certain,
And giveth it more desire.
Only doubt in mortal hushes the sound.
We have outsoared the doubt.
Man is a child of our younger heart.
Man is god in slow arising;
And betwixt his joy and his pain
Lies our sleeping, and the dreaming thereof.

FIRST GOD

Let the singer cry, and let the dancer whirl her feet
And let me be content awhile.
Let my soul be serene this night.
Perchance I may drowse, and drowsing
Behold a brighter world
And creatures more starry supple to my mind.

THIRD GOD

Now I will rise and strip me of time and space,
And I will dance in that field untrodden,
And the dancer's feet will move with my feet;
And I will sing in that higher air,
And a human voice will throb within my voice.
We shall pass into the twilight;
Perchance to wake to the dawn of another world.
But love shall stay,
And his finger-marks shall not be erased.

The blessed forge burns,
The sparks rise, and each spark is a sun.
Better it is for us, and wiser,
To seek a shadowed nook and sleep in our earth divinity,
And let love, human and frail, command the coming day.

THE END

BOOK FIVE.
THE WANDERER

HIS PARABLES AND HIS SAYINGS

THE WANDERER

I met him at the crossroads, a man with but a cloak and a staff, and a veil of pain upon his face. And we greeted one another, and I said to him, "Come to my house and be my guest."

And he came.

My wife and my children met us at the threshold, and he smiled at them, and they loved his coming.

Then we all sat together at the board and we were happy with the man for there was a silence and a mystery in him.

And after supper we gathered to the fire and I asked him about his wanderings.

He told us many a tale that night and also the next day, but what I now record was born out of the bitterness of his days though he himself was kindly, and these tales are of the dust and patience of his road.

And when he left us after three days we did not feel that a guest had departed but rather that one of us was still out in the garden and had not yet come in.

GARMENTS

Upon a day Beauty and Ugliness met on the shore of a sea. And they said to one another, "Let us bathe in the sea."

Then they disrobed and swam in the waters. And after a while Ugliness came back to shore and garmented himself with the garments of Beauty and walked away.

And Beauty too came out of the sea, and found not her raiment, and she was too shy to be naked, therefore she dressed herself with the raiment of Ugliness. And Beauty walked her way.

And to this very day men and women mistake the one for the other.

Yet some there are who have beheld the face of Beauty, and they know her notwithstanding her garments. And some there be who know the face of Ugliness, and the cloth conceals him not from their eyes.

THE EAGLE AND THE SKYLARK

A skylark and an eagle met on a rock upon a high hill. The skylark said, "Good morrow to you, Sir." And the eagle looked down upon him and said faintly, "Good morrow."

And the skylark said, "I hope all things are well with you, Sir."

"Aye," said the eagle, "all is well with us. But do you not know that we are the king of birds, and that you shall not address us before we ourselves have spoken?"

Said the skylark, "Methinks we are of the same family."

The eagle looked upon him with disdain and he said, "Who ever has said that you and I are of the same family?"

Then said the skylark, "But I would remind you of this, I can fly even as high as you, and I can sing and give delight to the other creatures of this earth. And you give neither pleasure nor delight."

Then the eagle was angered, and he said, "Pleasure and delight! You little presumptuous creature! With one thrust of my beak I could destroy you. You are but the size of my foot."

Then the skylark flew up and alighted upon the back of the eagle and began to pick at his feathers. The eagle was annoyed, and he flew swift and high that he might rid himself of the little bird. But he failed to do so. At last he dropped back to that very rock upon the high hill, more fretted than ever, with the little creature still upon his back, and cursing the fate of the hour.

Now at that moment a small turtle came by and laughed at the sight, and laughed so hard the she almost turned upon her back.

And the eagle looked down upon the turtle and he said, "You slow creeping thing, ever one with the earth, what are you laughing at?"

And the turtle said, "Why I see that you are turned horse, and that you have a small bird riding you, but the small bird is the better bird."

And the eagle said to her, "Go you about your business. This is a family affair between my brother, the lark, and myself."

THE LOVE SONG

A poet once wrote a love song and it was beautiful. And he made many copies of it, and sent them to his friends and his acquaintances, both men and women, and even to a young woman whom he had met but once, who lived beyond the mountains.

And in a day or two a messenger came from the young woman bringing a letter. And in the letter she said, "Let me assure you, I am deeply touched by the love song that you have written to me. Come now, and see my father and my mother, and we shall make arrangements for the betrothal."

And the poet answered the letter, and he said to her, "My friend, it was but a song of love out of a poet's heart, sung by every man to every woman."

And she wrote again to him saying, "Hypocrite and liar in words! From this day unto my coffin-day I shall hate all poets for your sake."

TEARS AND LAUGHTER

Upon the bank of the Nile at eventide, a hyena met a crocodile and they stopped and greeted one another.

The hyena spoke and said, "How goes the day with you, Sir?"

And the crocodile answered saying, "It goes badly with me. Sometimes in my pain and sorrow I weep, and then the creatures always say, 'They are but crocodile tears.' And this wounds me beyond all telling."

Then the hyena said, "You speak of your pain and your sorrow, but think of me also, for a moment. I gaze at the beauty of the world, its wonders and its miracles, and out of sheer joy I laugh even as the day laughs. And then the people of the jungle say, 'It is but the laughter of a hyena.'"

AT THE FAIR

There came to the Fair a girl from the country-side, most comely. There was a lily and a rose in her face. There was a sunset in her hair, and dawn smiled upon her lips.

No sooner did the lovely stranger appear in their sight than the young men sought her and surrounded her. One would dance with her, and another would cut a cake in her honour. And they all desired to kiss her cheek. For after all, was it not the Fair?

But the girl was shocked and started, and she thought ill of the young men. She rebuked them, and she even struck one or two of them in the face. Then she ran away from them.

And on her way home that evening she was saying in her heart, "I am disgusted. How unmannerly and ill bred are these men. It is beyond all patience."

A year passed during which that very comely girl thought much of Fairs and men. Then she came again to the Fair with the lily and the rose in her face, the sunset in her hair and the smile of dawn upon her lips.

But now the young men, seeing her, turned from her. And all the day long she was unsought and alone.

And at eventide as she walked the road toward her home she cried in her heart, "I am disgusted. How unmannerly and ill bred are these youths. It is beyond all patience."

THE TWO PRINCESSES

In the city of Shawakis lived a prince, and he was loved by everyone, men and women and children. Even the animals of the field came unto him in greeting.

But all the people said that his wife, the princess, loved him not; nay, that she even hated him.

And upon a day the princess of a neighbouring city came to visit the princess of Shawakis. And they sat and talked together, and their words led to their husbands.

And the princess of Sharakis said with passion, "I envy you your happiness with the prince, your husband, though you have been married these many years. I hate my husband. He belongs not to me alone, and I am indeed a woman most unhappy."

Then the visiting princess gazed at her and said, "My friend, the truth is that you love your husband. Aye, and you still have him for a passion unspent, and that is life in woman like unto Spring in a garden. But pity me, and my husband, for we do but endure one another in silent patience. And yet you and others deem this happiness."

THE LIGHTNING FLASH

There was a Christian bishop in his cathedral on a stormy day, and an un-Christian woman came and stood before him, and she said, "I am not a Christian. Is there salvation for me from hell-fire?"

And the bishop looked upon the woman, and he answered her saying, "Nay, there is salvation for those only who are baptized of water and of the spirit."

And even as he spoke a bolt from the sky fell with thunder upon the cathedral and it was filled with fire. And the men of the city came running, and they saved the woman, but the bishop was consumed, food of the fire.

THE HERMIT AND THE BEASTS

Once there lived among the green hills a hermit. He was pure of spirit and white of heart. And all the animals of the land and all the fowls of the air came to him in pairs and he spoke unto them. They heard him gladly, and they would gather near unto him, and would not go until nightfall, when he would send them away, entrusting them to the wind and the woods with his blessing.

Upon an evening as he was speaking of love, a leopard raised her head and said to the hermit, "You speak to us of loving. Tell us, Sir, where is your mate?"

And the hermit said, "I have no mate."

Then a great cry of surprise rose from the company of beasts and fowls, and they began to say among themselves, "How can he tell us of loving and mating when he himself knows naught thereof?" And quietly and in distain they left him alone.

That night the hermit lay upon his mat with his face earthward, and he wept bitterly and beat his hands upon his breast.

THE PROPHET AND THE CHILD

Once on a day the prophet Sharia met a child in a garden. The child ran to him and said, "Good morrow to you, Sir," and the prophet said, "Good morrow to you, Sir." And in a moment, "I see that you are alone."

Then the child said, in laughter and delight, "It took a long time to lose my nurse. She thinks I am behind those hedges; but can't you see that I am here?" Then he gazed at the prophet's face and spoke again. "You are alone, too. What did you do with your nurse?"

The prophet answered and said, "Ah, that is a different thing. In very truth I cannot lose her oftentime. But now, when I came into this garden, she was seeking after me behind the hedges."

The child clapped his hands and cried out, "So you are like me! Isn't it good to be lost?" And then he said, "Who are you?"

And the man answered, "They call me the prophet Sharia. And tell me, who are you?"

"I am only myself," said the child, "and my nurse is seeking after me, and she does not know where I am."

Then the prophet gazed into space saying, "I too have escaped my nurse for awhile, but she will find me out."

And the child said, "I know mine will find me out too."

At that moment a woman's voice was heard calling the child's name, "See," said the child, "I told you she would be finding me."

And at the same moment another voice was heard, "Where art thou, Sharia?"

And the prophet said, "See my child, they have found me also."

And turning his face upward, Sharia answered, "Here I am."

THE PEARL

Said one oyster to a neighbouring oyster, "I have a very great pain within me. It is heavy and round and I am in distress."

And the other oyster replied with haughty complacence, "Praise be to the heavens and to the sea, I have no pain within me. I am well and whole both within and without."

At that moment a crab was passing by and heard the two oysters, and he said to the one who was well and whole both within and without, "Yes, you are well and whole; but the pain that your neighbour bears is a pearl of exceeding beauty."

BODY AND SOUL

A man and a woman sat by a window that opened upon Spring. They sat close one unto the other. And the woman said, "I love you. You are handsome, and you are rich, and you are always well-attired."

And the man said, "I love you. You are a beautiful thought, a thing too apart to hold in the hand, and a song in my dreaming."

But the woman turned from him in anger, and she said, "Sir, please leave me now. I am not a thought, and I am not a thing that passes in your dreams. I am a woman. I would have you desire me, a wife, and the mother of unborn children."

And they parted.

And the man was saying in his heart, "Behold another dream is even now turned into mist."

And the woman was saying, "Well, what of a man who turns me into a mist and a dream?"

THE KING

The people of the kingdom of Sadik surrounded the palace of their king shouting in rebellion against him. And he came down the steps of the palace carrying his crown in one hand and his sceptre in the other. The majesty of his appearance silenced the multitude, and he stood before them and said, "My friends, who are no longer my subjects, here I yield my crown and sceptre unto you. I would be one of you. I am only one man, but as a man I would work together with you that our lot may be made better. There is no need for king. Let us go therefore to the fields and the vineyards and labour hand with hand. Only you must tell me to what field or vineyard I should go. All of you now are king."

And the people marvelled, and stillness was upon them, for the king whom they had deemed the source of their discontent now yielding his crown and sceptre to them and became as one of them.

Then each and every one of them went his way, and the king walked with one man to a field.

But the Kingdom of Sadik fared not better without a king, and the mist of discontent was still upon the land. The people cried out in the market places saying that they have a king to rule them. And the elders and the youths said as if with one voice, "We will have our king."

And they sought the king and found him toiling in the field, and they brought him to his seat, and yielded unto his crown and his sceptre. And they said, "Now rule us, with might and with justice."

And he said, "I will indeed rule you with might, and may the gods of the heaven and the earth help me that I may also rule with justice."

Now, there came to his presence men and women and spoke unto him of a baron who mistreated them, and to whom they were but serfs.

And straightway the king brought the baron before him and said, "The life of one man is as weighty in the scales of God as the life of another. And because you know not how to weigh the lives of those who work in your fiends and your vineyards, you are banished, and you shall leave this kingdom forever."

The following day came another company to the king and spoke of the cruelty of a countess beyond the hills, and how she brought them down to misery. Instantly the countess was brought to court, and the king sentenced her also to banishment, saying, "Those who till our fields and care for our vineyards are nobler than we who eat the bread they prepare and drink the wine of their wine-press. And because you know not this, you shall leave this land and be afar from this kingdom."

Then came men and women who said that the bishop made them bring stones and hew the stones for the cathedral, yet he gave them naught, though they knew the bishop's coffer was full of gold and silver while they themselves were empty with hunger.

And the king called for the bishop, and when the bishop came the king spoke and said unto his, "That cross you wear upon your bosom should mean giving life unto life. But you have taken life from life and you have given none. Therefore you shall leave this kingdom never to return."

Thus each day for a full moon men and women came to the king to tell him of the burdens laid upon them. And each and every day a full moon some oppressor was exiled from the land.

And the people of Sadik were amazed, and there was cheer in their heart.

And upon a day the elders and the youths came and surrounded the tower of the king and called for him. And he came down holding his crown with one hand and his sceptre with the other.

And he spoke unto and said, "Now, what would you do of me? Behold, I yield back to you that which you desired me to hold."

But they cried. "Nay, nay, you are our rightful king. You have made clean the land of vipers, and you have brought the wolves to naught, and we welcome to sing our thanksgiving unto you. The crown is yours in majesty and the sceptre is yours in glory."

Then the king said, "Not I, not I. You yourselves are king. When you deemed me weak and a misruler, you yourselves were weak and misruling. And now the land fares well because it is in your will. I am but a thought in the mind of you all, and I exist not save in your actions. There is no such person as governor. Only the governed exist to govern themselves."

And the king re-entered his tower with his crown and his sceptre. And the elders and the youths went their various ways and they were content.

And each and every one thought of himself as king with a crown in one hand and a sceptre in the other.

UPON THE SAND

Said one man to another, "At the high tide of the sea, long ago, with the point of my staff I wrote a line upon the sand; and the people still pause to read it, and they are careful that naught shall erase it."

And the other man said, "And I to wrote a line upon the sand, but it was at low tide, and the waves of the vast sea washed it away. But tell me, what did you write?"

And the first man answered and said, "I wrote this: 'I am he who is.' But what did you write?"

And the other man said, "This I wrote: 'I am but a drop of this great ocean.'"

THE THREE GIFTS

Once in the city of Becharre there lived a gracious prince who was loved and honoured by all his subjects.

But there was one exceedingly poor man who was bitter against the prince, and who wagged continually a pestilent tongue in his dispraise.

The prince knew this, yet he was patient.

But at last he bethought him; and upon a wintry night there came to the door of the man a servant of the prince, bearing a sack of flour, a bag of soap and a cone of sugar.

And the servant said, "The prince sends you these gifts in token of remembrance."

The man was elated, for he thought the gifts were an homage from the prince. And in his pride we went to the bishop and told him what the prince had done, saying, "Can you not see how the prince desires my goodwill?"

But the bishop said, "Oh, how wise a prince, and how little you understand. He speaks in symbols. The flour is for your empty stomach;

the soap is for your dirty hide; and the sugar is to sweeten your bitter tongue."

From that day forward the man became shy even of himself. His hatred of the prince was greater than ever, and even more he hated the bishop who had revealed the prince unto him.

But thereafter he kept silent.

PEACE AND WAR

Three dogs were basking in the sun and conversing. The first dog said dreamily, "It is indeed wondrous to be living in this day of dogdom. Consider the ease with which we travel under the sea, upon the earth and even in the sky. And meditate for a moment upon the inventions brought forth for the comfort of dogs, even for our eyes and ears and noses."

And the second dog spoke and he said, "We are more heedful of the arts. We bark at the moon more rhythmically than did our forefathers. And when we gaze at ourselves in the water we see that our features are clearer than the features of yesterday."

Then the third dog spoke and said, "But what interests me most and beguiles my mind is the tranquil understanding existing between dogdoms."

At that very moment they looked, and lo, the dog-catcher was approaching.

The three dogs sprang up and scampered down the street; and as they ran the third dog said, "For God's sake, run for your lives. Civilization is after us."

THE DANCER

Once there came to the court of the Prince of Birkasha a dancer with her musicians. And she was admitted to the court, and she danced before the prince to the music the lute and the flute and the zither.

She danced the dance of flames, and the dance of swords and spears; she danced the dance of stars and the dance of space. And then she danced the dance of flowers in the wind.

After this she stood before the throne of the prince and bowed her body before him. And the prince bade her to come nearer, and he said unto her, "Beautiful woman, daughter of grace and delight, whence comes your art?

And how is it that you command all the elements in your rhythms and your rhymes?"

And the dancer bowed again before the prince, and she answered, "Mighty and gracious Majesty, I know not the answer to your questionings. Only this I know: The philosopher's soul dwells in his head, the poet's soul is in the heart; the singer's soul lingers about his throat, but the soul of the dancer abides in all her body."

THE TWO GUARDIAN ANGELS

On an evening two angels met at the city gate, and they greeted one another, and they conversed.

The one angel said, "What are you doing these days, and what work is given you?"

And the other answered, "It was been assigned me to be the guardian of a fallen man who lives down in the valley, a great sinner, most degraded. Let me assure you it is an important task, and I work hard."

The first fallen angel said, "That is an easy commission. I have often known sinners, and have been their guardian many a time. But it has now been assigned me to be the guardian of the good saint who lives in a bower out yonder. And I assure you that is an exceedingly difficult work, and most subtle."

Said the first angel, "This is but assumption. How can guarding a saint be harder than guarding a sinner?"

And the other answered, "What impertinence, to call me assumptious! I have stated but the truth. Methinks it is you who are assumptious!"

Then the angels wrangled and fought, first with words and then with fists and wings.

While they were fighting an archangel came by. And he stopped them, and said, "Why do you fight? And what is it all about? Know you not that it is most unbecoming for guardian angels to fight at the city gate? Tell me, what is your disagreement?"

Then both angels spoke at once, each claiming that the work given him was the harder, and that he deserved the greater recognition.

The archangel shook his head and bethought him.

Then he said, "My friends, I cannot say now which one of you has the greater claim upon honour and reward. But since the power is bestowed in me, therefore for peace' sake and for good guardianship, I give each of you the other's occupation, since each of you insists that the other's task is the easier one. Now go hence and be happy at your work."

The angels thus ordered went their ways. But each one looked backward with greater anger at the archangel. And in his heart each was saying, "Oh, these archangels! Every day they make life harder and still harder for us angels!"

But the archangel stood there, and once more he bethought him. And he said in his heart, "We have indeed, to be watchful and to keep guard over our guardian angels."

THE STATUE

Once there lived a man among the hills who possessed a statue wrought by an ancient master. It lay at his door face downward and he was not mindful of it.

One day there passed by his house a man from the city, a man of knowledge, and seeing the statue he inquired of the owner if he would sell it.

The owner laughed and said, "And pray who would want to buy that dull and dirty stone?"

The man from the city said, "I will give you this piece of silver for it."

And the other man was astonished and delighted.

The statue was removed to the city, upon the back of and elephant. And after many moons the man from the hills visited the city, and as he walked the streets he saw a crowd before a shop, and a man with a loud voice was crying, "Come ye in and behold the most beautiful, the most wonderful statue in all the world. Only two silver pieces to look upon this most marvellous work of a master."

Thereupon the man from the hills paid two silver pieces and entered the shop to see the statue that he himself had sold for one spice of silver.

THE EXCHANGE

Once upon a crossroad a poor Poet met a rich Stupid, and they conversed. And all that they said revealed but their discontent.

Then the Angel of the Road passed by, and he laid his hand upon the shoulder of the two men.

And behold, a miracle: The two men had now exchanged their possessions.

And they parted. But strange to relate, the Poet looked and found naught in his hand but dry moving sand; and the Stupid closed his eyes and felt naught but moving cloud in his heart.

LOVE AND HATE

A woman said unto a man, "I love you." And the man said, "It is in my heart to be worthy of your love."

Ant he woman said, "You love me not?"

And the man only gazed upon her and said nothing.

Then the woman cried aloud, "I hate you."

And the man said, "Then it is also in my heart to be worthy of your hate."

DREAMS

A man dreamed a dream, and when he awoke he went to his soothsayer and desired that his dream be made plain unto him.

And the soothsayer said to the man, "Come to me with the dreams that you behold in your wakefulness and I will tell you their meaning. But the dreams of your sleep belong neither to my wisdom nor to your imagination."

THE MADMAN

It was in the garden of a madhouse that I met a youth with a face pale and lovely and full of wonder. And I sat beside him upon the bench, and I said, "Why are you here?"

And he looked at me in astonishment, and he said, "It is an unseemly question, yet I will answer you. My father would make of me a reproduction of himself; so also would my uncle. My mother would have me the image of her seafaring husband as the perfect example for me to follow. My brother thinks I should be like him, a fine athlete.

"And my teachers also, the doctor of philosophy, and the music-master, and the logician, they too were determined, and each would have me but a reflection of his own face in a mirror.

"Therefore I came to this place. I find it more sane here. At least, I can be myself."

Then of a sudden he turned to me and he said, "But tell me, were you also driven to this place by education and good counsel?"

And I answered, "No, I am a visitor."

And he answered, "Oh, you are one of those who live in the madhouse on the other side of the wall."

THE FROGS

Upon a summer day a frog said to his mate, "I fear those people living in that house on the shore are disturbed by our night-songs."

And his mate answered and said, "Well, do they not annoy our silence during the day with their talking?"

The frog said, "Let us not forget that we may sing too much in the night."

And his mate answered, "Let us not forget that they chatter and shout overmuch during the day."

Said the frog, "How about the bullfrog who that they clatter and shout overmuch during the day."

Said the frog, "How about the bullfrog who disturbs the whole neighbourhood with his God-forbidden booming?"

And his mate replied, "Aye, and what say you of the politician and the priest and the scientist who come to these shores and fill the air with noisy and rhymeless sound?"

Then the frog said, "Well, let us be better than these human beings. Let us be quiet at night, and keep our songs in our hearts, even though the moon calls for our rhythm and the stars for our rhyme. At least, let us be silent for a night or two, or even for three nights."

And his mate said, "Very well, I agree. We shall see what your bountiful heart will bring forth."

That night the frogs were silent; and they were silent the following night also, and again upon the third night.

And strange to relate, the talkative woman who lived in the house beside the lake came down to breakfast on that third day and shouted to her husband, "I have not slept these three nights. I was secure with sleep when the noise of the frogs was in my ear. But something must have happened. They have not sung now for three nights; and I am almost maddened with sleeplessness."

The frog heard this and turned to his mate and said, winking his eye, "And we were almost maddened with our silence, were we not?"

And his mate answered, "Yes, the silence of the night was heavy upon us. And I can see now that there is no need for us to cease our singing for the comfort of those who must needs fill their emptiness with noise."

And that night the moon called not in vain for their rhythm nor the stars for their rhyme.

LAWS AND LAW-GIVING

Ages ago there was a great king, and he was wise. And he desired to lay laws unto his subjects.

He called upon one thousand wise men of one thousand different tribes to his capitol and lay down the laws.

And all this came to pass.

But when the thousand laws written upon parchment were put before the king and he read them, he wept bitterly in his soul, for he had not known that there were one thousand forms of crime in his kingdom.

Then he called his scribe, and with a smile upon his mouth he himself dictated laws. And his laws were but seven.

And the one thousand wise men left him in anger and returned to their tribes with the laws they had laid down. And every tribe followed the laws of its wise men.

Therefore they have a thousand laws even to our own day.

It is a great country, but it has one thousand prisons, and the prisons are full of women and men, breakers of a thousand laws.

It is indeed a great country, but the people thereof are descendants of one thousand law-givers and of only one wise king.

YESTERDAY, TODAY AND TOMORROW

I said to my friend, "You see her leaning upon the arm of that man. It was but yesterday that she leaned thus upon my arm."

And my friend said, "And tomorrow she will lean upon mine."

I said, "Behold her sitting close at his side. It was but yesterday she sat close beside me."

And he answered, "Tomorrow she will sit beside me."

I said, "See, she drinks wine from his cup, and yesterday she drank from mine."

And he said, "Tomorrow, from my cup."

Then I said, "See how she gazes at him with love, and with yielding eyes. Yesterday she gazed thus upon me."

And my friend said, "It will be upon me she gazes tomorrow."

I said, "Do you not hear her now murmuring songs of love into his ears? Those very songs of love she murmured but yesterday into my ears."

And my friend said, "And tomorrow she will murmur them in mine."

I said, "Why see, she is embracing him. It was but yesterday that she embraced me."

And my friend said, "She will embrace me tomorrow."

Then I said, "What a strange woman."

But he answered, "She is like unto life, possessed by all men; and like death, she conquers all men; and like eternity, she enfolds all men."

THE PHILOSOPHER AND THE COBBLER

There came to a cobbler's shop a philosopher with worn shoes. And the philosopher said to the cobbler, "Please mend my shoes."

And the cobbler said, "I am mending another man's shoes now, and there are still other shoes to patch before I can come to yours. But leave your shoes here, and wear this other pair today, and come tomorrow for your own."

Then the philosopher was indignant, and he said, "I wear no shoes that are not mine own."

And the cobbler said, "Well then, are you in truth a philosopher, and cannot enfold your feet with the shoes of another man? Upon this very street there is another cobbler who understands philosophers better than I do. Go you to him for mending."

BUILDERS OF BRIDGES

In Antioch where the river Assi goes to meet the sea, a bridge was built to bring one half of the city nearer to the other half. It was built of large stones carried down from among the hills, on the backs of the mules of Antioch.

When the bridge was finished, upon a pillar thereof was engraved in Greek and in Aramaic, "This bridge was builded by King Antiochus II."

And all the people walked across the good bridge over the goodly river Assi.

And upon an evening, a youth, deemed by some a little mad, descended to the pillar where the words were engraven, and he covered over the graving with charcoal, and above it wrote, "The stones of this bridge were brought down from the hills by the mules. In passing to and fro over it you are riding upon the backs of the mules of Antioch, builders of this bridge."

And when the people read what the youth had written, some of them laughed and some marvelled. And some said, "Ah yes, we know who has done this. Is he not a little mad?"

But one mule said, laughing, to another mule, "Do you not remember that we did carry those stones? And yet until now it has been said that the bridge was builded by King Antiochus."

THE FIELD OF ZAAD

Upon the road of Zaad a traveller met a man who lived in a nearby village, and the traveller, pointing with his hand to a vast field, asked the man saying, "Was not this the battle-ground where King Ahlam overcame his enemies?"

And the man answered and said, "This has never been a battle-ground. There once stood on this field the great city of Zaad, and it was burnt down to ashes. But now it is a good field, is it not?"

And the traveller and the man parted.

Not a half mile farther the traveller met another man, and pointing to the field again, he said, "So that is where the great city of Zaad once stood?'

And the man said, "There has never been a city in this place. But once there was a monastery here, and it was destroyed by the people of the South Country."

Shortly after, on that very road of Zaad, the traveller met a third man, and pointing once more to the vast field he said, "Is it not true that this is the place where once there stood a great monastery?"

But the man answered, "There has never been a monastery in this neighbourhood, but our fathers and our forefathers have told us that once there fell a great meteor on this field."

Then the traveller walked on, wondering in his heart. And he met a very old man, and saluting his he said, "Sir, upon this road I have met three men who live in the neighbourhood and I have asked each of them about this field, and each one denied what the other had said, and each one told me a new tale that the other had not told."

Then the old man raised his head, and answered, "My friend, each and every one of these men told you what was indeed so; but few of us are able to add fact to different fact and make a truth thereof."

THE GOLDEN BELT

Once upon a day two men who met on the road were walking together toward Salamis, the City of Columns. In the mid-afternoon they came to a wide river and there was no bridge to cross it. They must needs swim, or seek another road unknown to them.

And they said to one another, "Let us swim. After all, the river is not so wide." And they threw themselves into the water and swam.

And one of the men who had always known rivers and the ways of rivers, in mid-stream suddenly began to lose himself; and to be carried away by the rushing waters; while the other who had never swum before crossed the river straight-way and stood upon the farther bank. Then seeing his companion still wrestling with the stream, he threw himself again into the waters and brought him also safely to the shore.

And the man who had been swept away by the current said, "But you told me you could not swim. How then did you cross that river with such assurance?"

And the second man answered, "My friend, do you see this belt which girdles me? It is full of golden coins that I have earned for my wife and my children, a full year's work. It is the weight of this belt of gold that carried me across the river, to my wife and my children. And my wife and my children were upon my shoulders as I swam."

And the two men walked on together toward Salamis.

THE RED EARTH

Said a tree to a man, "My roots are in the deep red earth, and I shall give you of my fruit."

And the man said to the tree, "How alike we are. My roots are also deep in the red earth. And the red earth gives you power to bestow upon me of your fruit, and the red earth teaches me to receive from you with thanksgiving."

THE FULL MOON

The full moon rose in glory upon the town, and all the dogs of that town began to bark at the moon.

Only one dog did not bark, and he said to them in a grave voice, "Awake not stillness from her sleep, nor bring you the moon to the earth with your barking."

Then all the dogs ceased barking, in awful silence. But the dog who had spoken to them continued barking for silence, the rest of the night.

THE HERMIT PROPHET

Once there lived a hermit prophet, and thrice a moon he would go down to the great city and in the market places he would preach giving and sharing to the people. And he was eloquent, and his fame was upon the land.

Upon an evening three men came to his hermitage and he greeted them. And they said, "You have been preaching giving and sharing, and you have sought to teach those who have much to give unto those who have little; and we doubt not that your fame has brought you riches. Now come and give us of your riches, for we are in need."

And the hermit answered and said, "My friends, I have naught but this bed and this mat and this jug of water. Take them if it is in your desire. I have neither gold nor silver."

Then they looked down with distain upon him, and turned their faces from him, and the last man stood at the door for a moment, and said, "Oh, you cheat! You fraud! You teach and preach that which you yourself do not perform."

THE OLD, OLD WINE

Once there lived a rich man who was justly proud of his cellar and the wine therein. And there was one jug of ancient vintage kept for some occasion known only to himself.

The governor of the state visited him, and he bethought him and said, "That jug shall not be opened for a mere governor."

And a bishop of the diocese visited him, but he said to himself, "Nay, I will not open that jug. He would not know its value, nor would its aroma reach his nostrils."

The prince of the realm came and supped with him. But he thought, "It is too royal a wine for a mere princeling."

And even on the day when his own nephew was married, he said to himself, "No, not to these guests shall that jug be brought forth."

And the years passed by, and he died, an old man, and he was buried like unto every seed and acorn.

And upon the day that he was buried the ancient jug was brought out together with other jugs of wine, and it was shared by the peasants of the neighbourhood. And none knew its great age.

To them, all that is poured into a cup is only wine.

THE TWO POEMS

Many centuries ago, on a road to Athens, two poets met, and they were glad to see one another.

And one poet asked the other saying, "What have you composed of late, and how goes it with your lyre?"

And the other poet answered and said with pride, "I have but now finished the greatest of my poems, perchance the greatest poem yet written in Greek. It is an invocation to Zeus the Supreme."

Then he took from beneath his cloak a parchment, saying, "Here, behold, I have it with me, and I would fain read it to you. Come, let us sit in the shade of that white cypress."

And the poet read his poem. And it was a long poem.

And the other poet said in kindliness, "This is a great poem. It will live through the ages, and in it you shall be glorified."

And the first poet said calmly, "And what have you been writing these late days?"

And the other another, "I have written but little. Only eight lines in remembrance of a child playing in a garden." And he recited the lines.

The first poet said, "Not so bad; not so bad."

And they parted.

And now after two thousand years the eight lines of the one poet are read in every tongue, and are loved and cherished.

And though the other poem has indeed come down through the ages in libraries and in the cells of scholars, and though it is remembered, it is neither loved nor read.

LADY RUTH

Three men once looked from afar upon a white house that stood alone on a green hill. One of them said, "That is the house of Lady Ruth. She is an old witch."

The second man said, "You are wrong. Lady Ruth is a beautiful woman who lives there consecrated unto her dreams."

The third man said, "You are both wrong. Lady Ruth is the holder of this vast land, and she draws blood from her serfs."

And they walked on discussing Lady Ruth. Then when they came to a crossroad they met an old man, and one of them asked him, saying, "Would you please tell us about the Lady Ruth who lives in that white house upon the hill?"

And the old man raised his head and smiled upon them, and said, "I am ninety of years, and I remember Lady Ruth when I was but a boy. But Lady Ruth died eighty years ago, and now the house is empty. The owls hoot therein, sometimes, and people say the place is haunted."

THE MOUSE AND THE CAT

Once on an evening a poet met a peasant. The poet was distant and the peasant was shy, yet they conversed.

And the peasant said, "Let me tell you a little story which I heard of late. A mouse was caught in a trap, and while he was happily eating the cheese that lay therein, a cat stood by. The mouse trembled awhile, but he knew he was safe within the trap.

"Then the cat said, 'You are eating your last meal, my friend.'

"'Yes,' answered the mouse, 'one life have I, therefore one death. But what of you? They tell me you have nine lives. Doesn't that mean that you will have to die nine times?'"

And the peasant looked at the poet and he said, "Is not this a strange story?"

And the poet answered him not, but he walked away saying in his soul, "To be sure, nine lives have we, nine lives to be sure. And we shall die nine times, nine times shall we die. Perhaps it were better to have but one life, caught in a trap -- the life of a peasant with a bit of cheese for the last meal. And yet, are we not kin unto the lions of the desert and the jungle?"

THE CURSE

And old man of the sea once said to me, "It was thirty years ago that a sailor ran away with my daughter. And I cursed them both in my heart, for of all the world I loved but my daughter.

"Not long after that, the sailor youth went down with his ship to the bottom of the sea, and with him my lovely daughter was lost unto me.

"Now therefore behold in me the murderer of a youth and a maid. It was my curse that destroyed them. And now on my way to the grave I seek God's forgiveness."

This the old man said. But there was a tone of bragging in his words, and it seems that he is still proud of the power of his curse.

THE POMEGRANATES

There was once a man who had many pomegranate trees in his orchard. And for many an autumn he would put his pomegranates on silvery trays outside of his dwelling, and upon the trays he would place signs upon which he himself had written, "Take one for aught. You are welcome."

But people passed by and no one took of the fruit.

Then the man bethought him, and one autumn he placed no pomegranates on silvery trays outside of his dwelling, but he raised this sign in large lettering: "Here we have the best pomegranates in the land, but we sell them for more silver than any other pomegranates."

And now behold, all the men and women of the neighbourhood came rushing to buy.

GOD AND MANY GODS

In the city of Kilafis a sophist stood on the steps of the Temple and preached many gods. And the people said in their hearts, "We know all this. Do they not live with us and follow us wherever we go?"

Not long after, another man stood in the market place and spoke unto the people and said, "There is no god." And many who heard him were glad of his tidings, for they were afraid of gods.

And upon another day there came a man of great eloquence, an he said, "There is but one God." And now the people were dismayed for in their hearts they feared the judgment of one God more than that of many gods.

That same season there came yet another man, and he said to the people, "There are three gods, and they dwell upon the wind as one, and they have a vast and gracious mother who is also their mate and their sister."

Then everyone was comforted, for they said in their secret, "three gods in one must needs disagree over our failings, and besides, their gracious mother will surely be an advocate for us poor weaklings."

Yet even to this day there are those in the city of Kilafis who wrangle and argue with each other about many gods and no god, and one god and three gods in one, and a gracious mother of gods.

SHE WHO WAS DEAF

Once there lived a rich man who had a young wife, and she was stone deaf.

And upon a morning when they were breaking their feast, she spoke to him and she said, "Yesterday I visited the market place, and there were exhibited silken raiment from Damascus, and coverchiefs from India, necklaces from Persia, and bracelets from Yamman. It seems that the caravans had but just brought these things to our city. And now behold me, in rags, yet the wife of a rich man. I would have some of those beautiful things."

The husband, still busy with his morning coffee said, "My dear, there is no reason why you should not go down to the Street and buy all that your heart may desire."

And the deaf wife said, "'No!' You always say, 'No, no.' Must I needs appear in tatters among our friends to shame your wealth and my people?"

And the husband said, "I did not say, 'No.' You may go forth freely to the market place and purchase the most beautiful apparel and jewels that have come to our city."

But again the wife mis-read his words, and she replied, "Of all rich men you are the most miserly. You would deny me everything of beauty and loveliness, while other women of my age walk the gardens of the city clothed in rich raiment."

And she began to weep. And as her tears fell upon her breast she cried out again, "You always say, 'Nay, nay' to me when I desire a garment or a jewel."

Then the husband was moved, and he stood up and took out of his purse a handful of gold and placed it before her, saying in a kindly voice, "Go down to the market place, my dear, and buy all that you will."

From that day onward the deaf young wife, whenever she desired anything, would appear before her husband with a pearly tear in her eye, and he in silence would take out a handful of gold and place it in her lap.

Now, it changed that the young woman fell in love with a youth whose habit it was to make long journeys. And whenever he was away she would sit in her casement and weep.

When her husband found her thus weeping, he would say in his heart, "There must be some new caravan, and some silken garments and rare jewels in the Street."

And he would take a handful of gold and place it before her.

THE QUEST

A thousand years ago two philosophers met on a slope of Lebanon, and one said to the other, "Where goest thou?"

And the other answered, "I am seeking after the fountain of youth which I know wells out among these hills. I have found writings which tell of that fountain flowering toward the sun. And you, what are you seeking?"

The first man answered, "I am seeking after the mystery of death."

Then each of the two philosophers conceived that the other was lacking in his great science, and they began to wrangle, and to accuse each other of spiritual blindness.

Now while the two philosophers were loud upon the wind, a stranger, a man who was deemed a simpleton in his own village, passed by, and when he heard the two in hot dispute, he stood awhile and listened to their argument.

Then he came near to them and said, "My good men, it seems that you both really belong to the same school of philosophy, and that you are speaking of the same thing, only you speak in different words. One of you is seeks the fountain of youth, and the other seeks the mystery of death. Yet indeed they are but one, and as they dwell in you both."

Then the stranger turned away saying, "Farewell sages." And as he departed he laughed a patient laughter.

The two philosophers looked at each other in silence for a moment, and then they laughed also. And one of them said, "Well now, shall we not walk and seek together."

THE SCEPTRE

Said a king to his wife, "Madame, you are not truly a queen. You are too vulgar and ungracious to be my mate."

Said his wife, "Sir, you deem yourself king, but indeed you are only a poor soundling."

Now these words angered the king, and he took his sceptre with his hand, and struck the queen upon her forehead with his golden sceptre.

At that moment the lord chamberlain entered, and he said, "Well, well, Majesty! That sceptre was fashioned by the greatest artist of the land. Alas! Some day you and the queen shall be forgotten, but this sceptre shall be kept, a thing of beauty from generation to generation. And now that you have drawn blood from her Majesty's head, Sire, the sceptre shall be the more considered and remembered."

THE PATH

There lived among the hills a woman and her son, and he was her first-born and her only child.

And the boy died of a fever whilst the physician stood by.

The mother was distraught with sorrow, and she cried to the physician and besought him saying, "Tell me, tell me, what was it that made quiet his striving and silent his song?"

And the physician said, "It was the fever."

And the mother said, "What is the fever?"

And the physician answered, "I cannot explain it. It is a thing infinitely small that visits the body, and we cannot see it with the human eye."

The physician left her. And she kept repeating to herself, "Something infinitely small. We cannot see it with our human eye."

And at evening the priest came to console her. And she wept and she cried out saying, "Oh, why have I lost my son, my only son, my first-born?"

And the priest answered, "My child, it is the will of God."

And the woman said, "What is God and where is God? I would see God that I may tear my bosom before Him, and pour the blood of my heart at His feet. Tell me where I shall find Him."

And the priest said, ""God is infinitely vast. He is not to be seen with our human eye."

Then the woman cried out, "The infinitely small has slain my son through the will of the infinitely great! Then what are we? What are we?"

At that moment the woman's mother came into the room with the shroud for the dead boy, and she heard the words of the priest and also her daughter's cry. And she laid down the shroud, and took her daughter's hand in her own hand, and she said, "My daughter, we ourselves are the infinitely small and the infinitely great; and we are the path between the two."

THE WHALE AND THE BUTTERFLY

Once on an evening a man and a woman found themselves together in a stagecoach. They had met before.

The man was a poet, and as he sat beside the woman he sought to amuse her with stories, some that were of his own weaving, and some that were not his own.

But even while he was speaking the lady went to sleep. Then suddenly the coach lurched, and she awoke, and she said, "I admire your interpretation of the story of Jonah and the whale."

And the poet said, "But Madame, I have been telling you a story of mine own about a butterfly and a white rose, and how they behaved the one to the other!"

THE SHADOW

Upon a June day the grass said to the shadow of an elm tree, "You move to right and left over-often, and you disturb my peace."

And the shadow answered and said, "Not I, not I. Look skyward. There is a tree that moves in the wind to the east and to the west, between the sun and the earth."

And the grass looked up, and for the first time beheld the tree. And it said in its heart, "Why, behold, there is a larger grass than myself."

And the grass was silent.

PEACE CONTAGIOUS

One branch in bloom said to his neighbouring branch, "This is a dull and empty day." And the other branch answered, "It is indeed empty and dull."

At that moment a sparrow alighted on one of the branches, and the another sparrow, nearby.

And one of the sparrows chirped and said, "My mate has left me."

And the other sparrow cried, "My mate has also gone, and she will not return. And what care I?"

Then the two birds began to twitter and scold, and soon they were fighting and making harsh noise upon the air.

All of a sudden two other sparrows came sailing from the sky, and they sat quietly beside the restless two. And there was calm, and there was peace.

Then the four flew away together in pairs.

And the first branch said to his neighbouring branch, "That was a mighty zig-zag of sound."

And the other branch answered, "Call it what you will, it is now both peaceful and spacious. And if the upper air makes peace it seems to me that those who dwell in the lower might make peace also. Will you not wave in the wind a little nearer to me?"

And the first branch said, "Oh, perchance, for peace' sake, ere the Spring is over."

And then he waved himself with the strong wind to embrace her.

SEVENTY

The poet youth said to the princess, "I love you." And the princess answered, "And I love you too, my child."

"But I am not your child. I am a man and I love you."

And she said, "I am the mother of sons and daughters, and they are fathers and mothers of sons and daughters; and one of the sons of my sons is older than you."

And the poet youth said, "But I love you."

It was not long after that the princess died. But ere her last breath was received again by the greater breath of earth, she said within her soul, "My beloved, mine only son, my youth-poet, it may yet be that some day we shall meet again, and I shall not be seventy."

FINDING GOD

Two men were walking in the valley, and one man pointed with his finger toward the mountain side, and said, "See you that hermitage? There lives a man who has long divorced the world. He seeks but after God, and naught else upon this earth."

And the other man said, "He shall not find God until he leaves his hermitage, and the aloneness of his hermitage, and returns to our world, to share our joy and pain, to dance with our dancers at the wedding feast, and to weep with those who weep around the coffins of our dead."

And the other man was convinced in his heart, though in spite of his conviction he answered, "I agree with all that you say, yet I believe the hermit is a good man. And it may it not well be that one good man by his absence does better than the seeming goodness of these many men?"

THE RIVER

In the valley of Kadisha where the mighty river flows, two little streams met and spoke to one another.

One stream said, "How came you, my friend, and how was your path?"

And the other answered, "My path was most encumbered. The wheel of the mill was broken, and the master farmer who used to conduct me from my channel to his plants, is dead. I struggled down oozing with the filth of laziness in the sun. But how was your path, my brother?"

And the other stream answered and said, "Mine was a different path. I came down the hills among fragrant flowers and shy willows; men and women drank of me with silvery cups, and little children paddled their rosy feet at my edges, and there was laughter all about me, and there were sweet songs. What a pity that your path was not so happy."

At that moment the river spoke with a loud voice and said, "Come in, come in, we are going to the sea. Come in, come in, speak no more. Be with me now. We are going to the sea. Come in, come in, for in me you shall forget you wanderings, sad or gay. Come in, come in. And you and I will forget all our ways when we reach the heart of our mother the sea."

THE TWO HUNTERS

Upon a day in May, Joy and Sorrow met beside a lake. They greeted one another, and they sat down near the quiet waters and conversed.

Joy spoke of the beauty which is upon the earth, and the daily wonder of life in the forest and among the hills, and of the songs heard at dawn and eventide.

And sorrow spoke, and agreed with all that Joy had said; for Sorrow knew the magic of the hour and the beauty thereof. And Sorrow was eloquent when he spoke of may in the fields and among the hills.

And Joy and Sorrow talked long together, and they agreed upon all things of which they knew.

Now there passed by on the other side of the lake two hunters. And as they looked across the water one of them said, "I wonder who are those two persons?" And the other said, "Did you say two? I see only one."

The first hunter said, "But there are two." And the second said, "There is only one that I can see, and the reflection in the lake is only one."

"Nay, there are two," said the first hunter, "and the reflection in the still water is of two persons."

But the second man said again, "Only one do I see." And again the other said, "But I see two so plainly."

And even unto this day one hunter says that the other sees double; while the other says, "My friend is somewhat blind."

THE OTHER WANDERER

Once on a time I met another man of the roads. He too was a little mad, and thus spoke to me:

"I am a wanderer. Oftentimes it seems that I walk the earth among pygmies. And because my head is seventy cubits farther from the earth than theirs, it creates higher and freer thoughts.

"But in truth I walk not among men but above them, and all they can see of me is my footprints in their open fields.

"And often have I heard them discuss and disagree over the shape and size of my footprints. For there are some who say, 'These are the tracks of a mammoth that roamed the earth in the far past.' And others say, 'Nay, these are places where meteors have fallen from the distant stars.'

"But you, my friend, you know full well that they are naught save the footprints of a wanderer."

THE END.

BOOK SIX.
THE GARDEN OF THE PROPHET

ALMUSTAFA, the chosen and the beloved, who was a noon unto his own day, returned to the isle of his birth in the month of Tichreen, which is the month of remembrance.

And as his ship approached the harbour, he stood upon its prow, and his mariners were about him. And there was a homecoming in his heart.

And he spoke, and the sea was in his voice, and he said: "Behold, the isle of our birth. Even here the earth heaved us, a song and a riddle; a song unto the sky, a riddle unto the earth; and what is there between earth and sky that shall carry the song and solve the riddle save our own passion?

"The sea yields us once more to these shores. We are but another wave of her waves. She sends us forth to sound her speech, but how shall we do so unless we break the symmetry of our heart on rock and sand?

"For this is the law of mariners and the sea: If you would freedom, you must needs turn to mist. The formless is for ever seeking form, even as the countless nebulae would become suns and moons; and we who have sought much and return now to this isle, rigid moulds, we must become mist once more and learn of the beginning. And what is there that shall live and rise unto the heights except it be broken unto passion and freedom?

"For ever shall we be in quest of the shores, that we may sing and be heard. But what of the wave that breaks where no ear shall hear? It is the unheard in us that nurses our deeper sorrow. Yet it is also the unheard which carves our soul to form and fashion our destiny."

Then one of his mariners came forth and said: "Master, you have captained our longing for this harbour, and behold, we have come. Yet you speak of sorrow, and of hearts that shall be broken."

And he answered him and said: "Did I not speak of freedom, and of the mist which is our greater freedom? Yet it is in pain I make pilgrimage to the isle where I was born, even like unto a ghost of one slain come to kneel before those who have slain him."

And another mariner spoke and said: "Behold, the multitudes on the sea-wall. In their silence they have foretold even the day and the hour of your coming, and they have gathered from their fields and vineyards in their loving need, to await you."

And Almustafa looked afar upon the multitudes, and his heart was mindful of their yearning, and he was silent.

Then a cry came from the people, and it was a cry of remembrance and of entreaty.

And he looked upon his mariners and said: "And what have I brought them? A hunter was I, in a distant land. With aim and might I have spent the golden arrows they gave me, but I have brought down no game. I followed not the arrows. Mayhap they are spreading now in the sun with the pinions of wounded eagles that would not fall to the earth. And mayhap the arrow-heads have fallen into the hands of those who had need of them for bread and wine.

"I know not where they have spent their flight, but this I know: they have made their curve in the sky.

"Even so, love's hand is still upon me, and you, my mariners, still sail my vision, and I shall not be dumb. I shall cry out when the hand of the seasons is upon my throat, and I shall sing my words when my lips are burned with flames."

And they were troubled in their hearts because he spoke of these things. And one said: "Master, teach us all, and mayhap because your blood flows in our veins, and our breath is of your fragrance, we shall understand."

The he answered them, and the wind was in his voice, and he said: "Brought you me to the isle of my birth to be a teacher? Not yet have I been caged by wisdom. Too young am I and too verdant to speak of aught but self, which is for ever the deep calling upon the deep.

"Let him who would have wisdom seek it in the buttercup or in a pinch of red clay. I am still the singer. Still I shall sing the earth, and I shall sing your lost dreaming that walks the day between sleep and sleep. But I shall gaze upon the sea."

And now the ship entered the harbour and reached the sea-wall, and he came thus to the isle of his birth and stood once more amongst his own people. And a great cry arose from their hearts so that the loneliness of his home-coming was shaken within him.

And they were silent awaiting his word, but he answered them not, for the sadness of memory was upon him, and he said in his heart: "Have I said that I shall sing? Nay, I can but open my lips that the voice of life may come forth and go out to the wind for joy and support."

Then Karima, she who had played with him, a child, in the Garden of his mother, spoke and said: "Twelve years have you hidden your face from us, and for twelve years have we hungered and thirsted for your voice."

And he looked upon her with exceeding tenderness, for it was she who had closed the eyes of his mother when the white wings of death had gathered her.

And he answered and said: "Twelve years? Said you twelve years, Karima? I measured not my longing with the starry rod, nor did I sound the depth thereof. For love when love is homesick exhausts time's measurements and time's soundings.

"There are moments that hold aeons of separation. Yet parting is naught but an exhaustion of the mind. Perhaps we have not parted."

And Almustafa looked upon the people, and he saw them all, the youth and the aged, the stalwart and the puny, those who were ruddy with the touch of wind and sun, and those who were of pallid countenance; and upon their face a light of longing and of questioning.

And one spoke and said: "Master, life has dealt bitterly with our hopes and our desires. Our hearts are troubled, and we do not understand. I pray you, comfort us, and open to us the meanings of our sorrows."

And his heart was moved with compassion, and he said: "Life is older than all things living; even as beauty was winged ere the beautiful was born on earth, and even as truth was truth ere it was uttered.

"Life sings in our silences, and dreams in our slumber. Even when we are beaten and low, Life is enthroned and high. And when we weep, Life smiles upon the day, and is free even when we drag our chains.

"Oftentimes we call Life bitter names, but only when we ourselves are bitter and dark. And we deem her empty and unprofitable, but only when the soul goes wandering in desolate places, and the heart is drunken with over-mindfulness of self.

"Life is deep and high and distant; and though only your vast vision can reach even her feet, yet she is near; and though only the breath of your breath reaches her heart, the shadow of your shadow crosses her face, and the echo of your faintest cry becomes a spring and an autumn in her breast.

"And Life is veiled and hidden, even as your greater self is hidden and veiled. Yet when Life speaks, all the winds become words; and when she speaks again, the smiles upon your lips and the tears in your eyes turn also into words. When she sings, the deaf hear and are held; and when she comes walking, the sightless behold her and are amazed and follow her in wonder and astonishment."

And he ceased from speaking, and a vast silence enfolded the people, and in the silence there was an unheard song, and they were comforted of their loneliness and their aching.

*

AND he left them straightway and followed the path which led to his Garden, which was the Garden of his mother and his father, wherein they lay asleep, they and their forefathers.

And there were those who would have followed after him, seeing that it was a home-coming, and he was alone, for there was not one left of all his kin to spread the feast of welcome, after the manner of his people.

But the captain of his ship counselled them saying: "Suffer him to go upon his way. For his bread is the bread of aloneness, and in his cup is the wine of remembrance, which he would drink alone."

And his mariners held their steps, for they knew it was even as the captain of the ship had told them. And all those who gathered upon the sea-wall restrained the feet of their desire.

Only Karima went after him, a little way, yearning over his aloneness and his memories. And she spoke not, but turned and went unto her own house, and in the garden under the almond-tree she wept, yet she knew not wherefore.

*

AND Almustafa came and found the Garden of his mother and his father, and he entered in, and closed the gate that no man might come after him.

And for forty days and forty nights he dwelt alone in that house and that Garden, and none came, not even unto the gate, for it was closed, and all the people knew that he would be alone.

And when the forty days and nights were ended, Almustafa opened the gate that they might come in.

And there came nine men to be with him in the Garden; three mariners from his own ship; three who had been his comrades in play when they were but children together. And these were his disciples.

And on a morning his disciples sat around him, and there were distances and remembrances in his eyes. And that disciple who was called Hafiz said unto him: "Master, tell us of the city of Orphalese, and of that land wherein you tarried those twelve years."

And Almustafa was silent, and he looked away towards the hills and toward the vast ether, and there was a battle in his silence.

Then he said: "My friends and my road-fellows, pity the nation that is full of beliefs and empty of religion.

"Pity the nation that wears a cloth it does not weave, eats a bread it does not harvest, and drinks a wine that flows not from its own winepress.

"Pity the nation that acclaims the bully as hero, and that deems the glittering conqueror bountiful.

"Pity the nation that despises a passion in its dream, yet submits in its awakening.

"Pity the nation that raises not its voice save when it walks in a funeral, boasts not except when its neck is laid between the sword and the block.

"Pity the nation whose statesman is a fox, whose philosopher is a juggle, and whose art is the art of patching and mimicking.

"Pity the nation that welcomes its new ruler with trumpetings, and farewells him with hootings, only to welcome another with trumpetings again.

"Pity the nation whose sages are dumb with years and whose strong men are yet in the cradle.

"Pity the nation divided into fragments, each fragment deeming itself a nation."

*

AND one said: "Speak to us of that which is moving in your own heart even now."

And he looked upon that one, and there was in his voice a sound like a star singing, and he said: "In your waking dream, when you are hushed and listening to your deeper self, your thoughts, like snow-flakes, fall and flutter and garment all the sounds of your spaces with white silence.

"And what are waking dreams but clouds that bud and blossom on the sky-tree of your heart? And what are your thoughts but the petals which the winds of your heart scatter upon the hills and its fields?

"And even as you wait for peace until the formless within you takes form, so shall the cloud gather and drift until the Blessed Fingers shape its grey desire to little crystal suns and moons and stars."

Then Sarkis, he who was the half-doubter, spoke and said: "But spring shall come, and all the snows of our dreams and our thoughts shall melt and be no more."

And he answered saying: "When Spring comes to seek His beloved amongst the slumbering groves and vineyards, the snows shall indeed melt and shall run in streams to seek the river in the valley, to be the cup-bearer to the myrtle-trees and laurel.

"So shall the snow of your heart melt when your Spring is come, and thus shall your secret run in streams to seek the river of life in the valley. And the river shall enfold your secret and carry it to the great sea.

"All things shall melt and turn into songs when Spring comes. Even the stars, the vast snow-flakes that fall slowly upon the larger fields, shall melt into singing streams. When the sun of His face shall rise above the wider horizon, then what frozen symmetry would not turn into liquid melody? And who among you would not be the cup-bearer to the myrtle and the laurel?

"It was but yesterday that you were moving with the moving sea, and you were shoreless and without a self. Then the wind, the breath of Life, wove you, a veil of light on her face; then her hand gathered you and gave you form, and with a head held high you sought the heights. But the sea followed after you, and her song is still with you. And though you have forgotten your parentage, she will for ever assert her motherhood, and for ever will she call you unto her.

"In your wanderings among the mountains and the desert you will always remember the depth of her cool heart. And though oftentimes you will not know for what you long, it is indeed for her vast and rhythmic peace.

"And how else can it be? In grove and in bower when the rain dances in leaves upon the hill, when snow falls, a blessing and a covenant; in the valley when you lead your flocks to the river; in your fields where brooks, like silver streams. join together the green garment; in your gardens when the early dews mirror the heavens; in your meadows when the mist of evening half veils your way; in all these the sea is with you, a witness to your heritage, and a claim upon your love.

"It is the snow-flake in you running down to the sea."

*

And on a morning as they walked in the Garden, there appeared before the gate a woman, and it was Karima, she whom Almustafa had loved even as a sister in his boyhood. And she stood without, asking nothing, nor knocking with her hand upon the gate, but only gazing with longing and sadness into the Garden.

And Almustafa saw the desire upon her eyelids, and with swift steps he came to the wall and the gate and opened unto her, and she came in and was made welcome.

And she spoke and said: "Wherefore have you withdrawn yourself from us altogether, that we may not live in the light of your countenance? For behold, these many years have we loved you and waited with longing for your safe return. And now the people cry for you and would have speech with you; and I am their messenger come to beseech you that you will show yourself to the people, and speak to them out of your wisdom, and comfort the broken of heart and instruct our foolishness."

And looking upon her, he said: "Call me not wise unless you call all men wise. A young fruit am I, still clinging to the branch, and it was only yesterday that I was but a blossom.

"And call none among you foolish, for in truth we are neither wise nor foolish. We are green leaves upon the tree of life, and life itself is beyond wisdom, and surely beyond foolishness.

"And have I indeed withdrawn myself from you? Know you not that there is no distance save that which the soul does not span in fancy? And when the soul shall span that distance, it becomes a rhythm in the soul.

"The space that lies between you and your near neighbour unbefriended is indeed greater than that which lies between you and your beloved who dwells beyond seven lands and seven seas.

"For in remembrance there are no distances; and only in oblivion is there a gulf that neither your voice nor your eye can abridge.

"Between the shores of the oceans and the summit of the highest mountain there is a secret road which you must needs travel ere you become one with the sons of earth.

"And between your knowledge and your understanding there is a secret path which you must needs discover ere you become one with man, and therefore one with yourself.

"Between your right hand that gives and your left hand that receives there is a great space. Only by deeming them both giving and receiving can you bring them into spacelessness, for it is only in knowing that you have naught to give and naught to receive that you can overcome space.

"Verily the vastest distance is that which lies between your sleep-vision and your wakefulness; and between that which is but a deed and that which is a desire.

"And there is still another road which you must needs travel ere you become one with Life. But of that road I shall not speak now, seeing that you are weary already of travelling."

*

THEN he went forth with the woman, he and the nine, even unto the market-place, and he spoke to the people, his friends and his neighbours, and there was joy in their hearts and upon their eyelids.

And he said: "You grow in sleep, and live your fuller life in you dreaming. For all your days are spent in thanksgiving for that which you have received in the stillness of the night.

"Oftentimes you think and speak of night as the season of rest, yet in truth night is the season of seeking and finding.

"The day gives unto you the power of knowledge and teaches your fingers to become versed in the art of receiving; but it is night that leads you to the treasure-house of Life.

"The sun teaches to all things that grow their longing for the light. But it is night that raises them to the stars.

"It is indeed the stillness of the night that weaves a wedding-veil over the trees in the forest, and the flowers in the garden, and then spreads the lavish feast and makes ready the nuptial chamber; and in that holy silence tomorrow is conceived in the womb of Time.

'Thus it is with you, and thus, in seeking, you find meat and fulfilment. And though at dawn your awakening erases the memory, the board of dreams is for ever spread, and the nuptial chamber waiting."

And he was silent for a space, and they also, awaiting his word. Then he spoke again, saying: "You are spirits though you move in bodies; and like oil that burns in the dark, you are flames though held in lamps.

"If you were naught save bodies, then my standing before you and speaking unto you would be but emptiness, even as the dead calling unto the dead. But this is not so. All that is deathless in you is free unto the day and the night and cannot be housed nor fettered, for this is the will of the Most High. You are His breath even as the wind that shall be neither caught nor caged. And I also am the breath of His breath."

And he went from their midst walking swiftly and entered again into the Garden.

And Sarkis, he who was the half-doubter, spoke and said: "And what of ugliness, Master? You speak never of ugliness."

And Almustafa answered him, and there was a whip in his words, and he said: "My friend, what man shall call you inhospitable if he shall pass by your house, yet would not knock at your door?

"And who shall deem you deaf and unmindful if he shall speak to you in a strange tongue of which you understand nothing?

"Is it not that which you have never striven to reach, into whose heart you have never desired to enter, that you deem ugliness?

"If ugliness is aught, indeed, it is but the scales upon our eyes, and the wax filling our ears.

"Call nothing ugly, my friend, save the fear of a soul in the presence of its own memories."

*

A<small>ND</small> upon a day as they sat in the long shadows of the white poplars, one spoke saying: "Master, I am afraid of time. It passes over us and robs us of our youth, and what does it give in return?"

And he answered and said: "Take up now a handful of good earth. Do you find in it a seed, and perhaps a worm? If your hand were spacious and enduring enough, the seed might become a forest, and the worm a flock of angels. And forget not that the years which turn seeds to forests, and worms to angels, belong to this Now, all of the years, this very Now.

"And what are the seasons of the years save your own thoughts changing? Spring is an awakening in your breast, and summer but a recognition of your own fruitfulness. Is not autumn the ancient in you singing a lullaby to that which is still a child in your being? And what, I ask you, is winter save sleep big with the dreams of all the other seasons."

And the Mannus, the inquisitive disciple, looked about him and he saw plants in flower cleaving unto the sycamore-tree. And he said: "Behold the parasites, Master. What say you of them? They are thieves with weary eyelids who steal the light from the steadfast children of the sun, and make fair of the sap that runneth into their branches and their leaves."

And he answered him saying: "My friend, we are all parasites. We who labour to turn the sod into pulsing life are not above those who receive life directly from the sod without knowing the sod.

"Shall a mother say to her child: 'I give you back to the forest, which is your greater mother, for you weary me, heart and hand'?

"Or shall the singer rebuke his own song, saying: 'Return now to the cave of echoes from whence you came, for your voice consumes my breath'?

"And shall the shepherd say to his yearling: 'I have no pasture whereunto I may lead you; therefore be cut off and become a sacrifice for this cause'?

"Nay, my friend, all these things are answered even before they are asked, and, like your dreams, are fulfilled ere you sleep.

"We live upon one another according to the law, ancient and timeless. Let us live thus in loving-kindness. We seek one another in our aloneness, and we walk the road when we have no hearth to sit beside.

"My friends and my brothers, the wider road is your fellow-man.

"These plants that live upon the tree draw milk of the earth in the sweet stillness of night, and the earth in her tranquil dreaming sucks at the breast of the sun.

"And the sun, even as you and I and all there is, sits in equal honour at the banquet of the Prince whose door is always open and whose board is always spread.

"Mannus, my friend, all there is lives always upon all there is; and all there is lives in the faith, shoreless, upon the bounty of the Most High."

*

And on a morning when the sky was yet pale with dawn, they walked all together in the Garden and looked unto the East and were silent in the presence of the rising sun.

And after a while Almustafa pointed with his hand, and said: "The image of the morning sun in a dewdrop is not less than the sun. The reflection of life in your soul is not less than life.

"The dewdrop mirrors the light because it is one with light, and you reflect life because you and life are one.

"When darkness is upon you, say: 'This darkness is dawn not yet born; and though night's travail be full upon me, yet shall dawn be born unto me even as unto the hills.'

"The dewdrop rounding its sphere in the dusk of the lily is not unlike yourself gathering your soul in the heart of God.

"Shall a dewdrop say: 'But once in a thousand years I am a dewdrop,' speak you and answer it saying: 'Know you not that the light of all the years is shining in your circle?' "

*

And on an evening a great storm visited the place, and Almustafa and his disciples, the nine, went within and sat about the fire and were silent.

Then one of the disciples said: "I am alone, Master, and the hoofs of the hours beat heavily upon my breast."

And Almustafa rose up and stood in their midst, and he said in a voice like unto the sound of a great wind: "Alone! And what of it? You came alone, and alone shall you pass into the mist.

"Therefore drink your cup alone and in silence. The autumn days have given other lips other cups and filled them with wine bitter and sweet, even as they have filled your cup.

"Drink your cup alone though it taste of your own blood and tears, and praise life for the gift of thirst. For without thirst your heart is but the shore of a barren sea, songless and without a tide.

"Drink your cup alone, and drink it with cheers.

"Raise it high above your head and drink deep to those who drink alone.

"Once I sought the company of men and sat with them at their banquet-tables and drank deep with them; but their wine did not rise to my head, nor did it flow into my bosom. It only descended to my feet. My wisdom was left dry and my heart was locked and sealed. Only my feet were with them in their fog.

"And I sought the company of men no more, nor drank wine with them at their board.

"Therefore I say unto you, though the hoofs of the hours beat heavily upon your bosom, what of it? It is well for you to drink your cup of sorrow alone, and your cup of joy shall you drink alone also."

*

AND on a day, as Phardrous, the Greek, walked in the Garden, he struck his foot upon a stone and he was angered. And he turned and picked up the stone, saying in a low voice: "O dead thing in my path!" and he flung away the stone.

And Almustafa, the chosen and the beloved, said: "Why say you: 'O dead thing'? Have you been thus long in this Garden and know not that there is nothing dead here? All things live and glow in the knowledge of the day and the majesty of the night. You and the stone are one. There is a difference only in heart-beats. Your heart beats a little faster, does it, my friend? Ay, but it is not so tranquil.

"Its rhythm may be another rhythm, but I say unto you that if you sound the depths of your soul and scale the heights of space, you shall hear one melody, and in that melody the stone and the star sing, the one with the other, in perfect unison.

"If my words reach not your understanding, then let be until another dawn. If you have cursed this stone because in your blindness you have stumbled upon it, then would you curse a star if so be your head should encounter it in the sky. But the day will come when you will gather stones and stars as a child plucks the valley-lilies, and then shall you know that all these things are living and fragrant."

*

AND on the first day of the week when the sounds of the temple bells sought their ears, one spoke and said: "Master, we hear much talk of God hereabout. What say you of God, and who is He in very truth?"

And he stood before them like a young tree, fearless of wind or tempest, and he answered saying: "Think now, my comrades and beloved, of a heart that contains all your hearts, a love that encompasses all your loves, a spirit that envelops all your spirits, a voice enfolding all your voices, and a silence deeper than all your silences, and timeless.

"Seek now to perceive in your self-fullness a beauty more enchanting than all things beautiful, a song more vast than the songs of the sea and the forest, a majesty seated upon the throne for which Orion is but a footstool, holding a sceptre in which the Pleiades are naught save the glimmer of dewdrops.

"You have sought always only food and shelter, a garment and a staff; seek now One who is neither an aim for your arrows nor a stony cave to shield you from the elements.

"And if my words are a rock and a riddle, then seek, none the less, that your hearts may be broken, and that your questionings may bring you unto the love and the wisdom of the Most High, whom men call God."

And they were silent, every one, and they were perplexed in their heart; and Almustafa was moved with compassion for them, and he gazed with tenderness upon them and said: "Let us speak rather of the gods, your neighbours, and of your brothers, the elements that move about your houses and your fields.

"You would rise up in fancy unto the cloud, and you deem it height; and you would pass over the vast sea and claim it to be distance. But I say unto you that when you sow a seed in the earth, you reach a greater height; and when you hail the beauty of the morning to your neighbour, you cross a greater sea.

"Too often do you sing God, the Infinite, and yet in truth you hear not the song. Would that you might listen to the song-birds, and to the leaves that forsake the branch when the wind passes by, and forget not, my friends, that these sing only when they are separated from the branch!

"Again I bid you to speak not so freely of God, who is your All, but speak rather and understand one another, neighbour unto neighbour, a god unto a god.

"For what shall feed the fledgling in the nest if the mother bird flies skyward? And what anemone in the fields shall be fulfilled unless it be husbanded by a bee from another anemone?

"It is only when you are lost in your smaller selves that you seek the sky which you call God. Would that you might find paths into your vast selves; would that you might be less idle and pave the roads!

"My mariners and my friends, it were wiser to speak less of God, whom we cannot understand, and more of each other, whom we may understand. Yet I would have you know that we are the breath and the fragrance of God. We are God, in leaf, in flower, and oftentimes in fruit."

*

And on a morning when the sun was high, one of the disciples, one of those three who had played with him in childhood, approached him saying: "Master, my garment is worn, and I have no other. Give me leave to go unto the market-place and bargain that perchance I may procure me new raiment."

And Almustafa looked upon the young man, and he said: "Give me your garment." And he did so and stood naked in the noonday.

And Almustafa said in a voice that was like a young steed running upon a road: "Only the naked live in the sun. Only the artless ride the wind. And he alone who loses his way a thousand times shall have a home-coming.

"The angels are tired of the clever. And it was but yesterday that an angel said to me: 'We created hell for those who glitter. What else but fire can erase a shining surface and melt a thing to its core?'

"And I said: 'But in creating hell you created devils to govern hell.' But the angel answered: 'Nay, hell is governed by those who do not yield to fire.'

"Wise angel! He knows the ways of men and the ways of half-men. He is one of the seraphim who come to minister unto the prophets when they are tempted by the clever. And no doubt he smiled when the prophets smile, and weeps also when they weep.

"My friends and my mariners, only the naked live in the sun. Only the rudderless can sail the greater sea. Only he who is dark with the night shall wake with the dawn, and only he who sleeps with the roots under the snow shall reach the spring.

"For you are even like roots, and like roots are you simple, yet you have wisdom from the earth. And you are silent, yet you have within your unborn branches the choir of the four winds.

"You are frail and you are formless, yet you are the beginning of giant oaks, and of the half-pencilled patterned of the willows against the sky.

"Once more I say, you are but roots betwixt the dark sod and the moving heavens. And oftentimes have I seen you rising to dance with the light, but I have also seen you shy. All roots are shy. They have hidden their hearts so long that they know not what to do with their hearts.

"But May shall come, and May is a restless virgin, and she shall mother the hills and plains."

*

AND one who had served in the Temple besought him saying: "Teach us, Master, that our words may be even as your words, a chant and an incense unto the people."

And Almustafa answered and said: "You shall rise beyond your words, but your path shall remain, a rhythm and a fragrance; a rhythm for lovers and for all who are beloved, and a fragrance for those who would live life in a garden.

"But you shall rise beyond your words to a summit whereon the stardust falls, and you shall open your hands until they are filled; then you shall lie down and sleep like a white fledgling in a white nest, and you shall dream of your tomorrow as white violets dream of spring.

"Ay, and you shall go down deeper than your words. You shall seek the lost fountain-heads of the streams, and you shall be a hidden cave echoing the faint voices of the depths which now you do not even hear.

"You shall go down deeper than your words, ay, deeper than all sounds, to the very heart of the earth, and there you shall be alone with Him who walks also upon the Milky Way."

And after a space one of the disciples asked him saying: "Master, speak to us of being. What is it to be?"

And Almustafa looked long upon him and loved him. And he stood up and walked a distance away from them; then returning, he said: "In this Garden my father and my mother lie, buried by the hands of the living; and in this Garden lie buried the seeds of yesteryear, bought hither upon the wings of the wind. A thousand times shall my mother and my father be buried here, and a thousand times shall the wind bury the seed; and a thousand years hence shall you and I and these flowers come together in this Garden even as now, and we shall be, loving life, and we shall be, dreaming of space, and we shall be, rising towards the sun.

"But now today to be is to be wise, though not a stranger to the foolish; it is to be strong, but not to the undoing of the weak; to play with young children, not as fathers, but rather as playmates who would learn their games;

"To be simple and guileless with old men and women, and to sit with them in the shade of the ancient oak-trees, though you are still walking with Spring;

"To seek a poet though he may live beyond the seven rivers, and to be at peace in his presence, nothing wanting, nothing doubting, and with no question upon your lips;

"To know that the saint and the sinner are twin brothers, whose father is our Gracious King, and that one was born but the moment before the other, wherefore we regard his as the Crowned Prince;

"To follow Beauty even when she shall lead you to the verge of the precipice; and though she is winged and you are wingless, and though she shall pass beyond the verge, follow her, for where Beauty is not, there is nothing;

"To be a garden without walls, a vineyard without a guardian, a treasure-house for ever open to passers-by;

"To be robbed, cheated, deceived, ay, misled and trapped and then mocked, yet with it all to look down from the height of your larger self and smile, knowing that there is spring that will come to your garden to dance in your leaves, and an autumn to ripen your grapes; knowing that if but one of your windows is open to the East, you shall never be empty; knowing that all those deemed wrongdoers and robbers, cheaters and deceivers are your brothers in need, and that you are perchance all of these in the eyes of the blessed inhabitants of that City Invisible, above this city.

"And now, to you also whose hands fashion and find all things that are needful for the comfort of our days and our nights--

"To be is to be a weaver with seeing fingers, a builder mindful of light and space; to be a ploughman and feel that you are hiding a treasure with every seed you sow; to be a fisherman and a hunter with a pity for the fish and for the beast, yet a still greater pity for the hunger and need of man.

"And, above all, I say this: I would have you each and every one partners to the purpose of every man, for only so shall you hope to obtain your own good purpose.

"My comrades and my beloved, be bold and not meek; be spacious and not confined; and until my final hour and yours be indeed your greater self."

And he ceased speaking and there fell a deep gloom upon the nine, and their heart was turned away from him, for they understood not his words.

And behold, the three men who were mariners longed for the sea; and they who had served in the Temple yearned for the consolation of her sanctuary; and they who had been his playfellows desired the market-place. They all were deaf to his words, so that the sound of them returned unto him like weary and homeless birds seeking refuge.

And Almustafa walked a distance from them in the Garden, saying nothing, nor looking upon them.

And they began to reason among themselves and to seek excuse for their longing to be gone.

And behold, they turned and went every man to his own place, so that Almustafa, the chosen and the beloved, was left alone.

*

A>ND when the night was fully come, he took his steps to the graveside of his mother and sat beneath the cedar-tree which grew above the place. And there came the shadow of a great light upon the sky, and the Garden shone like a fair jewel upon the breast of earth.

And Almustafa cried out in the aloneness of his spirit, and he said:

"Heavy-laden is my soul with her own ripe fruit. Who is there would come and take and be satisfied? Is there not one who has fasted and who is kindly and generous in heart, to come and break his fast upon my first yieldings to the sun and thus ease me of the weight of mine own abundance?

"My soul is running over with the wine of the ages. Is there no thirsty one to come and drink?

"Behold, there was a man standing at the cross-roads with hands stretched forth unto the passers-by, and his hands were filled with jewels. And he called upon the passers-by, saying: 'Pity me, and take from me. In God's name, take out of my hands and console me.'

"But the passers-by only looked upon him, and none took out of his hand.

"Would rather that he were a beggar stretching forth his hand to receive – ay, a shivering hand, and brought back empty to his bosom – than to stretch it forth full of rich gifts and find none to receive.

"And behold, there was also the gracious prince who raised up his silken tents between the mountain and the desert and bade his servants to burn fire, a sign to the stranger and the wanderer; and who sent forth his slaves to watch the road that they might fetch a guest. But the roads and the paths of the desert were unyielding, and they found no one.

"Would rather that prince were a man of nowhere and nowhen, seeking food and shelter. Would that he were the wanderer with naught but his staff and an earthen vessel. For then at nightfall would he meet with his kind, and with the poets of nowhere and nowhen, and share their beggary and their remembrances and their dreaming.

"And behold, the daughter of the great king rose from sleep and put upon her silken raiment and her pearls and rubies, and she scattered musk upon her hair and dipped her fingers in amber. Then she descended from her tower to her garden, where the dew of night found her golden sandals.

"In the stillness of the night the daughter of a ploughman, tending his sheep in a field, and returning to her father's house at eventide with the dust of the curving roads upon her feet, and the fragrance of the vineyards in the folds of her garment.

And when the night is come, and the angel of the night is upon the world, she would steal her steps to the river-valley where her lover awaits.

"Would that she were a nun in a cloister burning her heart for incense, that her heart may rise to the wind, and exhausting her spirit, a candle, for a light arising toward the greater light, together with all those who worship and those who love and are beloved.

"Would rather that she were a woman ancient of years, sitting in the sun and remembering who had shared her youth."

And the night waxed deep, and Almustafa was dark with the night, and his spirit was as a cloud unspent. And he cried again:

"Heavy-laden is my soul with her own ripe fruit;

Heavy-laden is my soul with her fruit.

Who now will come and eat and be fulfilled?

My soul is overflowing with her wine.

Who now will pour and drink and be cooled of the desert heat?

"Would that I were a tree flowerless and fruitless,

For the pain of abundance is more bitter than barrenness,

And the sorrow of the rich from whom no one will take

Is greater than the grief of the beggar to whom none would give.

"Would that I were a well, dry and parched , and men throwing stones into me;

For this were better and easier to be borne than to be a source of living water

When men pass by and will not drink.

"Would that I were a reed trodden under foot,

For that were better than to be a lyre of silvery strings

In a house whose lord has no fingers

And whose children are deaf."

*

NOW, for seven days and seven nights no man came nigh the Garden, and he was alone with is memories and his pain; for even those who had heard his words with love and patience had turned away to the pursuits of other days.

Only Karima came, with silence upon her face like a veil; and with cup and plate within her hand, drink and meat for his aloneness and his hunger. And after setting these before him, she walked her way.

And Almustafa came again to the company of the white poplars within the gate, and he sat looking upon the road. And after a while he beheld as it were a cloud of dust blown above the road and coming toward him. And from out the cloud came the nine, and before them Karima guiding them.

And Almustafa advanced and met them upon the road, and they passed through the gate, and all was well, as though they had gone their path but an hour ago.

They came in and supped with him at his frugal board, after that Karima had laid upon it the bread and the fish and poured the last of the wine into the cups. And as she poured, she besought the Master saying: "Give me leave that I go into the city and fetch wine to replenish your cups, for this is spent."

And he looked upon her, and in his eyes were a journey and a far country, and he said: "Nay, for it is sufficient unto the hour."

And they ate and drank and were satisfied. And when it was finished, Almustafa spoke in a vast voice, deep as the sea and full as a great tide under the moon, and he said: "My comrades and my road-fellows, we must needs part this day. Long have we climbed the steepest mountains and we have wrestled with the storms. We have known hunger, but we have also sat at wedding-feasts. Oftentimes have we been naked, but we have also worn kingly raiment. We have indeed travelled far, but now we part. Together you shall go your way, and alone must I go mine.

"And though the seas and the vast lands shall separate us, still we shall be companions upon our journey to the Holy Mountain.

"But before we go our severed roads, I would give unto you the harvest and the gleaning of my heart:

"Go you upon your way with singing, but let each song be brief, for only the songs that die young upon your lips shall live in human hearts.

"Tell a lovely truth in little words, but never an ugly truth in any words. Tell the maiden whose hair shines in the sun that she is the daughter of the morning. But if you shall behold the sightless, say not to him that he is one with night.

"Listen to the flute-player as it were listening to April, but if you shall hear the critic and the fault-finder speak, be deaf as your own bones and as distant as your fancy.

"My comrades and my beloved, upon your way you shall meet men with hoofs; give them your wings. And men with horns; give them wreaths of laurel. And men with claws; give them petals for fingers. And men with forked tongues; give them honey words.

"Ay, you shall meet all these and more; you shall meet the lame selling crutches; and the blind, mirrors. And you shall meet the rich men begging at the gate of the Temple.

"To the lame give your swiftness, to the blind of your vision; and see that you give of yourself to the rich beggars; they are the most needy of all, for surely no man would stretch a hand for alms unless he be poor indeed, though of great possessions.

"My comrades and my friends, I charge you by our love that you be countless paths which cross one another in the desert, where the lions and the rabbits walk, and also the wolves and the sheep.

"And remember this of me: I teach you not giving, but receiving; not denial, but fulfilment; and not yielding, but understanding, with the smile upon the lips.

"I teach you not silence, but rather a song not over-loud.

"I teach you your larger self, which contains all men."

And he rose from the board and went out straightway into the Garden and walked under the shadow of the cypress-trees as the day waned. And they followed him, at a little distance, for their heart was heavy, and their tongue clave to the roof of their mouth.

Only Karima, after she had put by the fragments, came unto him and said: "Master, I would that you suffer me to prepare food against the morrow and your journey."

And he looked upon her with eyes that saw other worlds that this, and he said: "My sister, and my beloved, it is done, even from the beginning of time. The food and the drink is ready, for the morrow, even as for our yesterday and our today.

"I go, but if I go with a truth not yet voiced, that very truth will again seek me and gather me, though my elements be scattered throughout the silences of eternity, and again shall I come before you that I may speak with a voice born anew out of the heart of those boundless silences.

"And if there be aught of beauty that I have declared not unto you, then once again shall I be called, ay, even by mine own name, Almustafa, and I shall give you a sign, that you may know I have come back to speak all that is lacking, for God will not suffer Himself to be hidden from man, nor His word to lie covered in the abyss of the heart of man.

"I shall live beyond death, and I shall sing in your ears

Even after the vast sea-wave carries me back

To the vast sea-depth.

I shall sit at your board though without a body,

And I shall go with you to your fields, a spirit invisible.

I shall come to you at your fireside, a guest unseen.

Death changes nothing but the masks that cover our faces.

The woodsman shall be still a woodsman,

The ploughman, a ploughman,

And he who sang his song to the wind shall sing it also to the moving spheres."

And the disciples were as still as stones, and grieved in their heart for that he had said: "I go." But no man put out his hand to stay the Master, nor did any follow after his footsteps.

And Almustafa went out from the Garden of his mother, and his feet were swift and they were soundless; and in a moment, like a blown leaf in a strong wind, he was far gone from them, and they saw, as it were, a pale light moving up to the heights.

And the nine walked their ways down the road. But the woman still stood in the gathering night, and she beheld how the light and the twilight were become one; and she comforted her desolation and her aloneness with his words: "I go, but if I go with a truth not yet voiced, that very truth will seek me and gather me, and again shall I come."

*

AND now it was eventide.

And he had reached the hills. His steps had led him to the mist, and he stood among the rocks and the white cypress-trees hidden from all things, and he spoke and said:

"O Mist, my sister, white breath not yet held in a mould,

I return to you, a breath white and voiceless,

A word not yet uttered.

"O Mist, my winged sister mist, we are together now,

And together we shall be till life's second day,

Whose dawn shall lay you, dewdrops in a garden,

And me a babe upon the breast of a woman,

And we shall remember.

"O Mist, my sister, I come back, a heart listening in its depths,

Even as your heart,

A desire throbbing and aimless even as your desire,

A thought not yet gathered, even as your thought.

"O Mist, my sister, first-born of my mother,

My hands still hold the green seeds you bade me scatter,

And my lips are sealed upon the song you bade me sing;

And I bring you no fruit, and I bring you no echoes

For my hands were blind, and my lips unyielding.

"O Mist, my sister, much did I love the world, and the world loved me,

For all my smiles were upon her lips, and all her tears were in my eyes.

Yet there was between us a gulf of silence which she would not abridge

And I could not overstep.

"O Mist, my sister, my deathless sister Mist,

I sang the ancient songs unto my little children,

And they listened, and there was wondering upon their face;

But tomorrow perchance they will forget the song,

And I know not to whom the wind will carry the song.

And though it was not mine own, yet it came to my heart

And dwelt for a moment upon my lips.

"O Mist, my sister, though all this came to pass,

I am at peace.

It was enough to sing to those already born.
And though the singing is indeed not mine,
Yet it is of my heart's deepest desire.
"O Mist, my sister, my sister Mist,
I am one with you now.
No longer am I a self.
The walls have fallen,
And the chains have broken;
I rise to you, a mist,
And together we shall float upon the sea until life's second day,
When dawn shall lay you, dewdrops in a garden,
And me a babe upon the breast of a woman."

THE END.

BOOK TWELVE
LAZARUS AND HIS BELOVED

THE CAST
Lazarus
Mary, his sister
Martha, his sister
The mother of Lazarus
Philip, a disciple
A Madman

THE SCENE

The garden outside of the home of Lazarus and his mother and sisters in Bethany

Late afternoon of Monday, the day after the resurrection of Jesus of Nazareth from the grave.

At curtain rise: Mary is at right gazing up towards the hills. Martha is seated at her loom near the house door, left. The Madman is seated around the corner of the house, and against its wall, down left.

THE PLAY

Mary: *(Turning to Martha)* You do not work. You have not worked much lately.

Martha: You are not thinking of my work. My idleness makes you think of what our Master said. Oh, beloved Master!

The Madman: The day shall come when there will be no weaver, and no one to wear the cloth. We shall all stand naked in the sun.

(There is a long silence. The women do not appear to have heard The

Madman speaking. They never hear him.)

Mary: It is getting late.

Martha: Yes, yes, I know. It is getting late.

(The mother enters, coming out from the house door.)

Mother: Has he not returned yet?

Martha: No, mother, he has not returned yet.

(The three women look towards the hills.)

The Madman: He himself will never return. All that you may see is a breath struggling in a body.

Mary: It seems to me that he has not yet returned from the other world.

Mother: The death of our Master has afflicted him deeply, and during these last days he has hardly eaten a morsel, and I know at night that he does not sleep. Surely it must have been the death of our Friend.

Martha: No, mother. There is something else; something I do not understand.

Mary: Yes, yes. There is something else. I know it, too. I have known it all these days, yet I cannot explain it. His eyes are deeper. He gazes at me as though he were seeing someone else through me. He is tender but his tenderness is for someone not here. And he is silent, silent as if the seal of death is yet upon his lips.

(A silence falls over the three women.)

The Madman: Everyone looks through everyone else to see someone else.

Mother: *(Breaking the silence)* Would that he'd return. Of late he has spent too many hours among those hills alone. He should be here with us.

Mary: Mother, he has not been with us for a long time.

Martha: Why, he has always been with us, only those three days!

Mary: Three days? Three days! Yes, Martha, you are right. It was only three days.

Mother: I wish my son would return from the hills.

Martha: He will come soon, mother. You must not worry.

Mary: *(in a strange voice)* Sometimes I feel that he will never come back from the hills.

Mother: If he came back from the grave, the surely he will come back from the hills. And oh, my daughters, to think that the One who gave us back his life was slain but yesterday.

Mary: Oh the mystery of it, and the pain of it.

Mother: Oh, to think that they could be so cruel to the One who gave my son back to my heart.

(A silence)

Martha: But Lazarus should not stay so long among the hills.

Mary: It is easy for one in a dream to lose his way among the olive groves. And I know a place where Lazarus loved to sit and dream and be still. Oh, mother, it is beside a little stream. If you do not know the place you could not find it. He took me there once, and we sat on two stones, like children. It was spring, and little flowers were growing beside us. We often spoke of that place during the winter season. And each time that he spoke of that place a strange light came into his eyes.

The Madman: Yes, that strange light, that shadow cast by the other light.

Mary: And mother, you know that Lazarus has always been away from us, though he was always with us.

Mother: You say so many things I cannot understand. *(Pause)* I wish my son would come back from the hills. I wish he would come back! *(Pause)* I must go in now. The lentils must not be overcooked.

(The mother exits through the door)

Martha: I wish I could understand all that you say, Mary. When you speak it is as though someone else is speaking.

Mary: *(Her voice a little strange)* I know, my sister, I know. Whenever we speak it is someone else who is speaking.

(There is a prolonged silence. Mary is faraway in her thoughts, and Martha watches her half-curiously. Lazarus enters, coming from the hills, back left. He throws himself upon the grass under the almond trees near the house.)

Mary: *(Running toward him)* Oh Lazarus, you are tired and weary. You should not have walked so far.

Lazarus: *(Speaking absently)* Walking, walking and going nowhere; seeking and finding nothing. But it is better to be among the hills.

The Madman: Well, after all it is a cubit nearer to the other hills.

Martha: *(After brief silence)* But you are not well, and you leave us all day long, and we are much concerned. What you came back, Lazarus, you made us happy. But in leaving us alone here you turn our happiness into anxiety.

Lazarus: *(Turning his face toward the hills)* Did I leave you long this day? Strange that you should call a moment among the hills a separation. Did I truly stay more that a moment among the hills?

Martha: You have been gone all day.

Lazarus: To think, to think! A whole day among the hills! Who would believe it?

(A silence. The mother enters, coming out from the house door.)

Mother: Oh, my son, I am glad you have come back. It is late and the mist is gathering upon the hills. I feared for you my son.

The Madman: They are afraid of the mist. And the mist is their beginning and the mist is their end.

Lazarus: Yes, I have come back to you from the hills. The pity of it, the pity of it all.

Mother: What is it Lazarus? What is the pity of it all?

Lazarus: Nothing, mother. Nothing.

Mother: You speak strangely. I do not understand you, Lazarus. You have said little since your home-coming. But whatever you have said has been strange to me.

Martha: Yes, strange.

(There is a pause.)

Mother: And now the mist is gathering here. Let us go into the house. Come, my children.

(The mother, after kissing Lazarus with wistful tenderness, enters the house.)

Martha: Yes, there is a chill in the air. I must take my loom and my linen indoors.

Mary: *(sitting down beside Lazarus on the grass under the almond trees, and speaking to Martha)* It is true the April evenings are not good for either your loom or your linen. Would you want me to help you take your loom indoors?

Martha: No, no. I can do it alone. I have always done it alone.

(Martha carries her loom into the house, then she returns for the linen, taking that in also. A wind passes by, shaking the almond tree, and a drift of petals falls over Mary and Lazarus.)

Lazarus: Even spring would comfort us, and even the trees would weep for us. All there is on earth, if all there is on earth could know our downfall and our grief, would pity us and weep for us.

Mary: But spring is with us, and though veiled with the veil of sorrow, yet it is spring. Let us not speak of pity. Let us rather accept both our spring and our sorrow with gratitude. And let us wonder in sweet silence at Him who gave you life yet yielded His own life. Let us not speak of pity, Lazarus.

Lazarus: Pity, pity that I should be torn away from a thousand thousand years of heart's desire, a thousand thousand years of heart's hunger. Pity that after a thousand thousand springs I am turned to this winter.

Mary: What do you mean, my brother? Why do you speak of a thousand thousand springs? You were but three days away from us. Three short days. But our sorrow was indeed longer than three days.

Lazarus: Three days? Three centuries, three aeons! All of time! All of time with the one my soul loved before time began.

The Madman: Yes, three days, three centuries, three aeons. Strange they would always weigh and measure. It is always a sundial and a pair of scales.

Mary: *(In amazement)* The one you soul loved before time began? Lazarus, why do you say these things? It is but a dream you dreamed in another garden. Now we are here in this garden, a stone's throw from Jerusalem. We are here. And you know well, my brother, that our Master would have you be with us in this awakening to dream of life and love; and He would have you an ardent disciple, a living witness of His glory.

Lazarus: There is no dream here and there is no awakening. You and I and this garden are but an illusion, a shadow of the real. The awakening is there where I was with my beloved and the reality.

Mary: *(Rising)* Your beloved?

Lazarus: *(Also rising)* My beloved.

The Madman: Yes, yes. His beloved, the space virgin, the beloved of everyman.

Mary: But where is your beloved? Who is your beloved?

Lazarus: My twin heart whom I sought here and did not find. Then death, the angel with winged feet, came and led my longing to her longing, and I lived with her in the very heart of God. And I became nearer to her and she to me, and we were one. We were a sphere that shines in the sun; and we were a song among the stars. All this, Mary, all this and more, till a voice, a voice from the depths, the voice of a world called me; and that which was inseparable was torn asunder. And the thousand thousand years with my beloved in space could not guard me from the power of that voice which called me back.

Mary: *(Looking unto the sky)* O blessed angels of our silent hours, make me to understand this thing! I would not be an alien in this new land discovered by death. Say more, my brother, go on. I believe in my heart I can follow you.

The Madman: Follow him, if you can, little woman. Shall the turtle follow the stag?

Lazarus: I was a stream and I sought the sea where my beloved dwells, and when I reached the sea I was brought to the hills to run again among the rocks. I was a song imprisoned in silence, longing for the heart of my beloved, and when the winds of heaven released me and uttered me in that green forest I was recaptured by a voice, and I was turned again into silence. I was a root in the dark earth, and I became a flower and then a fragrance in space rising to enfold my beloved, and I was caught and gathered by hand, and I was made a root again, a root in the dark earth.

The Madman: If you are a root you can always escape the tempests in the branches. And it is good to be a running stream even after you have reached the sea. Of course it is good for water to run upward.

Mary: *(To herself)* Oh strange, passing strange! *(To Lazarus)* But my brother it is good to be a running stream, and it is not good to be a song not yet sung, and it is good to be a root in the dark earth. The Master knew all this and He called you back to us that we may know there is no veil between life and death. Do you not see how one word uttered in love may bring together elements scattered by an illusion called death? Believe and have faith, for only in faith, which is our deeper knowledge, can you find comfort.

Lazarus: Comfort! Comfort the treacherous, the deadly! Comfort that cheats our senses and makes us slaves to the passing hour! I would not have comfort. I would have passion! I would burn in the cool space with my beloved. I would be in the boundless space with my mate, my other self. O Mary, Mary, you were once my sister, and we knew one another even when our nearest kin knew us not. Now listen to me, listen to me with your heart.

Mary: I am listening, Lazarus.

The Madman: Let the whole world listen. The sky will now speak to the earth, but the earth is deaf as you and I.

Lazarus: We were in space, my beloved and I, and we were all space. We were in light and we were all light. And we roamed even like the ancient spirit that moved upon the face of the waters; and it was forever the first day. We were love itself that dwells in the heart of the white silence. Then a voice like thunder, a voice like countless spears piercing the ether, cried out saying, "Lazarus, come forth!" And the voice echoed and re-echoed in space, and I, even as a flood tide became an ebbing tide; a house divided, a garment rent, a youth unspent, a tower that fell down, and out of its broken stones a landmark was made. A voice cried "Lazarus, come forth!" and I descended from the mansion of the sky to a tomb within a tomb, this body in a sealed cave.

The Madman: Master of the caravan, where are your camels and where are your men? Was it the hungry earth that swallowed them? Was it the simoom that shrouded them with sand? No! Jesus of Nazareth raised His hand, Jesus of Nazareth uttered a word; and tell me now, where are your camels and where are your men, and where are your treasures? In the trackless sand, in the trackless sand. But the moon will always come again.

Mary: Oh, it is like a dream dreamt upon a mountaintop. I know, my brother, I know the world you have visited, though I have never seen it. Yet all that you say is passing strange. It is a tale told by someone across a valley, and I can hardly hear it.

Lazarus: It is all so different across the valley. There is no weight there and there is no measure. You are with your beloved.

(A silence)

Lazarus: O my beloved! O my beloved fragrance in space! Wings that were spread for me! Tell me, tell me in the stillness of my heart, do you seek me, and was it pain to you to be separated from me? Was I also a fragrance and wings spread in space? And tell me now, my beloved, was there a double cruelty, was there a brother of His in another world who called you from life to death, and had you a mother and sisters and friends who deemed it a miracle? Was there a double cruelty performed in blessedness?

Mary: No, no, my brother. There is only one Jesus of one world. All else is but a dream, even as your beloved.

Lazarus: *(With great passion)* No, no! If He is not a dream then He is nothing. If He had not known what is beyond Jerusalem, then He is nothing. If He did not know my beloved in space then He was not the Master. O my friend Jesus, you once gave me a cup of wine across the table, and you said, "Drink this in remembrance of me." And you dipped a morsel of bread in the oil, and you said, "Eat this, it is my share of the loaf." O my friend, you have put your arm on my shoulder and called me "son." My mother and my sisters have said in their hearts, "He loves our Lazarus." And I loved you. And then you went away to build more towers in the sky, and I went to my beloved. Tell me now, tell me, why did you bring me back?

Did you not know in your knowing heart that I was with my beloved? Did you not meet her in you wandering above the summits of Lebanon? Surely you saw her image in my eyes when I came and stood before you at the door of the tomb. And have you not a beloved in the sun? And would you have a greater one than yourself separate you from her? And after separation what would you say? What shall I say to you now?

The Madman: He bade me also to come back but I did not obey, and now they call me mad.

Mary: Lazarus, Have I a beloved in the sky? Has my longing created a being beyond this world? And must I die to be with him? Oh, my brother, tell me, have I a mate also? If this thing be so, how good it is to live and die, and live and die again; if a beloved awaits me, to fulfil all that I am, and I to fulfil all that he is!

The Madman: Everywoman has a beloved in the sky. The heart of everywoman creates a being in space.

Mary: (Repeating softly as if to herself) Have I a beloved in the sky?

Lazarus: I do not know. But if you had a beloved, an other self, somewhere, somewhen, and you should meet him, surely there would not be one to separate you from him.

The Madman: He may be here, and He may call her. But like many others she may not hear.

Lazarus: (Coming to the centre of stage) To wait, to wait for each season to overcome another season; and then to wait for that season to be overcome by another; to watch all things ending before your own end comes-your end which is your beginning. To listen to all voices, and to know that they melt to silence, all save the voice of your heart that would cry even in sleep.

The Madman: The children of God married the children of men. Then they were divorced. Now, the children of men long for the children of God. I pity them all, the children of men and the children of God.

(A silence)

Martha: (Appearing in the doorway) Why don't you come into the house, Lazarus? Our mother has prepared the supper. (With a little impatience) Whenever you and Mary are together you talk and talk, and no one knows what you say.

(Martha stands for a sew seconds, then goes into the house.)

Lazarus: (Speaking to himself, and as though he has not heard Martha) Oh, I am spent. I am wasted, I am hungry and I am thirsty. Would that you could give me some bread and some wine.

Mary: (Going to him and putting her arm around him) I will, I will, my brother. But some into the house. Our mother has prepared the evening meal.

The Madman: He asks for bread which they cannot bake, and wine for which they have no bottles.

Lazarus: Did I say I was hungry and thirsty? I am not hungry for your bread, nor thirsty for your wine. I tell you I shall not enter a house until my beloved's hand is upon the latch of the door. I shall not sit at the feast till she be at my side.

(Mother peers from the house door.)

Mother: Now, Lazarus, why do you stay out in the mist? And you, Mary, why do you not come into the house? I have lit the candles and the food is upon the board, and yet you will stay out babbling and chewing your words in the dark.

Lazarus: Mine own mother would have me enter a tomb. She would have me eat and drink and she would even bid me sit among shrouded faces and receive eternity from withered hands and draw life from clay cups.

The Madman: White bird that flew southward where the sun loves all things, what held you in mid-air, and who brought you back? It was your friend, Jesus of Nazareth. He brought you back out of pity for the wingless who would not be along. Oh, white bird, it is cold here, and you shiver and the North wind laughs in your feathers.

Lazarus: You would be in a house and under a roof. You would be within four walls, with a door and a window. You would be here, and you are without vision. Your mind is here, and my spirit is there. All of you is upon the earth; all of me is in space. You creep into houses, and I flew beyond upon the mountaintop. You are all slaves, the one to the other, and you worship but yourselves. You sleep and you dream not; you wake but you walk not among the hills. And yesterday I was weary of you and of lives, and I sought the other world which you call death, and if I had died it was out of longing. Now, I stand here at this moment, rebelling against that which you call life.

Martha: (Who has come out of the house while Lazarus was speaking) But the Master saw our sorrow and our pain, and He called you back to us, and yet you rebel. Oh, what cloth, rebelling against its own weaver! What a house rebelling against its own builder!

Mary: He knew our hearts and He was gracious unto us, and when He met our mother and saw in her eyes a dead son, buried, then her sorrow held Him, and for a moment He was still, and He was silent. (Pause) Then we followed Him to your tomb.

Lazarus: Yes, it was my mother's sorrow, and your sorrow. It was pity, self-pity, that brought me back. How selfish is self-pity, and how deep. I say that I rebel. I say that divinity itself should not turn spring to winter. I had climbed the hills in longing, and your sorrow brought me back to this valley. You wanted a son and a brother to be with you through life. Your neighbours wanted a miracle. You and your neighbours, like your fathers and your forefathers, would have a miracle, that you may believe in the simplest things in life. How cruel you are and how hard are your hearts, and how dark is the night of your eyes. For that you bring down the prophets from their glory to you joys, and then you kill the prophets.

Martha: (with reproof) You call our sorrow self-pity. What is your wailing but self-pity? Be quiet, and accept the life the Master has given you.

Lazarus: He did not give me life, He gave you my life. He took my life from my own beloved, and gave it to you, a miracle to open your eyes and your ears. He sacrificed me even as He sacrificed Himself. (Speaking unto the sky) Father, forgive them. They know not what they do.

Mary: (In awe) It was He who said those very words, hanging upon the cross.

Lazarus: Yes, He said these words for me as for Himself, and for all the unknown who understand and are not understood. Did He not say these words when your tears begged Him for my life? It was your desire and not His will that bade His spirit to stand at the sealed door and urge eternity to yield me unto you. It was the ancient longing for a son and a brother that brought me back.

Mother: (Approaches him and puts her arm around his shoulders) Lazarus, you were ever an obedient son and a loving son. What has happened to you? Be with us, and forget all that troubles you.

Lazarus: (Raising his hand) My mother and my brothers and my sisters are those who hear my words.

Mary: These are also His words.

Lazarus: Yes, and He said these words for me as well as for Himself, and for all those who have earth for mother, and sky for father, and for all those who are born free of a people and a country and a race.

The Madman: Captain of my ship, the wind filled your sails, and you dared the sea; and you sought the blessed isles. What other wind changed your course, and why did you return to these shores? It was Jesus of Nazareth who commanded the wind with a breath of His own breath, and then filled the sail where it was empty, and emptied it where it was full.

Lazarus: (Suddenly he forgets them all, and he raises his head, and opens his arms.) O my beloved! There was dawn in your eyes, and in that dawn there was the silent mystery of a deep night, and the silent promise of a full day, and I was fulfilled, and I was whole. O my beloved, this life, this veil, is between us now. Must I live this death and die again that I may live again? Must needs linger until all these green things turn yellow and then naked again, and yet again? (Pause) Oh, I cannot curse Him. But why, of all men, why should I return? Why should I of all shepherds be driven back into the desert after the green pasture?

The Madman: If you were one of those who would curse, you would not have died so young.

Lazarus: Jesus of Nazareth, tell me now, why did you do this to me? Was it fair that I should be laid down, a humble lowly sorrowful stone leading to the height of your glory? Any one of the dead might have served to glorify you. Why have you separated this lover from his beloved? Why did you call me to a world which you knew in your heart you would leave? (Then crying with a great voice) Why – why – why did you call me from the living heart of eternity to this living death? O Jesus of Nazareth – I cannot curse you! I cannot curse you. I would bless you. (Silence. Lazarus becomes as one whose strength has gone out in a stream. His head falls forward almost upon his breast. After a moment of awful silence, he raises his head again, and with a transfigured face he cries in a deep and thrilling voice.) Jesus of Narareth! My friend! We have both been crucified. Forgive me! Forgive me. I bless you-now, and forevermore.

(At this moment the disciple appears running from the direction of the hills.)

Mary: Philip!

Philip: He is risen! The Master is risen from the dead and now He is gone to Galilee.

The Madman: He is risen, but He will be crucified again a thousand times.

Mary: Philip, my friend, what do you say?

Martha: (Rushes toward the disciple, and grasps him by the arms) How glad I am to see you again. But who has risen? Of whom are you speaking?

Mother: (Walking toward him) Come in, my son. You shall have supper with us tonight.

Philip: (Unmoved by any of their words) I say the Master has risen from the dead and has gone into Galilee.

(A deep silence falls.)

Lazarus: Now you shall all listen to me. If He has risen from the dead they will crucify Him again, but they shall not crucify Him alone. Now I shall proclaim Him, and they shall crucify me also.

(He turns in exaltation and walk in the direction of the hills.)

Lazarus: My mother and my sisters, I shall follow Him who gave me life until He gives me death. Yes, I too would be crucified, and that crucifixion will end this crucifixion.

(A silence)

Lazarus: Now I shall seek His spirit, and I shall be released. And though they bind me in iron chains I shall not be bound. And though a thousand mothers and a thousand thousand sisters shall hold my garments I shall not be held. I shall go with the East wind where the East wind goes. And I shall seek my beloved in the sunset where all our days find peace. And I shall seek my beloved in the night where all the mornings sleep. And I shall be the one man among all men who twice suffered life, and twice death, and twice knew eternity.

(Lazarus looks into the face of his mother, then into the faces of his sisters, the at Philip's face; then again at his mother's face. Then as if he were a sleepwalker he turns and runs toward the hills. He disappears. They are all dazed and shaken.)

Mother: My son, my son, come back to me!

Mary: My brother, where are you going? Oh come, my brother, come back to us.

Martha: (As if to herself) It is so dark I know that he will lose his way.

Mother: (Almost screaming) Lazarus, my son!

(A silence)

Philip: He has gone where we all shall go. And he shall not return.

Mother: (Going to the very back of the stage, close to where he has disappeared) Lazarus, Lazarus, my son! Come back to me! (She shrieks.)

(There is a silence. The running steps of Lazarus are lost in the distance.)

The Madman: Now he is gone, and he is beyond your reach. And now your sorrow must seek another. (He pauses) Poor, poor Lazarus, the first of the martyrs, and the greatest of them all.

THE END.